Godly Justice

By R. Darrell Wallace

Published by
Spiritbuilding Publishers
9700 Ferry Road, Waynesville, Ohio 45068

GODLY JUSTICE
By R. Darrell Wallace

ISBN: 978–1–964–80533–7

Scriptures are taken from the
KING JAMES VERSION (KJV), public domain.

Scripture taken from the New King James Version® (NKJV).
© 1982 by Thomas Nelson. Used by permission. All rights reserved.

Any similarity between fictional characters and actual persons, living or dead, is entirely coincidental. Some historical persons are mentioned within actual historical events. Fictional characters were added for dramatic effect, but do not alter historical events.

Spiritbuilding
PUBLISHERS

spiritbuilding.com

To my grandchildren

Brooks and Graysen

Preface

This story is a historical fiction that takes place at the end of the Civil War in Missouri, Kentucky, and Kansas. The main character, Gabe MacCallan, is a Kentuckian who served in the Confederate Army as a conscientious objector. He leaves Kentucky planning to travel north, but the apparent providence of God takes his life in a different direction when he arrives in Warrensburg, Missouri. His firm belief that those who sow the wind should reap the whirlwind, not out of revenge but of divine justice, lands him in a series of events that will shape his destiny.

I wrote this story for a couple of reasons. First, I love history and Western novels set in the American Frontier of the 1800s. Second, in the realm of fiction, most narratives take place within an imaginative setting where the presence of God is either nonexistent or merely hinted at, with no significant impact on the characters' lives. As a believer in God and His personal activity in our daily lives, I wanted to write something that had a historical setting while including God's providence in the characters' lives. I wanted to write this historical fiction with a biblical moral.

The main characters and the characters surrounding them in the story are fiction. However, newspaper articles, plat maps, and historical records from the Civil War period were researched for actual events, dates, historical people, and geographical locations.

Finally, the human heart seeks justice, but there is only one kind of true justice—godly justice with a Divine purpose. As we will see from this story, when we fear God and accept our calling, we genuinely become content, know peace, and find true justice and grace.

—*R. Darrell Wallace*

Part One

Sowing the Wind

"For whatsoever a man soweth, that shall he also reap."
Galatians 6:7

1

It was a cool Sunday morning in the early spring of 1865 in Southern Kentucky, and churchgoers filed out of the meeting house after worship.

"Good sermon, Brother Aaron, … as always," the elderly sister commented. "You really stepped on my toes this morning."

"Why, thank you, sister. You are too kind. I hope I wasn't too hard on you," he replied in his southern gentlemanly way.

"You remember now," she continued, "I want you to talk over me at my wake," she reminded.

"Yes, ma'am. I remember, but let's hope that ain't anytime soon."

Sister Cowan, now in her nineties and a widow, is one of the few people who remember the days after America gained its independence. She and her family were among five original families that began this congregation of the Disciples of Christ in the early 1800s when a pioneer preacher came through preaching the gospel. He was a preacher of the Restoration Movement, John "Racoon" Smith. Most people around those parts trace their family tree back to Scotland, and a few from Ireland. They were bred to be tough people, hard workers, and full of faith in their God and Savior, Jesus Christ. They were patriots for liberty to the core. They were sons and daughters of the American Revolution. When America declared independence from the King of England, going to war against England was like saying "sic 'em" to a dog. George Washington was their Sir William Wallace, and they rallied behind him. They lived their lives guided by principles of justice, mercy, humility, and faith in God and defended these beliefs with their musket rifles.

Gabe MacCallan was the son of Aaron MacCallan, a pioneer preacher, and one of three sons and two daughters. He had witnessed firsthand the hardships and trials that his parents went through. Being a good shepherd during hard times can leave a preacher wounded and alone. Now, America had entered into a great Civil War. When the War Between the States started, Confederate soldiers rode to the farm. The Confederate Army forced the three sons into service. The MacCallans were conscientious objectors to the war, but that made no difference to the Confederate Army. Gabe's oldest brother was tragically killed in Ringgold, Georgia, at the Battle of Chickamauga. He was part of the 2nd Kentucky Mounted Infantry. His middle brother deserted and came home. It wasn't long before a group of Confederate Home Guard rode to the farm. The Home Guard was a volunteer militia that went after deserters. They seized him, whipped him, laid him on a coffin they brought, and shot him through the head. His family was forced to witness in horror.

Gabe returned home on April 20, 1865. The news of Lee's surrender to Grant had spread rapidly throughout the South. Gabe was in the Kentucky 2nd Battalion Mounted Rifles that disbanded in Bowling Green, Kentucky. He turned in his weapons, refusing to be a Confederate rebel combatant, and returned home near Gamaliel. The Southern states faced complete collapse, with the banking system nearly nonexistent. Confederate currency was as worthless as scrap paper, and traditional cash crops like cotton and tobacco lost their reliability. Despite this turmoil, Kentucky was relatively spared from the worst effects, though not entirely without exceptions. In places like Gamaliel, residents faced raids from guerrilla bands that plundered, destroyed, and sometimes even killed. Confederate Brigadier General John Morgan instilled terror in the region. However, the MacCallan family, owning their small farm outright and free from debt, not only fared better than most but also managed to endure the severe hardships brought about by the War.

Gabe had experienced things in the War that he wanted to leave far behind. Coming home did not provide the healing he desperately needed. After a couple of weeks at home, Gabe decided to leave despite the pleas of his father and mother to stay. They had lost two sons and could not bear seeing him leave.

"If you must leave," his father said, "take this."

It was his Bible, the one from which he had preached for forty years. Between its cracked and worn leather cover was page after page of notes scribbled in the margins and scriptures underlined in pencil. The pages were worn thin and yellowed, and the edges of some pages were so thin that only memory could recall words that were now fading.

"This Bible is your only Bible. What will you preach from?" Gabe protested as he choked back tears.

"I have enough scripture and sermons in my head to last another forty years if the Lord's willin'. It's yours now. I want you to have it."

"You will also need this," his mother said as she entered the kitchen from the bedroom. Gabe turned to see his mother with something in her hand. "I've been saving this since before the war."

She handed him three gold coins and five silver coins. Confederate soldiers left the military without pay, and she knew that he would not get far without it. That evening, Gabe enjoyed his mother's southern cooking one more time. They sat and prayed together for God's blessing and guidance.

As the following day dawned, Gabe, his parents, and sisters exchanged tearful farewells. He walked along the dirt road past the old red oak tree that marked the entrance to the farm. Biscuits, bacon, and a few apples were flung over his shoulder in a flour sack. Tip, Gabe's faithful dog, trailed him to the ancient oak. Gabe shared one of his biscuits, but Tip left it untouched. For a decade, Tip had been Gabe's loyal companion, and now, Gabe sensed that Tip knew this was farewell and their final parting. With a heavy heart, he rested his hand on Tip's head, offering a comforting rub bchind his ear. It seemed as though Tip understood the gravity of the moment, sadness mirrored in his eyes. Gabe bid his beloved friend goodbye, setting off towards Glasgow Junction and onward to Nashville and from there to Memphis.

The journey to Memphis was a long one. Confederate soldiers who refused to accept reality were fleeing, often scavenging to survive. Lawlessness was setting in. Gabe made it to Memphis, where he bought a four-dollar ticket—not an easy task—on board a steam freighter going upriver. Gabe wasn't the only one trying to get away. People crowded the freighter, wanting to escape the harsh conditions of the South. His plan was to head for the Dakota and Lakota territories, believing he could escape the nightmares of the War haunting his mind. The freighter went as far as St. Louis. He disembarked, thanking God that he had made it this far and still had a little money left, but the biscuits, bacon, and apples only lasted a couple of days. Well-rested but hungry, alone, and vulnerable in a big city, he knew what to avoid, so he found a safe place to spend the night.

It was a Friday morning, May 12th, when he awoke to muddy streets from an overnight storm. The dampness sent a chill into his bones. *If only I could get a cup of hot coffee*, he thought to himself. The harsh smell of burning coal hung low in the air. He had never seen so many people, not even in Atlanta. The city they call the Gateway to the West was meeting its expectations. Two streets from the riverfront and running east to west were a row of shops and businesses, and the city was full of excitement and celebration. American flags were displayed everywhere. Above the streets, banners were hung, suspended from one building to another. Gabe managed to stop someone.

"Excuse me, sir," Gabe asked the passerby. "What is all this celebration about?"

"A New Constitution," the man said. "Slavery is finally being abolished in Missouri."

The MacCallans were never slave owners. Too poor, for one thing, but primarily because their convictions and conscience forbade them from considering another human being as property. Their reading of the Bible and the Declaration of Independence established that all men are created equal by one Creator in his image with certain inalienable rights.

After asking for directions to the Missouri Pacific Railroad Depot, he reached Seventh Street. The depot was alive with activity, though there seemed to be tension in the air. Union soldiers were posted at every entry point along the rail platform. Gabe walked past them to the clerk's window.

"How far will this rail take me?" Gabe asked.

"Well," the clerk said as he paused to put his pen in the inkwell, "if it hadn't been for Price's raid last fall, I would tell you Kansas City, but now I can only get you as far as Warrensburg."

"I reckon I'll take a ticket to Warrensburg then," Gabe said with frustration and disappointment.

"Yes, sir. One ticket to Warrensburg. That'll be $6.54. I would advise not to go beyond Warrensburg for a while."

"Why is that?" Gabe asked as he reached into his pocket for his money. The clerk put his hand on The Missouri Republican, a St. Louis newspaper, and slid it in front of Gabe. Pointing to the top left column, it read, *"…it is understood that the officers of Pacific Railroad have information that from 130 to 150 guerillas are in the counties in the vicinity of Lexington, where they have committed various depredations, among others, killing four men at Holden, Saturday night, and eight at Kingsville on Sunday night. These points are fifteen and twenty-two miles (respectively) west of Warrensburg."*

Above this notice was this mandate to the Union commander in Lexington, Missouri. The notice read,

Major Davis:

This is to notify you that I will give you until Friday, May 12th, 1865, to surrender the town of Lexington. If you surrender, we will treat you and all as prisoners of war. If we have to take it by storm, we will burn the town and kill the soldiery. We have the force and are determined to have it.

I am, sir, your obedient servant, A. Clement.

"Who is this 'A. Clement?'" Gabe asked.

"Why that's Archie Clement. Little Archie, they call him. He's taken command of a group of guerrilla rebels, and is the meanest bushwhacker you ever seen, the devil's son, he is. They say he'll cut your throat and scalp you, and laugh while doing it. I hope they finally get him this time."

The clerk took his watch from his vest pocket. "The train leaves the station in thirty minutes. Sign your name or make your mark here in the book," he said as he initialed and dated the ticket, then handed it to Gabe.

"Much obliged," Gabe said as he turned and walked toward the platform where he would wait to board. He could not help but think about what he had just read as he heard a train whistle in the distance.

2

The trip was uneventful when Gabe neared his destination on Friday, May 12, 1865. The train stopped to let people on and off at towns along the rail. As in St. Louis, Union soldiers were visible at every stop. Finally, the porter called out, "Next stop— Warrensburg!" The train pulled into the depot, which was still under construction. Gabe stepped onto the platform with the thought of finding the only person who could help him and give him the information he needed. He remembered what his father told him when he went into the military. "If you need help, find a local preacher."

He walked past a hotel to what appeared to be a main street. He looked to the west. A sign on a building up the road read, "Wholesale Grocer and General Commission Merchant, Samuel Clayton, Proprietor." Gabe walked into the establishment. It was lit with large display windows facing south at the front and one window in the back. On one side of the store were items that included housewares. There were ladies' apparel and fancy hats. To the left were grocery items, and behind the counter were firearms and ammo. Then, a gentleman came from the back. He was tall, slender, gray-haired, and unshaven. He was wearing wire-framed glasses and walked with a slight limp.

Gabe was admiring a Henry rifle across the counter when the old fella asked, "Can I help you, young man?"

"Yes, sir. Do you know a preacher in town I can talk to?"

"A preacher?" the man asked.

"Yes, sir."

"Where are you from, young fella?"

"Kentucky, sir."

"Thought so. I could tell by the accent. What's the preacher for?" the old gentleman asked.

"I'm passin' through, but I need a job for a little while to pay my way north," Gabe replied.

"Why north? North where?"

"The Dakotas."

The old gentleman rubbed his unshaven chin, spat into the spittoon on the floor, and wiped the tobacco juice from his mouth with a tobacco-stained bandana. Gabe could tell he was studying him. Why would a young man from Kentucky with nothing but the clothes on his back, no weapon, and a leather pouch strapped over his shoulder go north to the Dakotas?

"Are you a godly man?" The scruffy gray-bearded man asked with a little roughness in his voice.

"Sir?" Gabe inquired.

"You heard me. Are you a godly man? You said you were looking for a preacher."

"I try to be a good man, sir," Gabe replied.

"I didn't ask if you are a good man. I asked if you are a godly man," the old gentleman asked again, but more directly.

Gabe looked confused by the question, and then he reached slowly into his leather pouch, took out his father's Bible, and held it out to show the old man. The elderly man stuffed his bandana into his back pocket, approached Gabe, and examined him closely before turning his attention to the Bible Gabe was holding. He asked politely, "May I see it?" Confused by the man's request, Gabe handed the book over to him. With reverence in the older man's touch, Gabe handed him his Bible.

"This Bible is well-worn and older than you," the old gentleman remarked. "A well-worn Bible refreshes a worn-out soul," he said as he handled it with the care of a mother with a newborn. He opened it. Written on the inside cover was this inscription:

'Tis better to be forgotten whilst Christ is remembered than linger in memory whilst Christ is forgotten.

"This Bible ain't yorn. Whose is it?" The man asked with eyes now looking back at Gabe over his wire-framed glasses.

"It belonged to my father," Gabe replied.

"He's gone on to his reward, I take it?"

"No, sir, I mean—he gave it to me before I left home."

"He's a preacher of the gospel," the old gentleman observed. "I can tell," he remarked as he continued to flip through the pages.

"Yes, sir. My father is a gospel preacher."

The old gentleman thumbed through the pages, noting the numerous marginal notes, now faded. Closing the book, he said, "I know a preacher around here, and his name is Sam Clayton."

"Sam Clayton?" Gabe was perplexed now because the owner of this store was Samuel Clayton, according to the sign out front.

"That's right. Sam Clayton. You're lookin' at him."

"What's your name, son?"

"Gabriel MacCallan, son of Aaron MacCallan, a preacher for the Disciples of Christ."

Clayton handed the Bible back to him. "You're needin' a job. I'm needin' a store clerk and stock boy. I'll pay you six dollars a week and provide your room and board. Do you want the job?"

His offer was unusually generous, Gabe thought to himself.

"Yes, sir," Gabe said, but was almost speechless with disbelief.

"Good. There is a house down the street in Old Town that provides rooms and meals. The owner is a lady by the name of Alice Adair. Tell her I sent you and that I will take care of everything. She's a nice woman, and she'll care for you. You start first thing in the mornin'—six o'clock sharp."

Then Sam looked at Gabe from boot to hat.

"It looks like you haven't had a change of clothes in several days. Over there on that shelf, you will find some trousers and a shirt. I will deduct the cost from your pay."

"Thank you, sir." Gabe did as he was told.

After leaving the store with new shirts and trousers, and being thankful for God's providence, he found the house with the sign in front that read, *Adair's Room and Board*. It was a two-story Victorian-style house. A fence surrounded the yard and was soon to be shaded by huge, old, red maples and American chestnuts. American flags were draped across the porch railing as part of the Constitutional celebration. A gentle knock on the screen door summoned a kind and gracious lady, who promptly answered the door. "Pardon my appearance, dear," she said while wiping her hands on her apron. "How can I assist you?"

"Yes, ma'am. Sam Clayton sent me here to ask for a room. He graciously offered to take care of the expense for now," Gabe replied, a little embarrassed for having to rely on charity.

"He's such a good man," she replied, smiling and happy to help. "I'm not surprised. If Brother Sam trusts you, so can I. Come right in and have a seat while I get you some coffee."

She returned to the kitchen for coffee as Gabe walked into the drawing room. It was beautifully decorated, with everything in its place. The windows were opened, allowing the fragrance of the early blooming flowers in her garden to fill the room.

"I hope you don't mind your coffee black," she said as she returned to the room. "We are having a shortage of sugar, and I'm saving what I have for a couple of apple pies. The War has caused shortages in a lot of things. And prices keep going up."

"No, ma'am, I don't mind at all," Gabe responded, since he had little, if anything, to eat or drink in a while.

"Where are you from, dear? What brings you to Warrensburg?" She asked as she sat on the sofa across from him.

"I'm from Kentucky, on my way north to the Dakotas, ma'am."

"Hmm. We have a Civil War down here. They have Indian Wars up there. The country is coming apart at the seams. You just might be jumpin' from the fryin' pan into the fire if you go up there. It would be best if you stayed here for a while. Besides, it is too dangerous to take a stagecoach to Kansas City right now. Finish your coffee," she told him as she returned to the kitchen. "You can have the room at the top of the stairs on the right. It has a nice view of the street. Supper is at five. Breakfast is at five. I will have Lizzie bring you some fresh, warm water so you can clean up first. She will also place a fresh pitcher of water outside your door in the morning."

"Thank you, ma'am. That's very kind of you," Gabe gratefully replied, even though he caught only some of what she said as she walked to the kitchen.

Gabe finished his coffee and found his room, where he was able to get cleaned up. After having the best supper since leaving home, he returned to his room, still worn out from traveling. The leather pouch on the bed contained all of his belongings and his father's Bible. He took the

Bible out and opened it. The pages unfolded to Psalm chapter thirty-seven. He noticed a scripture that his father had underlined in pencil. Verse twenty-five reads, "I have been young, and now am old; yet have I not seen the righteous forsaken, nor his seed begging bread."

He turned the coal oil lamp wick down slowly, cupped his hand at the top of the chimney, and blew out the flame.

The next morning, Gabe awoke to the smell of bacon being fried. It was five o'clock, and compared to the previous days, the feather bed he was lying on provided a significantly more comfortable experience. He quickly put on his new shirt and trousers and went downstairs for breakfast. Lizzie had already set the table for him with fresh coffee.

"Did you sleep good, Mr. MacCallan?" Lizzie asked.

"Yes, ma'am, too good."

"My name is Lizzie," she said. "I have been with Miss Alice for many years now." She smiled and added, "If you need anything, I am your servant as well."

After enjoying biscuits and gravy, eggs, and bacon, Gabe began to make his way back to Clayton's store. The town was still quiet, and the air had a chill. There was a faint smell of wood smoke from kitchen stoves as the sun began showing its light from behind the hills. Only the robins and other songbirds were celebrating this Saturday morning. Gabe stepped up to the door at Clayton's store. As he raised his hand to knock on the door, it suddenly opened. The person who opened the door was an older lady.

"You must be Mr. MacCallan. I recognize the gray shirt and the black trousers," she said.

She welcomed him in with a smile. "I'm Mrs. Clayton. Brother Clayton isn't here because he had business in Jefferson City and gave me a list of things for you to do."

She led him around the store, including the back where they stored the dry goods and merchandise.

"Here's a broom. You can start by sweeping the front porch."

A few minutes later, a lady stepped up on the porch as Gabe swept. At first, she didn't notice him, but as if startled, she turned and looked at him with a curious look.

"Good morning, ma'am," he greeted with a cheerful note.

She just looked at him, then turned her head and walked into the store. The bell above the door let Mrs. Clayton know that someone had entered.

"Good morning, Clara," Mrs. Clayton greeted with a smile. Mrs. Clayton was always smiling.

"Good morning, Mrs. Clayton. Do you know a strange man is sweeping your front porch?"

"Yes. That's our new employee, Gabe MacCallan. Brother Clayton hired him yesterday." Looking toward the front, Miss Clara lowered her voice and asked, "Can he be trusted? You know there's a lot of mischief these days, with the War and all."

"If Brother Clayton trusts him, I will too."

Miss Clara was known as one of the prominent gossips in town and had appointed herself as the chairperson of the Christian Women's Association. Mrs. Clayton was very wise and aware of Miss Clara's manipulative nature, so she was always cautious about what she said around her, knowing it would be repeated.

"I was over at the Murrays' yesterday," Miss Clara started. "It seems Mr. Murray might be in some kind of financial trouble."

"Oh?" Mrs. Clayton expressed, pretending to be concerned.

"Well, when I approached Helen for a small donation to our Association, she said she would have to think about it."

"Why would you think they might be in financial straits?" Mrs. Clayton asked curiously.

Miss Clara acted surprised by her question. "Because who would not want to donate to such a worthy cause?" She replied. "Speaking of that," she continued, "can I depend on you for a small donation for our illustrious Christian Women's Association?"

Mrs. Clayton smiled and said, "Well, I'll have to think about it."

Miss Clara straightened her posture and didn't say anything for a moment.

"Very well then. I need two pounds of flour, please."

"That will be sixty cents." Mrs. Clayton told her.

"Sixty cents? Why so much?" Miss Clara thought of herself as someone who deserved special treatment.

"The War is coming to an end soon. Goods are in short supply, the times are changing, and so is the cost of living."

Reluctantly, Miss Clara agreed to pay the sixty cents. Annoyed that her initial expectations were not met and frustrated with the additional expense, she composed herself and curtly added, "I'll see you at worship in the morning, Mrs. Clayton." When she walked out the door, she paused and glanced at Gabe. With her nose in the air, she said, "Have a good day, sir."

To which Gabe smiled and responded, "Yes, ma'am. I'll think about it." That set Miss Clara's nose a little higher as she turned and stomped off. Gabe laughed to himself and stepped back inside.

"I can see you had the honor of meeting Miss Clara Wells."

"We had a 'Miss Clara' back home. I didn't know she lived here, too," Gabe replied with a smile.

Mrs. Clayton knew right then that she was going to like Gabe MacCallan.

"You can call me Emma."

"May I call you Miss Emma?" Gabe asked.

"Miss Emma will do fine," she replied.

Throughout the day, people came and went. Before long, Gabe was managing things. Everyone seemed to find Gabe pleasant and helpful. Emma went about her business as usual. When five o'clock came, she said he could quit for the day and would see him at church in the morning.

"Where is the church?" Gabe asked.

"It's near our farm. Mrs. Adair will bring you."

Gabe walked down the uneven street towards the Adair house, its surface marred by wagon ruts from the winter.

A few people were out and about, even though shops were closing for the day. This was his first survey of the town. *Several taverns to be such a small town*, he thought to himself. Suddenly, he heard gunfire and shouting coming from Market Street, just one block away. He became curious about the noise, so he walked over to see what it was. He saw two men riding on horseback, whooping and shooting into the air just to create mischief. They were not causing any harm until they reached the harness shop where they stopped. Gabe watched as both men dismounted and staggered into the shop. Struggling to make out the sounds, he ran across the street, reaching the west side of the building. He could hear the shop owner pleading with them to stop what they were doing. It sounded as if they were tearing the place apart when the door swung open, and the shop owner rolled onto the plank porch as if he had been thrown out.

"Please! Please!" The shop owner begged, "Don't do this."

One of the men had a leather strap, doubled it, and began whipping the poor fellow while the other man stood by, laughing. Just then, Gabe stepped from around the corner of the building.

"That will do!" he said with a voice of authority.

The menacing figure with the leather strap had his back turned to Gabe. He stopped whipping the shop owner when he heard the voice behind him and turned around red-faced with rage. Seizing the chance, the shop owner quickly scrambled into the shop. When the man turned to see Gabe, he saw a tall, lean, wide-shouldered, unarmed man. However, the tormenter could not make out Gabe's face, only his silhouette, because the sun was setting behind Gabe.

"Just who in tarnation are you?" the swine of a man growled as he walked up to within a few feet of Gabe.

"I said that will do!" Gabe repeated himself but with a little more force.

"Mister, maybe you need a lesson 'bout stickin' yer nose where it don't belong," the man replied angrily. With the tightly gripped leather strap in his hand, he unleashed its force upon Gabe. Gabe swiftly coiled the strap around his right wrist and forearm. In fluid, forceful motion, Gabe pulled the man to him, snatched his revolver from its holster with his left hand, and delivered a bone-breaking high kick to the man's rib section. The force of the blow sent him tumbling backward, gasping for breath, and crashing to the floor in front of the other man. It all happened so fast that the other fellow had no time to react. When they glanced up, Gabe had cocked the hammer on the revolver and was aiming the end of the barrel at the head of the one still standing.

"Get outta town!" Gabe demanded. As quick as a couple of scared cats, they mounted their horses.

"You ain't seen the last, mister!" one yelled as they rode away in a full gallop. Gabe went into the shop to check on the owner. By this time, several people were in the street, having witnessed the whole thing.

"Sir, are you alright?" Gabe asked the shop owner as he entered the shop.

"Just a few cuts and bruises," the owner replied, still trying to catch his breath. "You sure handled them two. What's your name, young man?"

"MacCallan. My name is Gabe MacCallan."

"Mr. MacCallan, I'm much obliged. There's been a lot of this sort'a thing going on for some time now."

"Who's the sheriff here?" Gabe asked.

"Sheriff Wells," he replied, "but his hands are full. Bushwhackers and outlaws claiming to be Confederate soldiers ride here occasionally, shooting up the place. The sheriff is a good, God-fearing man, but outnumbered."

"Those two weren't wearing uniforms," Gabe said as he examined the gun he had taken from them. "On the other hand, this revolver is standard Confederate issue, an 1851 Colt Navy." He turned his attention back to the shop owner. "I'll help you back home."

"I live behind the shop," the owner stated as he sat on a nearby stool. Just then, upset and frightened, a lady ran to him from the back of the shop.

"This man saved my life," he told her, explaining what happened. "My name is James Miller. This is my wife, Isabel."

"Thank you, thank you, young man," she said, wiping tears from her face.

Gabe turned to see a small crowd gathering outside. A few were beginning to come in to help. Gabe walked through the small crowd without saying a word. Whisperers were heard asking, "Who is he? Where did he come from?"

Gabe left the curious crowd and went back to the Adair House without looking back. Alice and Lizzie were seated on the porch. Alice asked, "Did you enjoy your day?"

"It was interesting," Gabe replied, concealing the revolver in his belt behind his back.

"We heard gunshots down toward the taverns. I hope you weren't nearby," Lizzie said with a voice of concern.

"It was just a couple of drunks that were run out of town. No one was seriously hurt," Gabe told them.

"Supper is ready if you're hungry," Lizzie said. "We were just waiting for you to arrive."

"That sounds good, ma'am. I've worked up a good appetite," Gabe replied.

After Supper and before turning in, he opened his father's Bible. The passage that lay open before him was Ezekiel 22:30. "And I sought for a man among them, that should make up the hedge, and stand in the gap before me for the land, that I should not destroy it: but I found none."

He laid the revolver next to his Bible and blew out the lamp flame.

3

Sundays were always busy for Gabe's family, so he was up and ready by five. The house was a little quieter than the day before, so he went into the dining room, sat at the table, and began reading his Bible. After a few minutes, Lizzie entered the dining room from the kitchen. She was tying her apron when she noticed Gabe.

"Mr. Gabe," she said, surprised to see him this early on a Sunday morning. "I apologize. Didn't figure on you being up this early today, and I didn't get you any fresh water this morning."

"That's okay, Miss Lizzie," Gabe said and smiled to ease her mind.

"I'll put on some coffee," she replied quickly. "Miss Alice will be in shortly. We'll have breakfast, then start Sunday dinner to take with us to church."

Shortly after, Mrs. Adair entered the room. "Good morning, Mr. MacCallan. You are certainly an early riser this morning."

"Good morning, Mrs. Adair."

"Please call me Alice."

"Sunday for my family was a busy day," Gabe said with a smile. "We always had to get an early start. Mrs. Clayton has invited me to worship this morning, and she said you could help me find the location."

"We will take you there," she replied. "We worship there, too."

As Gabe and Alice visited, Lizzie could be heard in the kitchen singing as she prepared breakfast.

"Lizzie loves to sing," Alice said.

Gabe listened to her sweet voice singing familiar hymns. "Tell me about Lizzie," Gabe inquired.

Alice glanced toward the kitchen. "Lizzie has been with me for ten years." Alice's expression changed from a smile to sadness as she gazed down at her coffee cup and recalled unpleasant days. "She and her mother were on the block for auction in St. Louis. Lizzie was about 12 years old. A buyer wanted Lizzie's mother, but he didn't want the child. Watching them take Lizzie from her mother's arms was heart-wrenching. Lizzie fought as any child would be expected. Gabe, I had a personal mission. I purchased negro slaves to buy their freedom. That's why I was there—to buy Lizzie and her mother's freedom. I approached the man who bought Lizzie. He agreed to sell her, but I had to pay three times the amount he paid. This left me unable to purchase her mother."

"Were you able to find her mother?" Gabe asked.

"She was taken to Arkansas. That's all I could find out," she replied.

"But Lizzie is your servant," Gabe said.

"Lizzie is a servant to everyone because she wants to be, not because she has to be," she replied as she proudly glanced toward the kitchen. "She's as much a daughter to me as I am a mother to her. I've taught her everything I know, and in return, she has taught me. I wish her mother could see her today. When I am gone, everything I have will go to her."

After having breakfast, with the food all prepared and everyone ready, they all rode together on a buckboard for a short distance south, beyond the railroad tracks near Sam Clayton's farm. By the time they arrived, several people were already there, including Miss Clara, who was always taking mental notes on who was or wasn't there. Emma welcomed everyone and was especially glad when she saw Gabe, Alice, and Lizzie.

"Good morning, Gabe, Alice, and Lizzie," Emma said as she greeted them.

"Good morning, Miss Emma," Lizzie replied.

"Gabe, let me show you around," Emma said. "This building is what we call the Tabernacle."

The Tabernacle was an open-air pole structure. At the center of the room was a coal-burning stove with a flue pipe extending through the center of the hip-style roof. Its design was shaped like an octagon, measuring about seventy feet wide. Tent canvas could be draped along the sides and secured to the ground using timber poles. Benches were placed in seven sections with sawdust covering the ground.

"There is a reason the Tabernacle is an octagon," Emma explained.

"Eight is the number for resurrection. There are seven sections of benches, and the men sit on one side and the women and children on the other. The number seven in the Bible represents the day the Lord rested after creation and is the number for completion. The east side of the Tabernacle is where we have the Lord's Supper table and the pulpit on a raised platform."

Gabe was fascinated with the way everything was laid out with a biblical pattern in mind.

"Brother Clayton won't be back until tomorrow, so Brother Carver will be speaking this morning," she said. "Brother Thompson will lead our singing, and our shepherds will lead us in observing the Lord's Supper. That's my brother-in-law, Silas Clayton, over there. He is one of the shepherds. His wife, Betsy, is around here somewhere. Afterward, we will have dinner on the ground. You will have to try my special sweet potato pie."

Gabe was being greeted by many in the crowd when he noticed a young lady who had also noticed him. It was Hannah Clayton, Silas, and Betsy Clayton's daughter. She was talking with two of her friends. Hannah was a beautiful young woman with dark brown wavy hair. Her dark eyes and dark-complected skin added to her beauty. When she smiled, a dimple appeared in her cheek. Her face flushed with shyness when she realized that Gabe had noticed her noticing him. They exchanged smiles before taking their respective seats. It was a full day of singing, preaching, and baptizing penitent sinners into Christ at a nearby creek.

Later, Alice, Gabe, and Lizzie returned to the house, where they rested on the front porch.

"I think I'll take a walk," Gabe said.

"Don't stay out long, Mr. Gabe. We will have leftover apple pie," Lizzie told him.

"Yes, ma'am. I won't."

Gabe crossed the street and made his way down toward the taverns where he had experienced an encounter with two bushwhackers. He found that only one of the taverns was open for business. Gabe had no intention of going there for a drink; he always steered clear of alcohol. The Sabbath Law, commonly known as the Blue Law, prohibited saloons and taverns from opening on Sundays. However, the law was sometimes ignored in western towns where the law was not heavily enforced. His purpose was to observe this den of iniquity that served as a haven for the kind of scoundrels he ran out of town the day before.

Gabe located a bench outside of a storefront and sat down, positioning himself across the street from the tavern. Laughter, cursing, and yelling poured from inside the tavern doors, mingled with dense tobacco smoke. As Gabe focused his gaze on those entering and leaving, a gentleman approached and tested the doorknob of the storefront. Gabe had been keeping an eye on him, too, watching his movements from one door to another. Acknowledging the man's presence, Gabe glanced at him as he settled himself at the opposite end of the bench.

"You're Gabe MacCallan, I hear," the man said as he looked toward the tavern.

"Yes, sir," Gabe responded, raising an eyebrow and casting a sidelong glance at the man. He pondered as to how this stranger knew his name.

"My name is Thomas Wells, the town sheriff," he said as he introduced himself. "I heard about what you did for the Millers yesterday, and they were grateful for your timely intervention. I believe you also met my wife yesterday, Clara." Gabe raised his eyebrow once more, this time with a sense of sympathy.

"Those two you ran out of town are probably from a camp gang between here and Columbus, some of Bloody Bill Anderson's men. Thank the Lord above, Anderson was killed a while back, but Little Archie Clement took his place. Some joined Clement, and some didn't."

The sheriff cut a plug of tobacco with his pocket knife, looked over to Gabe, and remarked, "You've certainly made yourself a reputation in a short amount of time, both good and bad, it seems. I'm looking for good men to help me clean out that thicket of bushwhackers." Gabe directed his gaze towards the sheriff, having a feeling about where he was going with his comment.

"I take it that you want me to help? You don't even know me," Gabe questioned.

"You chased those two murderers out of town without firing a single shot. That's enough for me," the sheriff responded. "Stay in Warrensburg a while. Take your time to think it over. I will be around."

With that, the sheriff stood up to leave. As he did, he tipped his hat. "Good meetin' you, Mr. MacCallan."

"You as well, Sheriff Wells," Gabe replied with slight confusion about this strange introduction.

Gabe maintained his watchful eye on the tavern, his mind occupied with his brief conversation. Not long after the sheriff's departure, four men rode up, tethered their horses to the hitching rail, and stepped onto the tavern's porch. One of the men looked up and down the street, then across the street. He caught sight of Gabe. Hard, shrewd eyes locked onto Gabe's. After a lingering gaze, Gabe rose to his feet and walked away. The man watched as Gabe rose from his seat and departed. He kept his eyes on Gabe for a minute and then entered the tavern.

The four men found an available table and sat down. The room wasn't large, only about twenty-four feet wide by thirty. The bar was half the length of the room. The proprietor was a German named Ben Werner. He sold beer and whiskey but specialized in moonshine. Women were never in the establishment due to the risky environment. There were ten men standing along the bar because most of the tables were filled. A few men were standing around, letting off steam. The air was thick with tobacco smoke and a stale odor.

"Jonah!" Ben shouted. Set four glasses and a jar of shine for those men over there."

Jonah was a slave that Ben won in a poker game in Jefferson City in '62. His former master was a gambler from New Orleans. He had too much to drink during a game and lost all of his cash. Ben laid down his winning hand and said, "I'll take that buck you brought with you instead of cash." Jonah has worked for Ben ever since.

Lane Shaw, Jim "Red" Kinsley, Earl Wilson, and William "Shorty" Harris were the men at the table. These men rode with Bloody Bill Anderson until he was killed last fall. After his death, they, and some others like Lane Shaw, splintered off into small bands of bushwhackers. It was Lane Shaw who spotted Gabe outside. Jonah set the table and overheard part of their conversation.

"Did you boys see that fella sittin' 'cross the street when we rode in?" Shaw asked them.

"I didn't see nobody," Wilson answered.

"You know that fella that ran Jones and Parker out of town yesterday? I think that was him," Shaw said.

"Well, let's go get him," Shorty said as he stood up.

"Sit down," Shaw demanded. "We need to learn more about him instead of going off with some half-cocked notion. If he's some kind of a Good Samaritan, we'll need to create an opportunity."

As they drank and talked over a plan, Jonah swept the floor and cleaned a nearby table, but he listened to every word.

Back at the Adair House, Gabe arrived just in time to savor a slice of apple pie with a steaming pot of coffee. He, Alice, and Lizzie spent the evening enjoying each other's company, sharing stories, and getting to know one another. Later, Gabe retired to his room and read his Bible. Lying in bed, he pondered the recent events, particularly his acquaintance with Sheriff Wells and the intriguing offer on the table. As the late-night songs of a mockingbird serenaded him, he drifted off to sleep. His Bible lay open at Psalm 122:1. The scripture his father had underlined read, "I was glad when they said unto me, let us go into the house of the Lord."

4

Sam Clayton had traveled to Jefferson City to participate in a delegation of preachers. They gathered to make an appeal to the state legislature against a "loyalty oath," a proposed amendment that would become part of the New Constitution of Missouri, soon to be put to a vote. While they were thrilled about the abolition of slavery as a part of the new law of the land, they were not thrilled about the loyalty oath. This new law would require all preachers, teachers, and public servants to take an oath to be loyal to the state. It would also require a person to swear that they had never taken up arms against the state of Missouri during the War. Anyone who refused to take the oath would be stripped of the right to hold public office, serve as a preacher, or teach in any capacity, public or private. To beat it all, they faced fines and imprisonment as felons. There was also a proposed restriction placed on property that churches could own.

Sam returned home frustrated with his delegation's lack of progress with the legislature. He arrived back in Warrensburg on the Missouri Pacific Railroad at about mid-afternoon. As he was walking past the clerk's office, he stopped when he noticed that the front page of the *Daily Missouri Republican* newspaper was tacked to the wall of the depot. In large bold print, it read, *Jeff Davis, Captured.*

"Finally," he said out loud. "I needed some good news today." Another man standing nearby commented, "Hopefully, that will be the last nail in the coffin for the Confederacy."

"I hope so," Sam replied, "but what lies ahead is going to be a hard row to hoe, I'm afraid."

Back at the store, Gabe was taking care of business. Emma had no worries about him because he had taken to being a merchant like a duck to water. A couple of young women were in the store doing what young women do. It's best to let them alone as they examine everything in the store. Once in a while, there would be a glance from Gabe to them and they to him. They giggled and whispered. The young lady in the blue dress was Sarah McGuire. Her family was quite prominent in the town. Her father's family came from Ireland during the potato famine. Although she was a native-born American, her accent still carried a distinct Irish lilt. Sarah was a beautiful redhead with blue eyes. Her blue dress made her eyes stand out even more. The other young lady was Hannah Clayton, who had caught Gabe's eye at church. Hannah came to the store primarily because of Gabe. He was all she had thought about since Sunday.

The Clayton family migrated from central Kentucky to Missouri around ten years ago. Hannah possessed that inherent Clayton-Kentuckian spirit, which Gabe found attractive. The two young ladies finished browsing and walked to the counter with the merchandise they wanted. Gabe was usually able to overcome his shyness, but not this time. No words were exchanged between him and the ladies, just glances, mostly between Hannah and Gabe. Gabe handed Hannah her change and offered to walk her and her friend to the door. She smiled and said yes. He held the door open for them. With one last smile and a glance from Hannah, she said, "I hope to see you at church next Sunday."

"I will? I mean… Yes. I'd like that," Gabe replied bashfully.

A few minutes later, Sam entered the store to find Gabe standing at the front, staring out the window. "What's the matter, son? You look like you lost somethin' and can't remember where you put it."

"No, sir. I may have just found her," he replied before he thought.

"Good," Sam responded, not catching all of what Gabe said. "Tell me how things have been for you the past couple of days." For the next few hours, Gabe and Sam restocked the back storage room, with Gabe having to endure Sam's complaining about what happened in Jefferson City.

Later that afternoon, at the Adair House, there was a knock on the rear door of the kitchen as Lizzie was getting supper ready. She opened the door, and to her surprise, it was Jonah, the servant who worked for

Ben at the tavern.

"Jonah?"

"Miss Lizzie," Jonah stammered urgently. "I ain't got much time. You need to warn Mr. Gabe."

"Mr. Gabe? Warn him about what?" Lizzie inquired.

"There's some bad men out to get him, Miss Lizzie. I overheard 'em talkin' yesterday."

"Are you saying Mr. Gabe was at Ben's tavern?" Lizzie asked, raising her voice.

"No! No! That ain't what I mean. He must've did somethin' to them men. They aim to hurt him, maybe kill him, Miss Lizzie." Jonah told her everything he had heard. "I got to go," Jonah said anxiously. "Please tell Mr. Gabe to be careful."

"I will, Jonah. You take care, too, you hear?" Lizzie told him.

"Yes, ma'am," he replied before hurrying away.

Lizzie closed the door, confused and not knowing what to do. *Miss Alice will know*, she said to herself. Lizzie quickly removed a pot of green beans from the wood stove, closed the flue damper, and hurried into the drawing room. As she rounded the dining room corner, Gabe stepped through the front door.

"Mr. Gabe!" He could tell that something serious was on her mind.

"What is it, Lizzie?"

"Come with me," she said as she hurried into the drawing room. Alice glanced up from her book as Lizzie and Gabe entered the room.

She said, "This must be important, from the looks of the two of you."

Wringing her hands in her apron, Lizzie began telling what had just happened. "Miss Alice, Jonah came to the back door a few moments ago. He was a terrible mess. He told me that he overheard some men yesterday, and they are planning to do some harm to Mr. Gabe."

"What?" Gabe asked with a tone of concern.

"What did Jonah say?" Alice asked as she stood up from her seat.

"They plan to send a message claiming that Mr. Miller and the sheriff wish to meet Mr. Gabe at Miller's harness shop. They intend to wait for him and plan to ambush him."

"When? Did he know?" Gabe asked.

"He said two days from now at closing time," Lizzie replied.

Alice looked at Gabe, seeing the concern in his eyes. "Gabe, is this about what happened with the Millers the day after you arrived? News travels quickly in this small town."

"Seems so," Gabe replied.

"We should alert Sheriff Wells," Lizzie insisted.

"No!" Gabe replied sharply. "I beg your pardon, Miss Alice and Miss Lizzie. I want the two of you to keep this to yourselves. Don't mention this to anyone, especially the Millers. If these fellas catch wind that the sheriff is involved, they will know they have been tipped off, and they might trace it back to Jonah, putting him and the Millers in danger."

"But surely you don't plan to face them alone, if at all?" Miss Alice asked, insisting that he change his mind.

Gabe's anger started to kindle. "These men have met their match this time," Gabe reassured with confidence.

"I don't like the sound of that, Gabe," Miss Alice remarked.

"Miss Alice, I started this. Who else is gonna finish it?"

The following day, Gabe finished his breakfast. Alice and Lizzie didn't say much until Alice couldn't stand it any longer. "What do you plan to do, Gabe?"

Gabe took a sip of his coffee and thought for a minute.

"I wish you would take this to Sam Clayton," Alice pleaded.

Gabe stood and put on his hat. "Alright, Miss Alice. I'll talk with Sam. Don't worry. This bunch isn't going to hurt anyone," Gabe reassured her.

Gabe arrived at work on time but had an obvious look of worry on his face. "Sam, I have something important to talk to you about and need your advice."

"I've already heard," Sam interrupted.

Gabe looked surprised at Sam's response. Sam motioned and said, "Come with me to the back." Emma was working the front of the store, and he didn't want her to hear their conversation.

"What have you heard?" Gabe asked.

"Jonah came by yesterday as I was closing just after you left. He was running an errand for that no-good scoundrel, Ben Werner. So, he came by here to warn you. He told me all about what he heard, and I told him to hurry to Miss Alice's to let you know. It appears that you got the message. It looks like you got yourself in some hot water, son."

Gabe asked, "What should I do?"

"We'll let Sheriff Wells know, but not today. Today and tomorrow, we go about business as usual." Sam moved a section of shelving out of the way, revealing a small door in the wall, and opened it. Reaching into the hidden compartment, he removed something wrapped in a linen cloth. As Sam unfolded the wrapping, he presented a holstered gun and belt. It was a .36 caliber Colt Paterson revolver, beautifully engraved with an ivory handle. The Paterson revolver helped win the war with the Comanches in Texas and the Mexican War. It had a five-shot revolving cylinder with a seven-and-a-half-inch barrel.

"That's a beautiful piece," Gabe said as he eased it from its finely crafted holster.

"Did you serve in the army during the Mexican-American War?" Gabe asked him.

"I was one of several thousand Kentuckians who volunteered for the war with Mexico," Sam replied as he turned toward the wall and reached for a sword, still belted and sheathed. Sam continued. "I was assigned to the Kentucky Cavalry unit," he said as he placed the blade on the table.

"Does your service explain the limp?" Gabe asked.

Sam nodded. "At the Battle of Cerro Gordo, led by Captain John Williams, I was hit by shrapnel, a piece of it is still in my leg," Sam said. He carefully placed the sword back on the wall and wrapped the gun and holster, but he didn't put the Paterson back into its safe place. Instead, he placed the gun under his arm. "It looks like I may need this," he said as they walked back into the store where Emma was tending to customers.

"There you both are," she said as Sam casually walked over to the counter near the guns and ammo. He placed the revolver under the counter and out of sight without her noticing.

Gabe went quietly about his business for the remainder of the day. His thoughts were consumed by the unwanted events that were unfolding. He wished he had not been so curious and minded his business that Saturday evening. But he also knew it could have ended tragically if he hadn't intervened. The Millers might have been killed if he had not investigated the commotion. He was struggling with the thought of how quickly things changed. Now, innocent people could get hurt or worse. The last thing he wanted was to make matters worse with his involvement. Yet, he knew that justice is never neutral, especially when the lives of the helpless are at risk. It was Abraham Lincoln who wisely said, "To sin by silence when people should protest makes cowards of men." Gabe MacCallan was one of those who refused to be silent and do nothing.

He was not a novice when it came to conflict. He had experienced several engagements during the War. Even as a conscientious objector, he would rise to the occasion, doing whatever was necessary to protect the lives of his fellow soldiers. He had taken lives to save others. All he wanted was to live a quiet life and mind his business. However, if conflict persisted, he was always prepared to settle it. And now, the moment had arrived to face yet another unwelcome challenge.

After a quiet supper, Gabe rested in his room, searching within himself about what to do. He opened his Bible for comfort and guidance. He found Romans 13:3-4 which read, "For rulers are not a terror to good works, but to the evil. Wilt thou then not be afraid of the power? Do that which is good, and thou shalt have praise of the same: for he is the minister of God to thee for good. But if thou do that which is evil, be afraid; for he beareth not the sword in vain: for he is the minister of God, a revenger to execute wrath upon him that doeth evil."

Gabe prayed, asking that he might act as God's avenger to execute wrath upon those who do evil, to give him the wisdom and strength he needed. Gabe slept, but not peacefully that night.

5

The news was beginning the trickle down to Warrensburg from Lexington that guerrillas had begun negotiations for their surrender. Although some refused to give up, many bushwhackers were tired of running. Those who refused to surrender fled to Texas. Even Little Archie Clement and his notorious bunch of cut-throats that included the James brothers, fled the state. This meant fewer hiding places and fewer allies to protect them. The camp gangs became outlaws on the run, turning their attention to bank and train robberies. Such were the likes of Lane Shaw and his murderous outfit.

It was mid-morning the day after Gabe was informed about the plot, and Shaw's men were preparing to ambush MacCallan. Jones and Parker were chomping at the bit. The night before, they nearly came to blows arguing over who would have the pleasure of killing him. Shaw managed to find out Gabe's full name, which wasn't difficult considering how townspeople gossip, but Shaw nicknamed him *the Samaritan*. Shaw made arrangements to have a message dropped off for Gabe. Wilson paid one of the boys in town ten cents to drop it off at Clayton's store. The note read,

Mr. MacCallan, your company is requested this afternoon, May 17th, after closing. I am your obedient servant, Mr. Miller.

Emma received it while Gabe and Sam were paying a visit with the Millers, as Gabe told them about Shaw's plan.

"What can I do?" Mr. Miller asked desperately.

"You need to leave the shop now," Sam told him. "You and Mrs. Miller can wait at the Adair House until all of this is over. We will come back here shortly and wait for them to show up."

"When you say *we*, does Sheriff Wells know about this?" Mrs. Miller asked. "He should be involved if this gets out of hand," Mr. Miller added.

"We plan to pay him a visit after we leave here, but we wanted you to know first," Sam reassured them. The Millers turned to each other with concern but with approval.

"Good," Gabe said. "Sam and I will be back as quickly as we can." The Millers closed the shop and hurried out the back way.

It was noon by the time Sam and Gabe mounted their horses and rode for the town square in Old Town, where the sheriff's office was located. Sheriff Wells was stepping out of the door. He had a routine of dining at the Bolton Hotel, a popular spot for locals and travelers passing through town.

"Sheriff Wells!" Gabe called out. "We need to have a word with you." The sheriff saw that it was Gabe and Sam.

"Join me at the hotel," the sheriff replied. They entered the hotel dining room, sat down, and told the sheriff everything.

"It sounds like Lane Shaw and his gang," the sheriff said. "Shaw is a mad dog, especially when he's on a hunt, and a clever fox, unlike those fools that run with him," the sheriff said as he leaned back in his chair. "He's the smart one. I've been hoping he would get tangled up in a clash with Union soldiers, meet his end, or be captured."

The sheriff took a sip of his black coffee. "It seems he knows your whereabouts, Gabe, which means he has had someone watching you since last Monday morning."

"If that's true," Gabe said, "then we've made a mistake by coming here with you. Shaw will be tipped off."

Sam took off his hat and mopped his head with his neck rag. "That changes everything," he said to Gabe.

"What now?" Gabe asked.

"Gabe, how many did you see at the tavern Sunday afternoon when Shaw showed up?" the sheriff asked.

"Three, not countin' Shaw," Gabe replied.

The sheriff stood and paced the floor, scratching his head and rubbing his brow. "Let's reckon there are at least six of 'em," the sheriff said as he sat back down. "Supposin' Shaw gets tipped off," he muttered, "They'll be expectin' an ambush at the Millers, so we gotta do what they'll never expect."

"Which is?" Sam asked.

"We won't show up," the sheriff said as he sat back down. "You said the Millers will be at the Adair House, right?"

"That's right," Gabe replied.

The sheriff continued. "Shaw would never put all of his eggs in one basket. When they discover no one is at Miller's store, I believe Shaw and his men will split up and show up at Sam's store and the Adair House. Sam, we'll need Silas. The two of you protect your property at the store. Make sure Miss Emma is safe. Gabe, you and I will go to the Adair House."

With that, Sam rose and quickly went out the door.

"Gabe, do you have a weapon?" the sheriff asked.

"I managed to take a Colt Navy from one of Shaw's men," Gabe said.

"Let's go back to my office," the sheriff said.

Right then, the waitress brought out his dinner. "That'll have to wait, Miss Abby," the sheriff said as he grabbed a piece of cornbread, and the two hurried back to his office. Once inside, the sheriff opened the gun case.

"Here's a box of .36 caliber balls, caps, powder, and a holster that will fit the Colt."

It was now 1:15 in the afternoon. Gabe and the sheriff rode quickly to the Adair house, tethered their horses at the rear of the house, and well out of sight. Lizzie met them at the kitchen door.

"Mr. Gabe! Sheriff Wells!" She was not pleasantly surprised to see them together.

"Where are the Millers and Miss Alice?" the sheriff asked.

"They are in the drawing room. I'm about to serve coffee."

Gabe and the sheriff hurried into the room with Lizzie close behind them. Alice and the Millers glanced up with surprise when they entered the room.

"Is it over?" Mrs. Miller asked.

"No, ma'am," Gabe said. "I am afraid there has been a change of plans. We have reason to believe that they will come here, and we also have reason to believe that they know Sheriff Wells is involved now. We need you all to move to safety. Do you have a place to go until this is over?"

Lizzie spoke up. "I do! The Tabernacle!"

"Quickly!" Gabe insisted, "Get to the buckboard and go to the Tabernacle." Lizzie hurried out to the carriage house as Gabe rushed upstairs to his room to retrieve the Colt Navy revolver. He descended the stairs to the dining room table, where Gabe emptied the gun and reloaded the cylinder with fresh caps and powder. He strapped on his gun belt and made sure that everyone made their way to safety.

In the meantime, Sam had arrived at Silas' farm west of town. Betsy, Silas' wife, had been working in the garden and was about to enter the house.

"Betsy, where's Silas?" Sam asked.

"He's at the corn crib," she replied, but noticed something was wrong. "Why?" she asked.

Without explaining, Sam swiftly spun his horse around toward the crib. Silas saw him coming in a hurry and walked out to greet him.

"Silas, we've got ourselves a heap of trouble. Come with me. I will explain on the way."

Silas saddled his horse as quickly as he could. From inside the house, Betsy heard the gallop of hooves rapidly going down the lane, and she ran to the door. *I wonder what's happened,* she said to herself. "Hannah!" She called toward the kitchen. "Watch Eli. I'll be back shortly."

It was about 2:30 in the afternoon when Sam and Silas arrived at the store. "Sister Clayton!" He always addressed his wife in such a way. "There might be trouble."

"Trouble? What trouble?" She asked as Sam went behind the counter to where he had placed his Paterson revolver a couple of days ago. But it wasn't there.

"Are you looking for this?" Emma walked over to the corner of the room and brought it out of a cupboard. "You didn't think I noticed the other day, did you?" she scolded. "Don't you know that after forty-three years, you can't pull the wool over my eyes?" She was not smiling this time, then handed him the gun with the note that had come earlier.

"This note did not come from the Millers," Sam told her. "It's a trap. There is a gang coming after Gabe," he said as he strapped on the gun belt. "You need to go home where it's safe. The Millers, Miss Alice, and Miss Lizzie might show up there."

"Why would that be? What's Gabe have to do with this?" she asked.

"It has something to do with what happened last week. We suspect the gang will split into two groups, one to show up here and the other at the Adair House. Gabe and the sheriff are there now, while Silas and I hunker down here."

While Gabe and the sheriff were at the Adair House, Red Kinsley walked into Ben's tavern and sat at a corner table. He and Earl Wilson had been tailing Gabe for a few days unnoticed. Kinsley came to the tavern to wait because Wilson had ridden back to warn Shaw about the sheriff's involvement and a possible ambush at Miller's harness shop. How Gabe and the preacher learned about their plans remained a mystery to him. Just then, Jonah set the table with a glass and a bottle of moonshine.

"Not right now, Jonah," he said, so Jonah took the glass and the moonshine back to the bar. "Jonah, where's Ben?"

"He's in the back, sir," Jonah replied. "Can I fetch him fer ya?"

"Jonah, you know the War is over," Kinsley said as he placed his hat on the table.

"Yes, sir," Jonah responded. "That's what I hear'd."

"You are free now. Do you know what you'll do?" Kinsley asked him.

"I reckon I ain't thought on it, sir," Jonah said as he took the broom and started sweeping the floor. Ben didn't allow him to stand and gab with the customers. At least with a broom in his hand, he appeared to be working.

Kinsley continued, "President Johnson is offering amnesty to any rebel who surrenders."

"Amnesty, sir?" Jonah asked.

"That's a fancy word meaning that if a man surrenders, he can go free, but only if he agrees to stop fightin'," Kinsley explained. He paused as if deep in thought for a moment. "I'm tired of fightin', Jonah. I'm tired of the killin'. I'm tired of runnin'. I want to be free of all of that."

Jonah stopped sweeping for a moment as he listened. He glanced at Kinsley from the corner of his eye and said, "Sounds like we both want to be free then."

Kinsley looked up at Jonah as he turned and walked to the bar. It was then that Kinsley realized who the informant was. He suddenly recalled how Jonah was sweeping the floor near them as Shaw talked openly about their plan to get Gabe. Kinsley took his hat, rose, and walked slowly to the bar.

"Jonah, I think I'll have that shot of shine you offered after all." Jonah poured Kinsley a drink. Kinsley threw it back in his throat and set the glass down hard on the bar. He looked up at Jonah with sternness in his face, a look of resolution. "Jonah," he said sternly.

"Yes, sir." Jonah could see a change in Kinsley's expression, sending a cold chill over him.

"You are a better man than I am." Then he paid for his drink, and without another word, he walked out the door, leaving Jonah puzzled by his behavior.

From Ben's tavern, Kinsley rode to Clayton's store, dismounted, and tied his horse to the rail. He stood outside and yelled, "Preacher! We need to talk. Just you and me."

Sam stepped out of the store and onto the front porch.

"When somebody comes needin' to talk to the preacher, most of the time, they're not intendin' to use a revolver," Sam said coolly and spat his chew of tobacco off the edge of the porch.

Kinsley raised his hands and said, "I'm not hostile. I mean no harm. Can I come in?" Sam was cautious but believed him and said, "Come inside."

Kinsley stepped onto the porch. He paused as Sam insisted on following him in. "Shaw knows," Kinsley said. "Wilson has gone back to tell him. The plan was to meet at the harness shop, but Shaw knows no one will be there. I'm done with this, Preacher. This ain't my fight, and I plan to take the amnesty deal offered by Commander Dodge."

"Alright then," Sam responded. "This is what you are goin' to do. This is called works of repentance." For the next few minutes, Sam laid out a new plan.

It was now 3:05 in the afternoon. Clouds were beginning to gather as a storm was brewing in the southwest. Wilson fired his pistol before he arrived near the camp to let the gang know he was coming.

"Something's up," Wilson told Shaw. "Me and Red saw the Samaritan and the preacher go to the harness shop and then to the sheriff. Then the preacher rode out of town in a hurry, while the Samaritan and the sheriff rode toward the house where he's a stayin'.'"

"They are on to us," Shaw said. "Where's Red?"

"He's goin' to meet us at the harness shop," Wilson replied.

"Jones, Parker, Shorty," Shaw summoned. "Once we meet up with Red, the three of you head to the preacher's store. If no one is there, meet us at the house where the Samaritan is stayin'," Shaw ordered. "Wilson, Red, and I will be there." Just then, Shaw heard the distant rumble of thunder. "A storm is coming," he remarked. "Let's get going!" They mounted and rode hard down Lexington Road toward Warrensburg.

At Clayton's store, Sam, Silas, and Kinsley agreed on what they would do. Kinsley would meet up with the gang as planned, but not reveal that Sam and Silas had gone to the Adair House to meet with Gabe and the sheriff. When they rode up, Sheriff Wells knew something was wrong.

"What is it?" the sheriff asked as he and Gabe stepped off the front porch.

"The tables have turned," Silas told them as he and Sam dismounted their horses. Then, Sam proceeded to tell them about their meeting with Kinsley and the revised plan concerning him.

"Kinsley? Can he be trusted? What if this is just another ambush? We'd be like fish in a barrel," Gabe said in a raised voice.

"We can trust him," Sam assured. "Otherwise, he'll either become a fugitive or get killed, and he wants neither one."

"How will we recognize Kinsley? What if he is accidentally killed?" Gabe asked.

"That's a chance he is willing to take," Silas replied.

"I know who Kinsley is," the sheriff said. "I can identify him. Bring your horses around back to the carriage house."

After taking care of the horses, they went into the house. Sam and Gabe positioned themselves in the kitchen near the back door. Silas and the sheriff set themselves upstairs in Gabe's room, where the windows faced the street. It was five o'clock in the afternoon when the gang rode into town to the harness shop where Kinsley was waiting.

"Anyone here?" Shaw wanted to know.

"No! They are on to us. They are either at Clayton's store or held up at the house where the Samaritan is stayin'," Kinsley told them. "The sheriff and the preacher are with him."

"Jones, Parker, Shorty, go check the store!" Shaw ordered, motioning for them to move out. Then the three of them took off to Clayton's store. Shaw told Kinsley, "You, me, and Wilson will go to the house."

The rain had begun to fall, and lightning flashed across the sky. Jones, Parker, and Shorty arrived at the store. Shorty positioned himself on one side of the door while Parker took the other. Jones kicked the door open, and the three of them stormed inside. With guns drawn, they searched the entire store, only to find no one there. They worked their way around to the back room.

"Ain't nobody here," Parker told the other two. "Let's grab some of them there weapons and ammo we seen out front before we leave."

As they rounded the corner toward the front, they were met with two 12-gauge double-barrel shotguns held by Emma and Betsy Clayton.

"Drop them guns!" Emma demanded.

Startled by seeing two armed women, they hesitated and froze. Suddenly, Betsy heard a click. Shorty drew his gun, but before he could get off a shot, Betsy unloaded one barrel into his chest with a deafening blast, sending him into the cupboard. Jones and Parker, the two men Gabe had driven out of town, suddenly realized these women were not bluffing.

"Well, that's a shame," Emma said. "Now, drop them there weapons!" she demanded again. "Or you two will be like your friend here who just met Jesus. Drop 'em slow and careful like."

"You heard what she said," Betsy added. "It's a fearful thing to fall into the hands of the Lord."

"*On the floor! Faces down! Hands on your heads!* I'd be praying to the Lord, if I were you," Emma demanded. "This might be your last chance to get right with Him. Betsy, me and the Lord can keep our eyes on these two while you go for help."

Betsy quickly placed her shotgun on the counter next to Emma and hurried out the door into the pouring rain. After a few minutes, Mr. Lowery came back with her.

"What in heaven's name!" Lowery remarked with shock and surprise.

"Mr. Lowery, I need you to hog-tie these two. There's some twine over yonder," Emma said.

While this was happening, Shaw, Wilson, and Kinsley had arrived at the front gate at the Adair House as the rain was pouring down. "Wilson, we'll try to draw 'em to the front. You go through the back."

"MacCallan!" Shaw called out.

"I'm here," Gabe hollered from within the house.

Shaw looked over at Kinsley and remarked that Jones, Parker, and Shorty should be here by now. The sheriff could see Shaw and Kinsley through the upstairs window of Gabe's room.

"Kinsley is on the left," he told Silas.

"Shaw! This is Sheriff Wells. All of you lay down your weapons."

"I ain't got no quarrel with you, sheriff," Shaw shouted. "Give us the Samaritan, and we'll go about our business. No one else will have to get hurt."

At the rear of the house, Gabe and Sam heard the creaking of the boards on the back porch deck.

"Someone is out there. Get ready," Sam whispered.

Suddenly, Wilson forcefully kicked in the back door. There was an eruption of gunfire, with multiple shots echoing throughout the house. Gabe rapidly discharged two rounds from his weapon, hitting Wilson and knocking him down. Sam managed to fire once before being struck. Silas and the sheriff hurriedly made their way to the staircase, cautiously descending to the now silent ground floor, when there was a flash of lightning and a loud clap of thunder, followed by gunshots from outside. Slowly, they went to the kitchen, where they discovered Wilson's lifeless body and Sam injured from a wound to his left side.

"I hope that wasn't Kinsley," Gabe said.

"No, Kinsley and Shaw are still outside. The other three are unaccounted for," the sheriff said.

"We heard gunshots from outside," Silas said.

From inside the house, they did not realize what had happened between Kinsley and Shaw. When gunfire erupted inside the house that killed Wilson, Shaw began to dismount, but Kinsley swiftly drew his gun and aimed it at Shaw's head.

"You no good, sorry…" Shaw cursed.

"Amnesty. I want amnesty, Shaw. Surrender, or this is not going to end in your favor."

"You know me by now, Kinsley. I will never surrender."

Suddenly, a flash of lightning and an instant clap of thunder rattled the horses. Shaw pulled his revolver, but Kinsley fired twice before Shaw could fully clear his holster. Shaw's gun discharged into the muddy street, and he fell from his horse, dead.

Gabe hurried out of the kitchen's back door and around to the front west corner of the house, still not sure of what had happened.

"Kinsley!" Gabe yelled.

"I'm Kinsley, MacCallan. All's clear."

Gabe peered from around the corner, cautiously, with his gun raised. Another flash of lightning lit up the sky, revealing Kinsley standing in the muddy street over the body of Lane Shaw.

"It looks like I misjudged you, Kinsley," Gabe said. "You turned out to be the smartest one in the bunch."

Sheriff Wells walked out of the house and onto the front porch.

Kinsley approached the sheriff with his hands up and attempted to surrender his weapons.

"I will have to take you to jail, Kinsley, but not yet."

"Buckle your gun belt back on," Gabe told him. "We still have three more to deal with. First, we need to get the Doc over here to tend to Sam's wound," the sheriff said. Kinsley and the sheriff rode to Clayton's store while Gabe remained at the house with Silas, tending to Sam. When they arrived, what they found cleared up a lot of confusion regarding the whereabouts of the other three. What surprised them the most was that the Clayton women had everything under control.

"Where's Brother Clayton, Silas, and Gabe?" Emma asked them, seeing only the two of them.

"They're safe. Sam is wounded, but he will be okay. Silas and Gabe are with him," the sheriff reassured. "We need to get the Doc over there. Mr. Lowery, can you go after the Doc? In the meantime, we will get these two to jail and the others ready for the cemetery."

6

The Confederacy was coming to terms with losing the war. Countless soldiers and bushwhackers were pursuing amnesty being offered by U.S. Commander Dodge on behalf of the President. Correspondence between Captain C. E. Rogers, Assistant Provost-Marshal in Warrensburg, and Colonel Chester Harding, Jr., commanding the district in Lexington, reported that one hundred Confederate soldiers were ready to surrender. A telegraph to Captain Rogers dated May 12th read,

> *Captain C. E. Rogers,*
> *Lexington:*
> *Accept the surrender. They will be treated as citizens. For their own protection, however, they should be kept together for a few days until the terms are made known throughout the country. Each man must take the oath and sign it in duplicate. One copy he will keep; it will be his safeguard as long as he honestly observes it. The other copy must be sent to the provost-marshal-general.*
> *Chester Harding, Jr.,*
> *Colonel, Commanding.*
> *Lexington, May 12th, 1865*

Kinsley was in a separate cell from his former partners, Jones and Parker. These two will not have the privilege of amnesty. They will be tried for crimes in Warrensburg and will likely be executed upon conviction.

"Let's go, Kinsley," the sheriff said.

It didn't take them long to reach the U.S. Army Post just west of town. The sheriff strode confidently past the post guard, flashing his badge as identification. Inside, near the entrance, a young Corporal stood ready to screen incoming visitors.

"I'm Sheriff Wells of Warrensburg," the sheriff declared. "I need to see the Provost-Marshal."

"State your business, sir," the Corporal requested.

"I'm here to seek amnesty and parole for a prisoner," the sheriff replied firmly.

The Provost-Marshal met with the sheriff, and after a brief discussion, the sheriff left the office, having received everything he came for.

The sheriff returned to where Kinsley was waiting, eager to hear some good news. "Kinsley, you've got a few papers to sign and an oath to take," the sheriff informed him. "I've got permission from the Provost-Marshal to keep you in my custody for ten days. After that, you're free to go."

Kinsley entered the building, joining a group of men waiting to undergo processing. As he stood among them, he overheard one of the men say, "He used to ride with Lane Shaw." Kinsley had hoped to slip through unnoticed and leave quietly. He kept his mouth shut and didn't say a word.

"You split off with Shaw after Anderson was killed. Where's Shaw?" one of the men asked Kinsley, but Kinsley never responded.

After an hour of processing, Kinsley completed the paperwork, took the oath, and stepped out of the building, aware of the eyes tracking his departure. Among those watching, he spotted Virgil Rennick, a name that rang a bell. Rennick was a friend of Lane Shaw, but he'd thrown in his lot with Little Archie Clement, unlike Shaw.

Word around the campfire was that Rennick ran with a rough bunch of 110 bushwhackers, including Little Archie. This gang had recently hit the bank in Kingsville, tearing up the town and leaving eight residents dead in their wake. Frank and Jesse James were said to be part of the mayhem too. The James brothers and Little Archie had taken to their heels, refusing to surrender, and were now outlaws on the run.

Rennick and several others gathered in a group, already looking for trouble. Kinsley paused and glanced in their direction to see that all eyes were still on him.

"Where's Shaw? Rennick repeated in a menacing tone.

Kinsley kept walking without saying a word. They continued to watch as Kinsley walked to where the sheriff was waiting.

It was the first Sunday since the shootout at the Adair House. Sam Clayton was on the mend, but the doctor had advised him to stay in bed for a couple of weeks due to the severity of his wound. Sam asked Gabe to preach in his absence. Gabe was hesitant. His reluctance stemmed from uncertainty about his own abilities, but Gabe was a man who stepped up his confidence when needed.

That morning and afternoon, he preached to a large crowd. Red Kinsley was there, making an honest effort to turn his life around. Sheriff Wells and Clara attended, with Alice sitting up front while Lizzie took a seat in the back with Jonah and the other black members. But Hannah Clayton continued to captivate Gabe's affection; her presence was like a beacon in the sea of faces.

After the singing, preaching, baptizing, and dinner on the ground, Gabe asked to escort Miss Hannah back home. She was thrilled that her parents had approved. Gabe felt more nervous around her than he did while preaching to two hundred people. Hannah had a little brother, Elisha, whom they called Eli. Naturally, he wanted to ride along, sitting between them. As they made their way to the farm, Eli kept things interesting by asking Gabe questions.

"I heard you shot them bad fellas," Eli blurted out.

"Elisha James!" Hannah scolded. "You apologize to Mr. Gabe! We don't discuss such things, especially on the Lord's Day!"

"That's alright," Gabe said. "Bad men reap what they sow. The Bible says that if we sow the wind, we reap the whirlwind, and those men reaped the whirlwind."

"Is that what you are, Mr. Gabe, a whirlwind to them outlaws?" Gabe smiled and glanced down at him. "If I have to be." He caught Hannah's gaze, who tried not to smile before looking away.

Pretty soon, they were at her family farm. Eli jumped to his feet and sprang from the buckboard, causing the dog to start barking and running after Eli.

"I apologize for him," Hannah said. "He can be a handful, I'm afraid," Hannah said embarrassingly. "Can you stay? Mother has leftover fried apple pies." Gabe wanted to accept her offer. To be with Hannah was more enticing than the pies.

"I enjoyed the day with you, Hannah," he replied. "Perhaps I should be heading back. I'd like to look in on Sam."

"Well," Hannah responded, clearly disappointed. "I will come by the store later this week," she perked up to say.

Gabe helped her down from the buckboard and walked her to the porch. "Tell your Pa and Ma I appreciate them letting me escort you home."

Gabe's horse was picketed at the side of the barn, with plenty of shade, grass, and water. Gabe whistled to let him know he was approaching. The chestnut raised his head and perked his ears up. Gabe laid his hand on his mane, grabbed the reins and saddle horn, and slid his boot into the stirrup. As he started toward Holden Road in a gallop, Eli was heard to shout, "See you, Gabe, the Whirlwind." Gabe smiled and waved. Hannah watched him leave from the front porch swing, waved and smiled back.

Before returning to town, Gabe stopped to visit Sam, who was still weak from blood loss. Gabe's visit had a purpose beyond socializing because he had something weighing heavily on his mind. Emma met him at the door.

"Gabe! Come in, dear. Make yourself at home. I'll tell Brother Clayton you are here," she said as she walked toward the bedroom. "Sam, Gabe is here!"

"Tell him to come in," Sam replied.

"You preached two wonderful sermons today, Gabe. We are so proud of you," Emma complimented.

"Thank you, Miss Emma."

"Go on back to the bedroom. Brother Clayton is expecting you."
Gabe stepped around the corner into the room.

"Gabe. I was expecting you sometime today. I heard how well you did. Pull up that chair and have a seat."

"How are you feeling?" Gabe asked.

"Sister Clayton won't let me do anything. I feel like an invalid. Don't be surprised if I'm not up and about tomorrow."

"Oh no, you won't," she demanded. Emma was eavesdropping and heard what Sam said.

"You see," he chuckled. "I'm a prisoner in my own home."

Gabe smiled. "Perhaps you should enjoy the peace and quiet."

"So you're here to side with Sister Clayton?" Sam teased, knowing Gabe was caught in the middle of their playful feud. "Changin' the subject," Sam said. "I heard that you've got eyes for my niece, Hannah."

"I wouldn't call it…," Gabe started to reply.

"She's a good girl," Sam interrupted. "You couldn't do any better." Gabe sat with his flat-rimmed slouch hat in his hands, appearing downcast. "Sam," Gabe paused for a moment, "I'm thinkin' of movin' on north like I planned just as soon as you get back on your feet."

"What's up there that you don't already have right here, Gabe?"

Gabe didn't say anything because he had no answer, and Sam was disheartened to hear it.

"You do what you have to do. I ask only one thing," Sam said. "I don't want you to break Hannah's heart. Don't lead her to some false hope. That wouldn't be doin' her right."

Gabe dropped his head once again and agreed. "Don't worry," Gabe said to calm his concerns.

Gabe visited a while longer, left the Clayton's, and made his way towards the Adair House. After securing his horse for the night and giving him plenty of hay, he entered through the kitchen's back door. Lizzie met him and welcomed him.

"Miss Alice is in the drawing room," she said. "I will bring you some coffee."

Gabe walked into the drawing room and sat down.

"You did well today, Gabe. The congregation was encouraged when they witnessed three more lost souls baptized into Christ."

Lizzie came in with the coffee.

"Thank you, Miss Lizzie," Gabe gratefully said.

"Is there something else I can get for the two of you?" Lizzie asked.

"No, Lizzie. We're fine. Thank you, dear. You may join us if you like."

"Thank you, but I have a few things to do," Lizzie replied.

Alice noticed Gabe appeared to be worried about something. "You should be walking on air, but I sense you are not content. Something is bothering you."

"Miss Alice, it seems that trouble follows me," Gabe said as he placed the cup and saucer on the table. "You saw what happened last week. It almost got Sam killed, and you and Miss Lizzie could have been hurt."

"Does trouble follow you, or has it something to do with your calling?" She posed a profound and unsettling question, leaving him unsure of its intended meaning. "I don't agree with the belief held by some that we have no control over the path our lives take, but I do believe that there is a purpose meant for us to accomplish. You, Lizzie, and I are beacons of light. Whenever light enters a dark room, the darkness flees. It flees and struggles to return. As long as light is present, darkness has to remain in places that light has not reached. As lights, we are called to expose what is in the darkness. The trouble you speak of that appears to follow you is the struggle that darkness causes when you expose what is in it."

Gabe listened uncomfortably, causing him to rise from his seat and walk to the window. He knew she was right, but he didn't want to hear it.

"You can move on if you want, Gabe, but your calling will follow you as long as there is light in you."

She laid a heavy burden on his conscience, letting it settle for a moment, and then remarked, "I don't see you extinguishing your light. Deep down, light is a part of who you are, Gabe. You chose it when you decided to follow Christ."

Gabe, still at the window, sighed. He knew she was right, even though he wanted to deny it.

"What should I do?" Gabe asked, still looking out the window.

"Don't follow your heart. Your heart will always want you to run. Let your calling give you direction. That's the only way you will find your peace."

"Somehow, that's what I thought you would say," Gabe replied.

"It's getting late for this old woman," she said. "I think I'll go to my room, get ready for bed, and read awhile. Have a good night, dear."

He did not respond, being lost in his thoughts. She left him alone. After a few minutes, he looked around to see she was no longer there. He went to his room and laid his father's Bible on the bureau. His thoughts were on the day, Hannah and Sam, but mostly on what Miss Alice said. He opened his Bible to a scripture that his father had underlined. It was Psalm 112:4. "Unto the upright there ariseth light in the darkness: he is gracious, and full of compassion, and righteous."

By morning light, Gabe decided to stay in Warrensburg.

7

Fourteen months had passed, and Warrensburg had become Gabe's adopted home, a refuge where he had grown a sense of belonging. He thanked Lizzie for yet another hearty breakfast as she cleared the table. In what was now a daily routine, Gabe went to the carriage house, picketed his horse while he cleaned the stall, and added fresh hay. Gabe named his horse *Whirlwind*. He was a remarkable horse. Gabe kept him after Lane Shaw was killed. In the lawless world of bushwhackers, if they saw horses or mules that were better stock than what they had, they took them, and at times, at the cost of the owner's life. Horses were also seized as spoils of war. Whirlwind's former owner was likely a fallen U.S. soldier, judging from the military brand on Whirlwind's shoulder. Gabe managed to purchase him from the U.S. Army for twenty dollars.

After Gabe led Whirlwind to the water trough and returned him to the stall, he left for Clayton's store. Emma would not be in that morning but planned to arrive later. Shortly after Gabe's arrival, Hannah walked through the door. Gabe and Hannah had become very close and made it a habit to see each other every morning. They had been spending time together almost every day since they first met.

"Good morning, Miss Hannah."

"Good morning, Mr. MacCallan." She smiled at the playful formality of their greetings. She put on her work apron as Gabe opened the window shades.

"Aunt Emma gave me a list of things she wants us to do," Hannah said, going through the list item by item. "She wants us to check the inventory, count credit receipts, and restock the shelves."

While she was reading through the list, Gabe was only paying attention to her eyes, the features of her face, the sound of her voice, and her wavy, dark brown hair.

"Do you think you can handle this list?" Her question snapped him back to the moment.

"Oh…, no problem at all," he replied, even though he hadn't heard a word she said.

"I'll start taking the inventory," she said. And before she could turn away, and without any warning, Gabe unexpectedly wrapped his arms around her, pulling her closer, and planted a kiss on her lips. Shocked and wide-eyed, she took a deep breath and slugged him with a hard right straight to the jaw. Gabe stepped back, a little dazed.

"Gabriel Aaron MacCallan!" She scolded. "Shame on you! What do you think you are doing? What if a customer had walked in? Lord, help us if it happened to be Miss Clara. What if my mother had walked in with Eli? What if…? And this early in the morning?"

Right then, she grabbed Gabe by the ears, pulled him to her, and laid a big kiss square on the lips. She then shoved him away, grabbed the broom handle, whacked him with it across the upper arm, and stomped out the front door. She was heard fussing all the way out. Gabe just smiled as he rubbed his sore jaw and returned to work.

"It was worth it," he said to himself.

Fifteen minutes passed, and she still hadn't returned to the store. Gabe decided he had better go and see about her. When he stepped onto the porch, he found she wasn't sweeping, only moving the broom around. She quickly turned her back to him when he walked out the door, turning only slightly to see if he was approaching her.

"I'm sorry for slugging you so hard and whacking you with the broom handle," she said, still with her back to him.

"I deserved it," Gabe admitted as he rubbed his jaw and arm.

"I'm not apologizin' for sluggin' you," she turned and replied with a frown. "I'm just sorry I hit you so hard."

That made him smile, although it hurt a little.

"Sheriff Wells wants to meet with me this morning," Gabe told her. "Can you mind the store by yourself for a while?" She glanced up at him with her piercing dark eyes, which seemed to cut through him like daggers.

"I reckon you can," he said. "I'll be back in a little while." Gabe put on his hat. As he walked down the street, Hannah watched him. She had fallen in love with him. A smile gradually replaced her frown, and she returned to the store.

It was about half a mile to the sheriff's office in Old Town of Warrensburg. Gabe gently rubbed his jaw, impressed by Hannah's right hook, and couldn't help but smile at what had happened. The township was awake now. Shops were open by this time, and many of the townspeople had come to know him. The occasional "Good morning, Gabe" would occur along the way. He arrived at the sheriff's office and entered. The sheriff glanced up from his desk.

"Gabe. Have a seat," Sheriff Wells invited, then noticed that Gabe's jaw was red." What happened to your jaw?"

"If you don't mind, sheriff, I can't stay long," Gabe said without commenting.

"Alright. I'll get down to business. Have you given any thought about my offer?"

A little more than a year ago, the sheriff asked him to consider joining him to clean up the outskirts of the township.

"Is this that deputy position you offered last year?" Gabe was afraid to ask.

"It is, but first, I need to ask you a question," the sheriff said, as he picked up a letter from the Governor and stepped around his desk.

"This letter outlines the New State Constitution adopted last year. I don't like this part of it, but it's the law of the land for now. The law requires all public servants, includin' preachers and teachers, to take an oath of loyalty to the state. In this oath, a person must swear they have never taken up arms against the U.S. Government. Would you be able to take that oath?"

"No, sir," Gabe replied.

"Why not?" The sheriff asked.

"I was a Confederate soldier. Even though I was a conscientious objector, I served nonetheless. If I take this oath, I would perjure myself and violate my oath to the Almighty."

"That's what I hoped you would say," the sheriff said, surprisingly to Gabe.

"Will you still work with me to clean up the outskirts of this town? I won't require you to take the oath."

Gabe paused for a moment, then said, "I reckon there's more than one way to break a stubborn mule," Gabe replied, referring to the job he was being asked to do. Sheriff Wells was pleased to hear it.

"You've known for a long time," the sheriff began, "that Ben's tavern is a haven for gang members and troublemakers. I aim to shut him down by cuttin' off his supply of moonshine. I know of two suppliers, but he's got his own stills hidden somewhere, and I haven't been able to track them down. Once I locate those stills, I can nail him for producin' and sellin' moonshine without payin' taxes, and that'll give me the grounds to close his place for good."

Shortly after the war began, Congress created the Internal Revenue Service to collect taxes on the sale of alcohol and tobacco, aiming to recoup war expenses. Moonshiners, however, were dodging these taxes.

Meanwhile, a Temperance Movement, popular among law-abiding citizens, emerged to curtail the flow of alcohol into their town.

The sheriff continued. "I can't officially appoint you as my deputy, but you can work with me as a private citizen."

"What's your plan?" Gabe asked.

The sheriff proceeded to outline the initial phase of their operation.

Following their conversation, Gabe made his way back to the store. As he entered the store, Hannah looked up to see Gabe as he entered. She smiled when she saw him.

"Can you help Mrs. Mayes with her things?" she asked.

Mrs. Mayes cast a curious glance toward Gabe and then to Hannah, noticing the communication they made to each other with their eyes.

"Glad to," Gabe said, smiling still with a bit of a swollen jaw.

"We've been hearing a lot about you, Mr. MacCallan, some good things I must say," Mrs. Mayes said kindly, then leaned closer to Gabe to ensure her words remained between them. "You know," she whispered, "I've noticed how the two of you look at each other. Hannah would make a wonderful wife."

"Yes, ma'am, thank you," he replied awkwardly, extending a helpful hand to her buckboard with her groceries.

"You have a wonderful day," Gabe said as he bid her farewell with a warm smile. Gabe walked back into the store and over to where Hannah was working.

"What was she whispering about?" Hannah asked curiously.

"Oh, it was nothing. Have you been busy?" Gabe asked her.

"A little," she replied. "Most have been asking for something that wasn't here."

"What would that be?"

"You," she said with a smirk. "I've lost track of how many ladies have come by just to see you. You've certainly made a name for yourself over these last few months, Mr. MacCallan," she teased, stepping closer. He gazed into her smiling, dark eyes as she looked around to see if anyone was watching them. Then, rising on her toes, she gently kissed his sore cheek.

"Hannah Clayton," he said, "you sure are full of surprises."

She smiled. "Mother was here earlier. Even she was asking where you were. She wants you to come over for supper tonight."

"And you?" he asked as he put his arms around her. "Do you want me to come for supper?"

Hannah responded with a big smile. "What do you think?"

Emma arrived that afternoon. The rest of the day was busy attending to customers. Some wanted to visit with Gabe, which Hannah found amusing, but he loved the attention, and that's what she found more entertaining. When closing time came, Emma told them to run along.

"See you at supper, Mr. Celebrity," Hannah said, poking fun. He glanced at her without responding while she laughed and started on her way home.

Summer had arrived with long and hot days. The humidity was heavy, causing thunderstorms to pop up in the evenings. Hannah and her mother prepared supper and set the table. Silas and Eli milked their three cows and fed the calves before bringing the horses and the mule into their stalls for the night. A couple of cats playfully evaded Eli as he tried to catch one of them.

"Eli!" Hannah hollered out the back door toward the barn. "Run to the hen house and get us four fresh eggs."

"Ahhh," he protested. "I'm scared of the rooster."

"Four eggs—now!" Hannah demanded. "I don't want to hear none of your excuses."

Silas came in to clean up. He was a quiet man by nature, God-fearing, and hardworking. "Did you say Gabe was coming over tonight?" he asked.

"Yes, Pa," Hannah said.

"I'm glad it's not that Baldwin boy who came a-courtin' a couple of years ago," he muttered.

Hannah shot him a frown. "Oh, Pa, will you forget about him. I sure have."

Just then, Eli came in with four eggs gathered in his shirt. "I took a t'baccy stick in the hen house. That ole rooster knew better than to mess with me then."

"If you hurt that rooster," his mother warned. "I'll take that stick to your behind. Now, go get yourself cleaned up. Mr. Gabe will be here soon."

"Oh boy! The Whirlwind is comin'!"

"What's that about?" Silas asked.

"Oh, Gabe told him something a while back, and Eli started calling him the Whirlwind," Hannah explained.

It wasn't long before Gabe rode up. He stood on the porch with his hat in his hands, a little nervous, and wiping sweat from his brow. He knocked, and Hannah came to the door, smiling with a smile that now belonged only to him, and invited him inside. They entered the main room side by side, her arm affectionately wrapped around his.

"Gabe!" Silas rose from his chair, extending his hand for a firm shake. "Come in, Gabe. Have a seat."

Just then, Betsy came from the kitchen with the last dish to be laid on the dining room table. "We can visit at the table. Now, come on before supper gets cold."

The table was spread with enough food for an army. Gabe was asked to give thanks, which he did very well.

"Gabe, we've known you for more than a year but have not heard very much about your family. What about your folks?" Betsy asked. Gabe began telling them about his upbringing in Kentucky, recounting the joys and sorrows that shaped his life. They listened to every detail, asked questions, and were endeared to him even more.

"Have you heard from your parents lately?" Betsy asked.

"I wrote to them a couple of months ago, Gabe said, and heard from them recently. Everyone seems to be doing fine."

"I hope you've made Warrensburg your new home now," Eli said.

Gabe glanced at Hannah, who sat beside him, and replied, "I reckon I have. Feels like there's nowhere else I'd rather be." She blushed and smiled.

After supper, Gabe and Hannah sat on the front porch swing. They had been together all day, but it felt right to both of them to end their day here. They talked some but mostly enjoyed the quietness together. There was an unspoken connection between them that transcended words. Hannah slipped her hand into his. The creaking sway of the swing, the call of a whippoorwill, and the serenade of katydids in the trees created a tranquil evening. Hannah kissed him and laid her head on Gabe's shoulder. Even though they didn't want the evening to end, it was getting late, so Gabe thanked Hannah's parents for a wonderful supper and their hospitality. Then Hannah walked him to where Whirlwind was picketed.

"I'm glad you came tonight," Hannah whispered in his ear. "I'll see you tomorrow. You're a good man, Gabriel Aaron MacCallan," she said, giving him one last kiss before walking back to the house. Eli had been playing with his dog behind the house when he noticed Gabe was about to leave.

"See you later, Gabe, the Whirlwind," Eli shouted.

Gabe tapped his heels into Whirlwind's sides. Whirlwind reared his head and leaped into a gallop. It wasn't long before Gabe was back at the Adair House. Alice was sitting in her usual favorite chair reading when he walked into the drawing room.

"Good evening, Gabe," Alice said as she removed her glasses and set them on the table beside her. "I'm sure you had a good supper at the Claytons."

"I did indeed," Gabe replied as he glanced around the cozy room, "but it's always good to end the day here," Gabe added. He sat on the sofa across from Alice and leaned back with a feeling of contentment. "I never thanked you for the words of wisdom you gave many months ago," he told her.

"What words of wisdom," she asked, unable to remember.

"I've thought long and hard about what you said. I've found my peace."

She smiled as if to say that she knew he had.

Before turning in, after opening his Bible to Proverbs 3:5-6, he retired after a long and memorable day. "Trust in the Lord with all thine heart; and lean not unto thine own understanding. In all thy ways acknowledge him, and he shall direct thy paths."

Thank you, God, for bringing me to Warrensburg, he prayed, and he drifted to sleep.

8

The following morning at Clayton's store, Gabe approached and greeted Hannah. She returned his greeting with an affectionate glance, her eyes bright with a smile. He then walked to where Sam had settled himself near the spittoon.

"I hope you are preaching this Sunday," Gabe said.

Sam spat and wiped his chin. "Lord willin'," he replied.

"Can you preach on reaping what you sow?" Gabe asked.

"I suppose," Sam replied. "Why?"

"I think there's about to be a whirlwind," Gabe responded without explanation. Sam rubbed his chin, trying to imagine what that meant, but was afraid to ask. Hannah cast a disapproving look, knowing the implication of the "whirlwind" comment.

Gabe and Hannah carried on their day as always, sneaking in playful flirtatious behavior between them. The weather had cleared, but the air was hot and hung heavy with humidity. The day was coming to a close when Hannah woke her uncle, who had fallen asleep in his chair.

"Good night, you two! I'll close up," Sam told them.

They walked out of the store together. Hannah remembered what Gabe said early that morning, was still troubled by Gabe's comment, and decided to get to the bottom of it.

"I don't know what you and the sheriff are up to, but you had better show up in the morning in one piece," she sternly warned him.

"I will," he reassured her, easing her mind. "Don't worry."

Then she looked warmly into his eyes as if looking into his soul. "Promise me?" she asked.

"I promise," he replied, but she sensed apprehension. She kissed him and made her way home.

As she made her way home, Gabe made his way to the Sheriff's Office, where he and Kinsley met to review their plan. Sheriff Wells chose to remain in town to dispel any rumor that he was involved with what was about to happen. When night came, Gabe and Kinsley traveled north of town to Amos McPherson's place. Amos lived alone on the banks of the Black Water River. His father was a Scotsman who married an Osage Indian woman. She and her tribe had converted to Christianity and were taught to read and write in English. When their son was born, she named him after her great-grandfather, Chief Gray Horse, but the child's father gave him the Christian name Amos.

The Osage Indians are native to Missouri, dating back hundreds of years. They are tall, with many standing at least six feet in height, and have red skin. Amos was more Osage than Scottish-American and preferred the name Gray Horse. He adopted the cultural practices and appearance of his Osage people. Like the men of his mother's people, he was over six feet tall. His face, eyebrows, and head were shaven, except for the top of his head, where his coal-black hair was roached and extended down his back. His skin was tattooed, and he wore animal skins for clothing. He knew their oral history, the land, the river, and how to survive, unnoticed if necessary. The Osage were known for their fierce and fearless nature, which earned them a reputation that struck fear into the hearts of many. Bushwhackers and Confederate soldiers called Gray Horse the *Black Water Ghost* and left him alone.

One story about the Black Water Ghost was well-known. One night, a gang rode to his place while he was away on the river. They murdered his family and burned down his home. When Gray Horse saw smoke and light in the sky, he hurried home. He found his wife abused and murdered. His boy had tried to run to find him but was discovered by the river, shot twice in the back. The gang stole horses and robbed his meat supplies. A few nights later, Gray Horse tracked the cutthroats to a camp two miles downriver. Silently, he approached, his body covered in black charcoal. Like a shadow, he slipped into their camp and killed them one by one as they slept. Since that night, whenever a gang came near, Gray Horse left one man alive to warn others. They say he moves as silently as the fog, unseen and unheard, earning the name Black Water Ghost. Bushwhackers have a saying, "Better to sleep next to your worst enemy than to camp near the Black Water Ghost."

The evening grew darker as Gabe and Kinsley rode into Gray Horse's land. "How do we find him?" Kinsley asked.

"The sheriff said that he will find us," Gabe replied. When they located the cabin, there was a silence that gave them an uneasy feeling. Nothing was heard to move, not even the rustling of a branch.

Gabe called out to him. "Gray Horse! Sheriff Wells sent us! He needs your help!"

Sheriff Wells was a good friend of Gray Horse's father, who died about ten years ago.

Gabe called again, and then they heard a voice behind them.

"What do you want?" They had ridden past him without knowing. They turned, and there he was, tall, broad in the shoulders, dark, imposing, and holding a rifle.

"Sheriff Wells said you could help us," Gabe informed him. "We need to get upriver to resolve a problem."

Gray Horse remained silent for a moment, then asked, "What problem?"

"Moonshiners' camps, two of them," Gabe answered.

Gray Horse was well aware of these two camps. He had been watching them closely and wanted them gone, but he had left them alone because they were on the north side of the river. They would encounter trouble if they ever crossed over, and the moonshiners were well aware of it. Gray Horse invited Gabe and Kinsley into his cabin. It was a log cabin. Bear skins, deer and elk skins, and other hides of fur-bearing creatures covered the walls. There was a fire pit in the center of the room. The roof was not gabled but hipped with an opening at the center, which drew like a chimney without filling the cabin full of smoke. For lighting, he made candles from bees' wax. The floor was dry dirt, but the seating area was covered with animal skins like the walls.

"Sit," Gray Horse motioned to them. "If you are friends of Wells, you are friends and guests of mine. You will wait until midnight before going to these camps. These men are killers," Gray Horse said as he hung his

Kentucky rifle on the wall. "How will you deal with these men?" Gray Horse asked.

"That's what we hoped you'd help us with," Kinsley said.

"You are called the Black Water Ghost," Gabe added. "Your land is on the southeast side of the river, and everyone knows not to cross the river from the north. We need to make everyone believe that you have crossed the river."

"In other words," Kinsley interrupted, "if you take care of the men, we will do the rest." Gray Horse needed little to persuade him.

"I will take care of the murderers," he replied. "Leave your guns here. You will not need them."

They did as Gray Horse recommended by waiting until midnight to start downstream on a raft that Gray Horse had made. Because it was a new moon, the night was pitch black. The air was cold, and the fog sent a chill to the bone, even in July. Only the sound of the water and the occasional fish splashing were heard nearby. A horned owl and a whippoorwill could also be heard in the distance. They drifted downriver for approximately three miles until they reached the first camp. They maneuvered the raft silently towards the steep bank just below the camp.

"Stay here until I call you," Gray Horse whispered. He then stepped into the thick darkness and foliage barefoot, without making a sound. Several minutes passed, and no sound was heard from the camp.

After an hour, they heard Gray Horse whistle from a rock ledge above the riverbank. Gabe and Kinsley secured the raft and made their way up the bank.

"There were six men," Gray Horse said. "Now, no more."

Gabe and Kinsley quickly demolished the stills, dumping the corn, sour mash, and moonshine into the river. Then, they drifted downstream for about a mile and a half to the second camp. As with the six at the first camp, the Black Water Ghost descended like the Angel of Death upon the five unsuspecting drunk men at the second camp. The mission was completed, and they returned to Gray Horse's cabin to retrieve their weapons and horses. By this time, dawn was breaking. They thanked him for his help.

"You are welcome here," Gray Horse said.

"We are in your debt," Gabe told him. "If you need us for anything, you can count on us. I never forsake a friend." They rode back to Warrensburg.

9

Gabe was exhausted, but there was no time to rest. He made his way back to the Adair House. Lizzie met him at the kitchen's back door, and was glad to see him because they were worried about him.

"Mr. Gabe!"

Alice overheard Lizzie and hurried into the kitchen. "While you clean up," Alice said, "Lizzie and I will set the table and have fresh coffee ready for you. It looks like you need lots of it."

After washing up and changing into clean clothes, Gabe joined them downstairs, feeling much better. Alice poured him a cup of strong coffee. "I know it's none of our business," she said, "but do you care to tell us where you were last night?"

"I apologize for not telling you, but Sheriff Wells needed help with something," Gabe replied as he sipped his coffee.

"Nothing like a hot cup of coffee," he said as it knocked the chill off from being on the river all night.

He turned to Lizzie, seated at the end of the table. "Miss Lizzie, is there a way I can talk to Jonah privately?"

"The only time I know of is when Ben allows him to attend worship on Sunday morning," she replied. "But he has to return to the tavern right after. He never stays for dinner."

"That's why we always have a special plate made just for him so he can take it with him. We even give Jonah some extra fried chicken for Ben. We figure Ben will be more likely to let him come to worship," Miss Alice added. "What's this about, Gabe?"

"Another storm is brewing with Ben and his tavern, and I want Jonah to be safe," Gabe said. He thanked them for the breakfast and coffee, then hurried to the store. Arriving a bit later than usual, he found Sam and Hannah there, both wondering where he'd been.

"Hannah, Gabe's here," Sam hollered from the front. Hannah was in the back restocking goods that arrived yesterday afternoon.

"She's been wondering where you were for the past thirty minutes. I could hear her fussin' from out here," Sam said, giving Gabe a wink over his wire-rimmed glasses.

"That is *not* true," Hannah protested, "but it's about time you showed up! I had to restock everything by myself."

She tried to act frustrated with Gabe, but her act wasn't convincing. Gabe just grinned and got to work as customers started to trickle in. Sam couldn't help but have a little fun with them.

"I declare," he chuckled. "You two act like an old married couple."

Gabe ambled over to where Hannah was arranging the freshly delivered merchandise.

"Did you and the sheriff finish your business last night?" Hannah asked without looking up from what she was doing.

"We did."

"Is that the end of it?" Hannah continued.

Gabe hesitated to answer, and she glanced at him from the corner of her eye with a raised eyebrow.

"There's one more thing we have to do," Gabe sheepishly replied, suspecting what her reaction would be, but she remained quiet.

Meanwhile, as Sam enjoyed the banter between Gabe and Hannah, Kinsley was reporting everything to the sheriff. Phase One had been accomplished.

"Now," the sheriff began, "we need to track down Ben's still."

"There is someone who might know," Kinsley replied.

"Who?"

"Jonah," Kinsley said.

"Why hadn't I thought about him? See what you can find out," the sheriff responded.

Later that Saturday afternoon, Kinsley made a visit to Ben's tavern. Several of the regulars were there, but no familiar faces. He found a table and sat down. Jonah noticed him as he came in, brought a glass to the table, and poured him a drink. He hadn't seen Kinsley around in a good while. He smiled and said in a low voice, "Looks like you be free."

Kinsley smiled, raised his glass, and nodded. "Looks like we both are," he replied. Jonah grinned and made his way back to the bar, where Ben was cursing and yelling, clearly upset about something. Kinsley knew exactly why. Word had gotten around that Ben's suppliers had been put out of business last night.

On the far side of the room, three men were deep in conversation, their voices low but carrying just enough for Kinsley to overhear.

"Did you hear what happened last night?" one of them asked. "On the north side of the Black Water River, eleven men were killed as they slept. Not a trace of a struggle, not a single shot fired. Nope. Them poor fellas were all found with a knife wound to the temple."

The second man sat up straight, terror washing over his face. "That's the sign of that half-breed, the Black Water Ghost. He's never crossed the river before. His land is on the southeast side. Wonder why he crossed the river?"

"It's a mystery," the first man replied as he took the last swallow from his glass of shine. "After the Black Water Ghost killed them, he destroyed their stills."

The men glanced over at Ben, who was far from his usual good-humored self. "I'd say most of his moonshine supply just got cut off," one of them remarked.

"Jonah!" Ben yelled. "Go to the back and bring out what we have left."

Jonah did as he was told, and Kinsley rose from his chair, laid ten cents on the bar for the drink, and went out the door. He quickly ran to the back of the tavern and tapped on the rear door. Jonah cracked it open to see who it was.

"Jonah, we need your help again." Jonah glanced toward the front to make sure no one was behind him.

"Do you know where Ben's still is located?"

At first, Jonah thought it was a strange question, but suddenly he realized that Kinsley had something to do with what happened last night.

"Jonah!" Ben yelled again. "Where you at? Bring what we have out here!"

"Stay put," Jonah told Kinsley. He quickly grabbed a wooden box with six jars of moonshine, hauled it to the front, and returned to Kinsley.

"I don't know the place, but I know the runner. No time to talk," Jonah told him urgently.

As he shut the door behind him and returned to the front of the tavern, a pair of men strolled inside. One had a couple of Colt Navy revolvers strapped on and was wearing Confederate grays. He was a filthy and foul-smelling fellow. The other man didn't fare much better, and he, too, was well-armed. They walked past Jonah to where Ben stood behind the bar.

"We're lookin' for a fella that might be around here," one of the men said to Ben.

"If you want to know anything around here, you gotta buy a drink," Ben replied. "Dependin' on the question, the charge might be double. Who you lookin' for?"

"We're lookin' for a fella named Kinsley. They call him Red, Red Kinsley. He's a deserter," the man said.

"The war's over, last I heard," Ben replied as he poured their drinks. "Union's been handin' out amnesty like it's Christmas candy."

"It ain't over!" the foul-smelling one shot back, his voice rising in defiance.

"Red, you say?" Ben mused as he poured each of them a glass of whiskey. "I don't know the man, but there was a fella in here a few minutes ago, red-headed, a slim fella. Come to think of it, I believe he ran with Lane Shaw a while back," Ben said, shaking his head. "Shaw met his Maker over a year ago. Had a run-in with the sheriff and some of the town folk."

"We knew Shaw," one of them said. "He was a friend until he joined up with Red."

Jonah was at the end of the bar wiping shot glasses and listening.

"We will be around for a while," the man said. "If you see him again, let us know."

"That'll cost you triple for that drink," Ben said firmly. The men scowled but paid up and turned to leave. As one strode past the end of the bar, he paused, casting a hateful gaze at Jonah. With disdain, he spat on the bar top, the spittle splashing on Jonah's shirt, then continued out the door. Jonah did not look at them and remained silent, wiping away the disgusting tobacco spit with his towel.

Back at Clayton's store, Gabe and Hannah were closing up after a long day. As Hannah was locking the door, Kinsley rode up. "Gabe, I know how to find what we're lookin' for, and Jonah can help us," he said urgently. Hannah turned at the sound of Kinsley's voice. He quickly removed his hat and said, "I beg your pardon, Miss, for my impolite intrusion."

"Kinsley, this is Hannah," Gabe introduced.

"It's a pleasure, Miss Hannah. Gabe speaks of you quite fondly."

"Very nice to meet you, Mr. Kinsley," she replied, wondering what he had shared with Gabe about her.

"Meet me tomorrow morning at the Tabernacle," Gabe told him. "Jonah should be there. Let the sheriff know." Kinsley agreed and tipped his hat to Hannah before leaving.

Gabe started to step off the porch when Hannah stepped in front of him.

"Gabe, what's going on that I should be aware of?"

"We are about to put Ben out of business. For now, that's all I can tell you."

"If it involves you, I want to know more, whether you like it or not," she insisted as she pressed her finger to his chest and would not be satisfied until he told her.

"Kinsley and I are working with the sheriff to do some housecleaning. There's one more thing we have to do to shut down Ben's tavern."

"It sounds too dangerous, Gabe. Why do you always have to be involved?" she protested.

He didn't answer her question. He didn't really know how. As they made their way to the buckboard, helping her up in the buckboard, he replied, "Hannah, we've known one another for over a year. It feels like we've known each other all of our lives. I'm not going to be reckless because I want us to be together from now on," he expressed sincerely.

She sat and listened, but her heart wasn't entirely at ease. But Gabe's words did provide some reassurance, revealing that he shared the same feelings for her as she had for him.

"I'll see you tomorrow," she responded, "but I still don't like it." Then she kissed him more tenderly than she had before. "Now, go home and get some sleep," she said, trying to smile. "You look tired."

She was right. Gabe was utterly exhausted. He hadn't slept for over twenty-four hours. That night, he opened his Bible. The pages unfolded to James chapter four. The scripture underlined in pencil was verse seventeen, which read, "Therefore to him that knoweth to do good, and doeth it not, to him it is sin." He prayed that God would give him the strength to do what was needed as he blew out the lamp. Thunder in the distance and the gentle sound of rain lulled him into a deep sleep.

10

Gabe arrived at Hannah's home on Whirlwind the following day, fortunate to have traveled in between rain showers. The older folks said it had been the rainiest July since 1819. Hannah was ready and waiting on the front porch as always.

"Miss Clayton, you look as radiant as a morning glory," Gabe remarked with a playful grin and coaxing a warm smile from her.

"And you look very handsome yourself, Mr. MacCallan," she replied with a playful tone.

He picketed Whirlwind under a shade tree, removed the saddle, and stored it in the barn. He then hitched the Clayton's mare to the buckboard. Eli rushed from the front door, his mother calling for him to slow down. He wanted to ride with Gabe, but Hannah wanted Gabe to herself. When she was about to say "No!" to Eli, Gabe said, "Climb on." As expected, she shot a frustrated look toward Gabe as Eli found his seat between them. Eagerly, Eli asked, "Can I ride Whirlwind sometime?" Gabe chuckled. "We'll see."

Upon reaching the Tabernacle, Gabe looked around to see who had arrived. Several people walked up to greet them. He was becoming well-known, and Hannah stayed close by his side. It was obvious to everyone that these two were a couple now.

Gabe noticed Kinsley with Sheriff Wells and his wife, Miss Clara. After a brief wait, Jonah finally arrived. Gabe, Kinsley, and the sheriff met Jonah as he was about to enter the Tabernacle.

"Jonah, I owe you more than my thanks," Gabe gratefully told him. "But I need to ask you a favor."

"Yes, sir," Jonah replied. "The man you is looking for who delivers the shine is Mr. Lile; he always has a rider with him."

"Do you mean Noah Lile?" the sheriff asked.

"Yes, sir," Jonah affirmed.

"I know who he is," the sheriff said. "He runs with two others just like him. It was suspected that he was responsible for hanging a man last year, but there wasn't enough proof."

"Yes, sir," Jonah replied.

"Jonah, do you know when the next delivery will be?" Gabe asked.

"He comes on different days, at different times, but now that Mr. Ben's suppliers is gone, I expect he will be here this afternoon."

For the next few minutes, Jonah gave them more details about how the shine was delivered.

"There's another problem, Mr. Gabe," Jonah added.

"Two men be lookin' for Mr. Kinsley, and they say they is lookin' for him 'cause he be a deserter."

"What did they look like?" Kinsley asked. "Did one of them have a scar down the left side of his face? "Yes, sir," Jonah responded. "He don't like black folk at all, I'll tell you that for sho."

"The man you are talking about is Virgil Rennick. I saw him at the Army Post when I received my amnesty papers. He's lookin' for revenge because I encouraged Shaw to split off from the gang after the death of Bloody Bill Anderson and likely because I killed Shaw. Rennick and Shaw were friends at one time."

Just then, singing could be heard inside the Tabernacle as the call to worship began.

"Jonah, we owe you. Thank you for your help," the sheriff said gratefully. "Gabe, you and Kinsley meet me at my office at three o'clock this afternoon."

The rest of the morning, Gabe tried to focus on worship and the sermon, but felt distracted and uneasy. When worship ended, he had no appetite, which Hannah noticed.

"We can leave whenever you are ready," she told him. "I can tell something heavy is weighing on you."

"I will be meeting the sheriff this afternoon," Gabe replied. He then looked at Hannah with seriousness in his eyes, making her worry even more. "It looks like we will be making our raid tonight," he said.

"Where are you going?" she asked. "What do you mean?"

"Shutting down Ben's tavern isn't going to be as easy as we thought. There is a web that this spider has woven that must be taken down first to get to him," Gabe explained.

"Gabe, you aren't helping me feel any better," she responded, her expression filled with concern. "I don't like this. Let the sheriff handle this. Stay out of it. This isn't your concern."

"I can't. You know the scriptures," Gabe reminded her. "Evil men wax worse and worse."

With aggravation heard in her voice, she said, "I'm starting to learn how stubborn you can be when you've set your mind. Just promise me that you won't do anything foolish?"

Gabe took Hannah home, but neither of them said a word. She knew he was determined, and there was no changing his mind. He was loyal to a fault, a quality she admired in him, but also one that worried her. They arrived at her home, and he helped her down from the buckboard. She looked into his eyes, but this time without a smile.

"I'll see you in a couple of days," he reassured her.

He rode as quickly as he could to the sheriff's office. Kinsley joined him shortly after. They entered the office where the sheriff was waiting. The sheriff set a couple of chairs around a table. "Have a seat, gentlemen," the sheriff said.

Gabe kicked off the meeting, his voice steady and resolute. "According to Jonah, Lile won't make a delivery at the rear of the tavern unless he knows everything is clear. This means his partner is holed up somewhere nearby with the moonshine. Lile always enters the tavern first to let Ben know he's arrived. Once Lile gets the all-clear from Ben, he rides to his partner. If it's not clear, Ben will direct him to a secondary location for the drop. Sheriff, this is where you come in. You'll show up at the tavern, mingle with the customers, and keep Ben on edge. Kinsley and I will be ready to follow Lile to wherever his partner is waiting after he finds out he can't deliver at the tavern."

"How will you and I know who Lile is?" Kinsley asked.

"If Ben does what I expect," Gabe explained, "he'll signal Lile that it's not safe to deliver there. Before Jonah left this morning, I told him to follow Lile out, and that will be our sign. We'll stay out of sight but keep an eye on the front. When Lile rides away, we follow. Sheriff, you stay behind, but make sure Ben doesn't suspect anything."

With their plan in place, the trio headed to the tavern. The street was a mire of mud, and the stifling humidity made every breath feel thick. Gabe ran through every possible scenario in his mind, but none ended well. His thoughts drifted to Hannah. He wondered if involving her in his life was exposing her to dangers she didn't deserve. She deserved better than he could give her. Deep down, a part of him whispered that he should have moved on long ago.

As they approached the tavern, Gabe's heart pounded. He knew the risks, but there was no turning back now. Gabe and Kinsley rode past the tavern. They hitched their horses at a shop on the opposite side, far enough to be out of sight but close enough to watch the tavern. The sheriff tethered his horse to the rail outside the tavern. He walked up to the door, paused before entering, glanced down the street to where Gabe and Kinsley were set, and entered the tavern. Jonah noticed him immediately, as did Ben. Several men were gathered at the bar. Seven others were seated at tables.

"Sheriff Wells," Ben said with surprise in his voice.

"What brings you here on a rainy Sunday afternoon?"

"I heard a couple of Home Guard soldiers were in town looking for someone. The War is over, and I want to know their business. Do you know anything about them?" the sheriff asked.

"Can't recall nobody that I know of," Ben lied nervously.

The sheriff began making himself comfortable and talking to the customers. Time dragged on. Thirty minutes turned into an hour, and Ben's nerves wound tighter than a hangman's noose with the sheriff's lingering presence. Just as the tension reached a peak, the doors swung open, and the men he had been waiting for walked in. It was Noah Lile, followed closely by Virgil Rennick. Since their last visit, Rennick and his partner had found gainful employment.

Jonah, stationed behind the bar, quickly noted their arrival. He set out two glasses.

"Whiskey, as usual, Jonah," Lile requested. Lile always ordered whiskey because he knew how the rot-gut moonshine was made.

"Same here," Rennick said hatefully to Jonah. Jonah poured them their whiskey.

"Now get yourself down yonder at the other end of the bar," Rennick snarled. "I don't want no smelly buck negro around while I'm tryin' to enjoy my whiskey."

The insult didn't bother Jonah any. Rennick hadn't bathed in three months and smelled worse than a wet dog. Even the men at the bar saw the ignorant irony in his vile slander. They just turned away and laughed to themselves at his stupidity. Rennick hated black folks, not just because of their color, but because the Union Army freed slaves and enlisted volunteers as scouts. The Union couldn't depend on white citizens to be scouts, so they created a unit called the U.S. Colored Troops. The U.S. Army provided them protection and paid ten dollars a month. They served honorably, proudly, and fiercely. They were called "Black Devils" by Confederate soldiers who feared them. The War may have ended, but as far as Rennick and his ilk were concerned, it was far from over.

Ben eased over to Lile and spoke in a lowered voice, almost whispering, "The sheriff is in the house. You will need to deliver at the other location."

"Which one is the sheriff?" Rennick asked almost loud enough to be heard by everyone there.

"Keep your voice down, you fool!" Lile demanded.

"He's the fella sitting at the far table… gray mustache… smoking a cigar," Ben whispered without looking his way.

Rennick turned and strutted over to the sheriff. "Sheriff," Rennick said, trying to appear cordial, but his arrogance wouldn't let him.

"I'm lookin' for a friend of mine. His name is Red Kinsley, and I wondered if you seen him."

The sheriff looked up. "Who are you?" he asked.

"The name's Virgil Rennick."

The sheriff dismissed him, saying, "If I see this fella you are lookin' for, I'll tell him you're lookin' for him." The sheriff looked away and returned to his conversation with the men at the table, deliberately ignoring Rennick, whose face flushed with anger.

"I think you know Red Kinsley," Rennick said with a raised voice. "I saw him leave with you when he got his amnesty papers at the Army Post," he added, pointing his finger at the sheriff.

"Rennick!" Lile bellowed, his voice cutting through the tension like a whip crack. He knew Rennick would get out of hand if he didn't stop him. Rennick glanced back toward Lile, turned, and walked back to the bar, but kept his eye on the sheriff, giving him a cold stare. The sheriff remained unflinching. He just leaned back in his chair, tucked his thumbs in his vest pockets, and took a draw from his cigar with a wry grin across his face. Lile finished off his whiskey and promptly left.

As they went out the door, Jonah picked up a spittoon from the floor at the end of the bar, followed them out, and emptied it at the end of the porch. That was his signal for Gabe and Kinsley. Kinsley had already recognized Rennick as he entered the tavern. Lile and Rennick mounted their horses, veered west to Clinton Street, and then turned southwest toward the outskirts of town.

After the incident with Rennick, the sheriff didn't follow them as he planned to prevent raising suspicions with Ben. Gabe and Kinsley were on their own and followed at a safe distance. Staying well out of sight, they watched as Lile and Rennick rode to a farm. Though the farmhouse had been reduced to ashes in a skirmish three years prior, the log barn still stood, weathered but sturdy. It was here that the third man awaited them, the moonshine loaded onto a pack mule.

Gabe and Kinsley secured their horses roughly seventy-five yards from the barn, hidden amidst a dense thicket of trees and elder bushes. With weapons at the ready, they advanced cautiously, their every step calculated to minimize noise on the damp grass and brush.

"I'll circle 'round to the back while you cover the front," Kinsley whispered to Gabe.

As a seasoned marksman, Gabe had no equal when it came to using a rifle, having honed his skills as a rifleman in the 2nd Kentucky

Battalion.

"When they come out," Gabe said. "I'll take the lead rider."

"Just remember, we need Lile alive," Kinsley reminded.

They moved to their positions as quickly and quietly as possible. Lile could be heard from inside the barn cursing and yelling at Rennick for his foolishness at the tavern involving the sheriff. As Kinsley moved to his position behind the barn, he could see the fourth man. *This is not going to be an easy fight,* he thought as he slowly inched closer. Kinsley surveyed the barn, looking for every possible hiding place. It had been used to house tobacco and keep livestock. Haylofts were above the log pens on each side of the gangway.

While Kinsley settled into his position, Gabe slowly moved through the tall brush and tree saplings about ten yards away, trying not to be detected. Once in a better position, he had a good view into the gangway of the barn where the men were. The doors on the old double-pen log barn were about to fall apart, which helped his view.

One of the men had mounted the horse leading the mule. He started leaving the barn ahead of the others as they mounted their horses. When the lead rider exited the barn, Gabe shouted, "Don't move! Drop your weapons!"

This startled the lead rider. He drew his revolver and fired in the direction of the voice. Gabe reacted swiftly and fired his rifle, knocking the rider off his horse. The crack of the rifle was so loud that the sound reverberated around the woods and back. The chaos and seeing the rider fall lifeless from his horse made the others so confused that they scrambled back into the barn to take cover. One tried to escape through the back door, and another thunderous roar came from the woods. This time, it was from Kinsley's rifle. Now, two men lay wounded, if not dead.

"Sheriff! That you out there?" Lile's voice echoed from within the barn.

Gabe's response was firm and unwavering. "Two of your men are down, Lile. You two had best come out with your hands raised. No weapons!"

"Ok. You win, sheriff, but you know it ain't illegal to run shine," Lile called back.

"That's a matter for a judge to decide," Gabe replied. "You and Rennick will save yourselves a heap'a trouble. Surrender, and this will be easier on all of us. There's been enough bloodshed."

There was a brief moment of silence, but during Gabe's negotiations, Kinsley quietly and carefully crept closer to the rear entrance of the barn. The horse that belonged to the man he just shot was still nearby, so his movements were slow and easy to prevent the horse from exposing him. A whinny or a snort would draw unwelcome attention. He knew that Rennick had no intention of surrendering because he had violated his amnesty oath.

"We are coming out!" Lile yelled. "This shine ain't worth dying for."

Lile dropped his sidearm and holster, but Kinsley could see well enough to notice Rennick slipping a revolver into his belt behind his back. They walked out together with their hands raised. Gabe stepped out of the brush with his rifle leveled on Rennick. He figured he would be more foolish than Lile and try something stupid.

"You ain't the sheriff," Lile said.

"Never said I was," Gabe replied.

In a sudden burst of action, Kinsley yelled, "Gabe!" as he saw Rennick making a move for his gun. Kinsley had him square in his sights, but Gabe quickly saw Rennick's action. In a split second, both rifles fired together as Rennick fired his revolver. Kinsley's round struck Rennick first in the rib section, knocking him off balance and spinning him around. Gabe's shot found its mark in the center of Rennick's chest. However, Rennick's revolver had discharged, sending a hot .36 caliber lead ball grazing Gabe's left shoulder. Kinsley's well-placed shot had knocked Rennick off his target, saving Gabe's life. The smoke of spent gunpowder settled low in the air over Rennick's body lying face down on the wet grass. He died instantly. Lile stood frozen in his boots, afraid to blink with his hands over his ears. The other two men were severely wounded. Kinsley disarmed them and tied their hands and feet. Gabe, gritting his teeth against the pain, fashioned a makeshift bandage from his bandana, stopping the flow of blood from his wound. Lile was forced to pour forty-eight quarts of moonshine onto the ground.

"You ride into town for the sheriff," Kinsley told Gabe. "I will keep an eye on these three."

A few hours later, all three were in jail. It turned out that one of them was wanted in Kingsville for murder, and the other one violated his parole. No mercy was granted to parole violators seeking a second chance. Provost-Marshal Captain Rogers promptly executes parole violators, as he did in Warrensburg a month prior.

"Lile," Gabe said. "Tell us where Ben's shine is being made."

"If you tell us what we need to know," the sheriff added, "then we will do what we must, and you can go free. If not, you will be at the mercy of a jury full of God-fearing people. And let me tell you, there ain't no mercy when God-fearing people want justice."

"What am I bein' charged for, Sheriff?" Lile wanted to know.

"I haven't charged you yet, but you will be processed in court first thing tomorrow. The charge will be aiding and abetting two murderers."

Lile didn't need much persuasion. Cowards want to live as much as anyone else. He told them all they needed to know. As Gabe, Kinsley, and the sheriff discussed their next move, Kinsley asked Gabe, "How's your arm?"

"I'll manage," Gabe replied, trying to keep it loosened up.

"Let's strike while the iron is hot," the sheriff ended.

11

The mood at Ben's tavern could not have been more unsettling. Two of his sources were mysteriously destroyed. He was running out of shine. However, as far as he knew, Lile had delivered his supply at the alternate location. Little did he know, Sheriff Wells, Gabe, and Kinsley were braving a torrential rain as they made their way northwest toward Devil's Branch. The sheriff was familiar with the location, but the encroaching darkness meant it would be harder to find. Lile revealed that Ben owned a modest twenty-acre farm where the shine was secretly made. Ben doesn't just have one still there. He has two.

Devil's Branch served as the property line on the west and north sides. To get to the stills, they must get past the farmhouse where a tenant lives. Lile told them that the tenant works the stills with two brothers. After a grueling thirty-minute ride in the pouring rain, they arrived at Devil's Branch.

"Lile said there is only one way in or out," the sheriff told them, his voice raised enough to be heard over the pouring rain. "We need to find another way."

They rode across a narrow bridge that spanned the swollen branch, its waters surging from the relentless downpour of the past few days. From there, they rode towards a farmhouse nestled in the woods on the western side of the branch, and upon their arrival, a dog began barking. The dog's barking alerted the homeowner, who promptly appeared at the door and warned the three strangers to halt or face being shot, suspecting them to be bushwhackers. The sheriff called out and identified himself.

"Mr. Skaggs, this is Sheriff Wells of Warrensburg. May we come in?"

"What brings you here, sheriff? If you are the sheriff, I can't see 'cause it's too dark," the man said from his front porch, reluctant to lower his 12-gauge double-barrel.

"We are here to raid an illegal moonshine operation on the east side of Devil's Branch."

"I know the one you speak of," Skaggs replied. "Come on in, Sheriff, where it's dry. I'll have the Mrs. put on a pot." They dismounted their horses and entered the porch to get out of the rain.

"Much obliged for the offer, Mr. Skaggs, but we are short on time. May we have your permission to pass through your property so we can get across Devil's Branch?" the sheriff asked.

"You are welcome to do whatever you need, but most of my property lies on the lower side of the branch. The bottom's flooded right now, and you'd never get across."

The group exchanged worried glances, pondering their next move.

"There is another way," Skaggs offered. "The branch hooks east at the north end of my property, and the ground is higher there and ain't flooded. I have a walk-bridge across the branch, three good-sized poplar logs tied together."

"That's what we'll use to get across," Gabe told them. "Can you take us there?"

"I won't just show it to you; I'll cross over with you," he said with a toothless grin. "I've been wantin' that side of the branch cleaned up for a good while now. Let me grab my coat."

On horseback and wearing rain-soaked clothing, they were led through a path to the north side of the branch. It was pitch dark, but Mr. Skaggs knew the way so well he could have led them with his eyes closed if he wanted. The land was mostly in timber. Huge, tall, straight poplars were mixed with oaks and American Chestnuts as ancient as the Osage Indians who once occupied the land. As Skaggs had described, three large poplar logs lay together across the branch to the other side. There was also a guide rope tied from side to side. They tied the horses and grabbed their rifles.

The branch was swollen, deep, swift, flowing like a river, but still well below the walk-bridge. If a man were to fall in, there would be no hope. With cautious steps in the darkness, they carefully placed their feet on the damp logs, ensuring each step was secure until finally they reached the other side of Ben's property. The roaring current drowned out any noise they might have made as they approached, so they quickly ran up the bank to the ridgeline.

Pausing to look things over and catch their wind, they couldn't see any evidence of anyone being around. They were against a tree line on the edge of a clearing with several acres of corn reaching shoulder-high and tasseling. In the darkness, they could make out what looked like the opening to the clearing toward the south. The corn and the tree line provided them the perfect cover. The noise from the rushing swollen branch still covered any sound from their approach, but that could also be said for anyone who might approach them, so they remained cautious. The element of surprise was hopefully on their side.

They moved slowly along the tree line toward the opening, pausing about every twenty feet to survey and listen. The rain had finally stopped, but rainwater continued to fall from trees overhead. The air resonated with the chorus of katydids and tree frogs. There was no movement they could discern, only the flickering lights of lightning bugs that danced in the darkness. Moving closer, they headed southward toward the clearing's entrance, with Gabe taking the lead. Suddenly, he raised his hand, signaling for everyone to halt. He placed his index finger over his lips and then his ear and directed their attention by pointing to their ten o'clock position. The faint echoes of men's voices were heard, indistinct, but their presence was unmistakable. They cautiously pressed forward to pinpoint the exact location, with their senses sharpened as they remained vigilant.

"Stay here," Gabe said, his voice barely a whisper when he turned to the others. He then made his way to where there was an open gate in a split-rail fence. Beyond the fence lay a thicket of trees, dense and foreboding. Inside a dense grove of trees, there was a cabin situated to the south about fifty yards away, he estimated. There was a soft glow of light in the windows. Gabe's gaze was drawn to the silhouette of a man on the front porch, but his focus quickly shifted as he heard voices again. The voices didn't come from the cabin. He turned his attention to his left, away from the cabin, where there was an open-air shelter he had not noticed. He could smell wood smoke as it lingered low to the ground. This had to be where both stills were located. Gabe could only see shadows in the dim lighting and promptly returned to the others to relay his findings.

"A fence line runs parallel with the location of the stills," he reported. "At least two men are there. There is a cabin about fifty yards from the gate to the southeast. There's at least one at the cabin." Gabe continued to map out the plan. "Kinsley, you and I will take care of the two at the stills. Sheriff, you and Mr. Skaggs hold back at the gate. When we have secured the perimeter, we will signal for you to advance."

With a plan in mind, Kinsley and Gabe moved quickly along the edge of the cornfield. When they reached a safe distance from the still to get a closer look, they discovered that the men were gone.

"They must have gone to the cabin," Kinsley said in frustration with a choice word or two.

"This might work to our advantage," Gabe said as he quickly re-evaluated the situation. He turned to Kinsley. "Go back to the sheriff and bring them back here."

"Wait!" Kinsley whispered. "Someone is coming back."

They watched as a man returned and checked the still, stoked the fire, and returned to the cabin. "New plan," Gabe said. "They are making a new batch. Follow me."

When the man returned to the cabin, Gabe and Kinsley crossed the fence and maneuvered their way to the stills. The shelter was cluttered with barrels, sacks of corn, firewood, and boxes of empty jars and jugs. The pungent smell of sour mash mingled with wood smoke. Gabe made his way behind one of the stills and managed to remove a hot copper line from the seething tank, causing steam to spew.

"Now, what do we do?" Kinsley asked.

"We hide and bide our time," Gabe replied.

After a few minutes, one of the men came out to check on the stills again. He noticed the steam and that the copper pipe had been removed.

"What in tha—!"

The man started to curse but was abruptly silenced by the distinct click of a revolver that was pressed against his ear.

"Stay quiet. I'm not the only one with a gun pointed at you. Do as we say," Gabe told him in a low monotone voice.

"How many men are here?" Gabe asked him.

"There's three of us," the man nervously answered.

Gabe grabbed the suspender straps behind his back. "You're going to lead us into the cabin. Is there a back way in?"

"Yes, sir," he said. "Mister, I ain't done nothing against you. Them two in yonder is my brothers. We don't want no trouble."

"Shut your mouth!" Gabe ordered him. "You make a sound and all of you will die!"

"Kinsley, you take the back door," Gabe said, ignoring the man's whimpering pleas. With his hands on his head and the cold end of a revolver barrel at the base of his skull, he walked in front of Gabe to the front door of the cabin that had been left open.

"Tom, Joe, we got trouble!" he yelled as he and Gabe walked in.

The sheriff and Mr. Skaggs were watching the cabin and could see against the dim light from the cabin door that either Gabe or Kinsley had one of the men restrained and was going in, so they ran to the cabin.

"Don't move, or he dies, then you die," Gabe ordered the two in the cabin. "You two, walk real slow like over to the fireplace with hands on your head!"

They did as they were told, and the one Gabe brought in with him was shoved across the floor and made to join them. Kinsley had entered the cabin from the back, and the sheriff and Mr. Skaggs came through the front.

"Good job, boys," the sheriff said. "I'm Sheriff Wells from Warrensburg. You fellas are now under arrest. But perhaps we can reach a mutually beneficial agreement, provided you are willing to cooperate."

Right then, Mr. Skaggs, who had stepped back outside, rushed back inside. "Somebody's comin' up the lane, and it sounds like more than one."

"Quickly! the sheriff said. Shut the door. Let's get these three tied up. Gabe, you go out the back and take the north side; Kinsley, you take the south. Mr. Skaggs, you might want to get safely out of the way."

"Out of the way?" Skaggs protested. "I didn't bring this here rifle for a coon hunt. This is the most fun I've had in a long time," he said as he grinned with a big chew of tobacco in his jaw and spat on the floor.

A band of four riders emerged from the wooded lane, one of them being Ben Werner. Upon discovering that Lile had failed to make the delivery, Ben quickly realized what the sheriff was up to at the tavern. Finding three volunteers was no challenge for Ben, as those who frequented his establishment jumped at such opportunities. As they drew nearer, Ben and his companions saw nothing outside of the cabin that made them suspicious. However, Ben's instincts made him proceed with caution.

"Joe, Clint, Tom!" Ben called out. There was no reply. "Take cover," Ben told his men. They dismounted, unholstered their guns, and found cover behind the trees.

"Ben, this is Sheriff Wells." Ben's fears were now confirmed.

"I thought you were up to somethin', Sheriff."

"Ben, there is no need to take this any further. Y'all lay down your weapons."

"This has gone too far, Sheriff," Ben replied. "Let's compromise and make a deal between us." He knew that the sheriff was more of a politician than a fighter.

"I'm shuttin' you down, Ben. I have to take you to jail for tax evasion, and any deal will have to be between you and the U.S. Government."

While the sheriff was keeping Ben occupied, Gabe and Kinsley took their positions in case things went badly. Because Gabe was on the north side, he could venture out wider into the trees, and from his vantage point, he had a more precise line of sight.

"Alright, Sheriff. I'm comin' in."

Sheriff Wells turned to Mr. Skaggs. "Mr. Skaggs, have you ever been a deputy?"

"No, sir," he replied.

"You are now. If these three so much as scratch, you consider it a hostile act against a law officer."

"Don't worry, Sheriff. If there's any scratchin' it'll be from my itchy trigger finger," Skaggs said, laughing in a sinister way.

"Ben, walk out toward me to the porch," the sheriff hollered from inside the cabin. The sheriff opened the door and stepped onto the porch. His gun was holstered, and he set his rifle against the outside wall. *This is either brave, stupid, or both*, he thought to himself. Ben stepped out and walked toward the porch.

"Boys, lower your weapons," Ben ordered. "I'll make a deal with the sheriff and we can leave." He made his way to the front porch.

"Ben, we've known each other a long time, but you know the law, and you also know that I have to enforce it."

While they were hashing out their detail, one of the bushwhackers Ben had brought along started getting antsy. He and the other misfits were former camp gang members, outlaws, and murderers who still had an ax to grind. Their bloodlust to kill a lawman was eager to be satisfied.

Gabe and Kinsley watched in the darkness for any movement among the trees. Against the backlight from the cabin door, the sheriff and Ben combined into a single silhouette, unable to distinguish one from the other. Suddenly, Gabe noticed movement. A figure raised his rifle, but the bushwhacker fired toward the cabin before Gabe could get a shot. The bushwhacker missed the sheriff, and Ben moaned and collapsed. Gabe shot toward the flash of the bushwhacker's gun barrel. Kinsley replied with a round in the bushwhacker's direction. Chaos erupted.

Seizing his rifle with one hand, the sheriff gripped Ben's arm with the other and forcefully hauled him into the cabin. He was severely wounded but alive. Guns from both sides blazed with flashes of light, and deafening roars echoed throughout the woods. Bark exploded off trees as rounds of lead tore through them, sending bark and wood fragments flying like shrapnel. One of their horses caught a stray bullet and went down. It was as chaotic as a battlefield for the first few minutes. Kinsley and Gabe were the only ones not pinned down and could maneuver freely to flank on the right and the left. Gabe found a clear shot and took it. One was now down, but Gabe's shot exposed his position. A shot sent a round past his head, and another cut his shirt sleeve. *That was too close,* he said to himself as he ducked behind a huge poplar and then quickly moved to another position. Kinsley followed immediately with his shot, hitting the tree trunk and splintering pieces of wood into the face of the gunman. Reacting in pain, he stumbled back. Kinsley chambered another round and put a bullet into the man's chest. Now, two were down. Suddenly, everything was silent until the remaining gunman couldn't stand it any longer and ran like a scared rabbit toward the horses. Gabe never wanted to shoot a retreating enemy, so he unloaded his Colt into the mud behind him as he ran. The coward's rear end found the saddle of his horse. Kinsley wasn't as merciful and shot the fool, dropping him into the mud as his horse ran away. It was over. Three men were dead, Ben was severely wounded, and he was out of business.

The Drake brothers were ordered to destroy the stills while Mr. Skaggs kept a gun on them. Ben was made as comfortable as possible. Before leaving for Warrensburg, the sheriff thanked Mr. Skaggs for his service and dismissed him from his duties as a deputy. Back in Warrensburg, the Drake brothers were put behind bars, and the doctor was summoned to tend to Ben's wound.

"Sheriff," Doc said. "If you keep getting me up before my morning coffee to patch up wounded prisoners, I will have to start chargin' you."

"Hopefully, this will be the last of it, Doc," the sheriff responded. "I'll put on some coffee."

"Make it strong," Doc replied. "From the looks of Ben, I may be here a while."

Gabe arrived home drenched, exhausted, sore, and wounded, but grateful to finally be in a warm, dry place. His head throbbed from stress and the onset of a fever. Lizzie and Alice were alarmed by the sight of his blood-soaked shirt sleeve and his wet, muddy clothes. They quickly cleaned and dressed his wound, then helped him into dry clothes and made sure he was well-fed.

"You need to see the doctor this morning," Alice insisted.

"I left him at the jail tending to Ben Werner," Gabe replied, wincing from his throbbing arm. "I will have Hannah take a look at it." He told them all about what had happened involving Ben. The most satisfying thing he said was, "Ben's tavern has been shut down for good."

Gabe couldn't wait to see Hannah in the morning.

12

The eastern sky wasn't as red this morning as it had been. Gabe slept more peacefully than in days, even though it had been only a few hours. It was just about dawn when he awoke. Afraid he had overslept, he jumped out of bed with a growl. His muscles were stiff, and he could barely raise his arm because of the pain, but he was eager to see Hannah. Determined, he made his way to Whirlwind as quickly as he could.

"Whirlwind, my friend," he murmured, patting the horse's neck, "maybe we'll finally have some fair weather. Today might be the perfect day to ask a pretty girl's father for her hand in marriage."

After a hearty breakfast, he headed to Clayton's store. The moment he stepped inside, he spotted Hannah, looking as radiant as ever. Her face lit up as if her prayers had been answered. She rushed over, throwing her arms around him so tightly that he winced from the pain in his arm.

"Ow! Not so tight!" he groaned. But she didn't listen. She kissed and hugged him anyway with all the affection she could give. Suddenly, she realized he was hurt. She stepped back, giving him a look that instantly reminded him of his mother's stern gaze right before he got into trouble.

"You've been shot, haven't ya?" she scolded, her voice laced with worry, shock, and frustration.

"It's not that bad," he replied as if that would make her feel better. She spun around and grabbed the broom as he placed his hand over his wound, in case she had in mind to use the broom handle, as she had done in the past.

"Gabriel Aaron MacCallan!" she chastised as she pointed the end of her broom handle at him. "I won't have you making me worry that you have been shot or worse every day! I'm not about to be a young widow with three small children."

He stepped closer to her and wiped the tears from her cheeks. "Does this mean that you will have me as your husband?" She looked at him with tear-filled eyes and whispered, "Yes."

Two months later, in September 1866, Gabe and Hannah were married at the Tabernacle. There was a large crowd. Sam gave Gabe the Henry rifle that he had admired for so long at the store as a gift. Hannah received a lot of nice things from the ladies of the church. There was a special guest there that day. Gabe invited Gray Horse to the wedding, who sat next to Sheriff Wells and Miss Clara, who was visibly uncomfortable.

Thanks to Gabe and Kinsley, Sheriff Wells enjoyed a period of calm in Warrensburg. A couple of years later, he retired, leaving behind a town that was in a better state of affairs. Jonah found freedom and a new home among former slaves in Mt. Olive, thanks to the generous donation of land by a former slave owner. He married and started a family. Ben faced fines and time in jail, but his friendship with the sheriff remained unbroken. He never reopened his tavern. Red Kinsley said his goodbyes after being Gabe's best man at the wedding. Before leaving for Kansas City, Gabe gave him a Bible as a gift. Inside the cover, he wrote,

I will never forsake a friend.
Your friend,
Gabe MacCallan

Gabe and Hannah left for Kentucky before winter. Everyone was saddened to see them go, but all bid them Godspeed until they met again. Alice Adair passed away one year later. She left everything to Lizzie. The house remained *Adair's Room and Board*. Gabe never forgot how she guided his life when he needed it most. He mourned her passing when he heard the news.

Part Two

Awaking Vindication

"Stir up thyself, and awake to my judgment,
even unto my cause, to my cause, my God and my Lord."
Psalm 35:23

13

Families were typically large and often lived very close to one another. It was common for parents to live with one of the children until the parents' deaths. Gabe's grandparents lived their final years with Gabe's parents and died before the War. They were buried in the family cemetery next to his brothers. Death and tragedy were not strangers to any family in those days.

It was the fall of the year when Gabe and Hannah arrived at his boyhood home in Kentucky. The leaves on the shagbark hickory and the tulip poplar trees were a bright yellow. The days were still hot, but all signs pointed to a change in the season. The long shadows of the evening were beginning to signal shorter days and cooler nights.

Gabe stood inside the wrought iron fence of the family cemetery between the gravestones of his two brothers. The body of his oldest brother was never brought home from Ringgold, Georgia, where he was killed in battle and laid to rest. His stone was on Gabe's right, erected in his memory. His youngest brother was buried on his left. He will forever be seventeen. Gabe's eyes looked beyond the fence, where there was an old maple tree that he and his brothers used to climb. A gentle breeze swayed its branches as he watched a flock of sparrows fly to the tree. His mind drifted back to more innocent times. He could still hear his brothers' voices and see them as they played together as boys.

"Why were they taken? Why not me instead of them?" Gabe muttered aloud with the weight of grief heavy in his voice.

"I've asked the Lord a thousand questions," came a voice from behind him. Gabe turned to see his father standing outside the fence. He hadn't realized he'd spoken out loud or that anyone else was around.

"Why them instead of me?" asked his father, his voice weakened with sorrow. "But heaven has been silent." Gabe had no answer. There was none to offer.

"A flood of scriptures flows through my mind, searching for answers," his father continued with pain in every word. "I still don't understand. I never will, I suspect, this side of glory."

Gabe could see that his father seemed much more frail now. Though he was worn, he was not defeated. Yet, his voice expressed weariness. His hard, calloused hands gripped the tops of the balusters of the fence because his posture was no longer as straight and steady, and his footing was not as secure as it once was.

"Your mother still mourns. I suppose she always will. Thankfully, the passing of time has helped her tears to be fewer."

For a few minutes, Gabe and his father stood silently next to the fence, wishing for words of comfort, but only the rustling of leaves in the trees and the calls of a couple of crows in the distance broke the silence. Finally, his father said, "Perhaps we should go. Your mother told me to fetch you for supper." So, Gabe and his father made their way back to the house. As they walked together, Gabe's father said, "I think Hannah is going to fit the family very well," as he laid his hand on Gabe's shoulder. "I'm glad you two are home."

The house was filled with the warm, comforting aroma of freshly baked biscuits and fried chicken. All six family members gathered around the large table, big enough to seat eight. Aaron led them in giving thanks. After a few minutes of filling their plates and sampling everything on the table, Aaron turned to Gabe and asked, "Have you been keeping up with Kentucky politics, Gabe?"

Anna, the youngest, quickly responded, "Father, let's not talk politics at the table."

Gabe replied anyway. "No, I've had plenty to keep me busy in Missouri," he said, glancing at Hannah, who blushed.

Mama MacCallan then turned to Hannah. "Hannah, we'd love to hear more about your people."

For the next hour, they enjoyed their meal while listening to Hannah talk about her home in the Show Me State. She also reminisced about living near Danville, Kentucky, where she was born, and wondered aloud if her childhood friends might still be there.

After supper and washing the dishes, they spent the rest of the evening on the front porch. The MacCallans lived in a two-story log house built by Gabe's grandfather. The farm was situated outside of Freetown, off Gamaliel Road. The poplar logs used to construct the house were nearly twice as wide as a man's waist and hewn to a narrow twelve inches. On both ends of the house stood two sturdy stone chimneys. A dogtrot connected the main house to the kitchen. Above the kitchen was a separate room that formerly belonged to his grandparents but now belonged to Gabe and Hannah. The front porch that spanned the entire length of the house was a favorite gathering place for neighbors and friends.

After long, hot summer days, it was a regular pastime to have neighbors come to the MacCallans after supper. They would bring banjos, fiddles, and guitars, turning the front porch into a lively place for entertainment. In those days, the community worked, worshiped, and raised their children together. Families intermarried. They cared for one another during lean years. In the fall, they harvested and housed one another's tobacco crops and hay. When someone finished stripping tobacco to prepare the crop for the market earlier than expected, he would go to his neighbor to help with theirs. They celebrated the birth of children, offered comfort during mourning, and nursed each other back to health during sickness. Loving your neighbor as yourself was a way of life.

Pretty soon, everyone had heard about Gabe's arrival back home with a pretty wife and were gathering to welcome them home. The women ran the men and the children off the porch to the yard beneath the large maples that Gabe's grandfather planted when the house was built. The York clan came with the Ritters and the Allens. The Grays were there with their new grandbabies. The women brought quilts and doilies as gifts to Hannah.

The big news among the menfolk was about President Johnson's visit to Louisville the month before and the recent changes that had everyone in an uproar over the increasing power from Washington. The newly established Freedmen's Bureau, organized by the U.S. Government following the Civil Rights Act passed last April, didn't begin operations in Kentucky until June. Much like during the War, the county's residents were deeply divided on the issue of slavery. When the talk of politics wore thin, the conversation naturally shifted to the weather, the tobacco crops, and local news. Gabe listened intently to it all, absorbing the familiar sounds of home. His father, ever the storyteller, kept everyone entertained with a tale or two, weaving memories and laughter into the evening.

Aaron MacCallan was an extraordinary man. He healed people's souls with God's word and had a gift for curing animals. Gabe wasn't sure where his father gained his veterinary knowledge, but he was often called to help with a sick mule, a cow down with milk fever, or to help pull breeched calves. He always knew the right plants and herbs to use for poultices. He had a way about him that animals seemed to understand. It was amazing to watch, people would say.

Most of all, Aaron was wise. He had a gift from God to turn the scriptures into everyday living. It was not uncommon for him to be seen walking with someone to the Rock. The Rock was a place that overlooked the hollow. It was his sanctuary, a place where he often meditated and prayed. It provided a peaceful refuge for a troubled soul. He began preaching when he was ordained in the Presbyterian church. However, when John "Raccoon" Smith came preaching at what is now called the Mulkey Meeting House, Aaron was there to listen. By the end of the meetings, Aaron and several other preachers had joined a movement committed to being known simply as Christians and the Disciples of Christ. They sought a simpler form of faith that followed more closely with the first-century church.

As the moon rose higher in the clear starlit sky, everyone bid their goodbyes and returned home. Gabe was thankful to God that Hannah was there with him. He would not have returned had it not been for marrying her. When Gabe and Hannah finally turned out the light, Hannah felt less homesick for her home in Warrensburg. Hannah missed her family deeply. It was her first time away from home, and despite being brought up by tough frontier women, she felt homesick and longed for the comfort of her family. Though she tried to hide her feelings, Gabe's mother noticed. A mother always knows. Gabe's two sisters also sensed her sorrow and comforted her with their warm, new relationships.

14

It was Sunday, October 14, 1866, when a series of events would begin to change Gabe and Hannah's lives.

The church that called themselves the Disciples of Christ was planted in the community after several revival meetings that sparked controversy. Because they walked away from what was considered the Christian norm, which was riddled with traditions that began with the Reformers, critics labeled them as heretics, water dogs, and Campbellites. A fire had destroyed the church building during the War, but that did not discourage the believers from worshiping, as they did each week. The makeshift meeting place was filled with people thrilled to see Gabe and meet Hannah, but most of all, to listen to his sermon, "Ye are Lights in the World." In a pond nearby, two more souls were immersed in water with faith in Christ.

One of Gabe's childhood friends was there, Quinn Howard from Freetown. Freetown was established by a former slaveowner who expected slavery to be abolished in Kentucky twenty years sooner than it was. He was a generous man who cared for his slaves but had become convinced that slavery needed to end. When he freed them, he gave them four hundred acres for their settlement.

Like Gabe, Quinn had tied the knot with a young lady since the last time he and Gabe had seen each other. Quinn and his wife-to-be had just started courting before Quinn joined the army and married after he came home. His wife was a former slave and the granddaughter of Ezekiel Coe, a man of both Cherokee and African descent. His mother had two sons by her Cherokee master in North Carolina, which gave Zeke and his family Cherokee features. They had high cheekbones and dark reddish-brown skin. After emancipation, the Coe family granted several hundred acres of land on Coe Ridge, situated along the Cumberland River, to their freed slaves. The colony at Coe Ridge was known for being hardworking, honest, and God-fearing. They never stirred up trouble and peacefully coexisted with their neighbors. The same was true for those living in Freetown. Quinn had heard that Gabe had returned home, and he and his wife came to visit him.

"Quinn!" Gabe called to him excitedly as they shook hands and embraced each other like long-lost brothers. As they visited with each other, the wives became acquainted. The last time Gabe and Quinn saw one another was before the War. Because Quinn was free, he joined the Union Army the year after Gabe was forced into the Confederate Army. Quinn talked about his service in the Army, and Gabe talked about his in the Confederacy.

"I joined the 115th U.S. Colored Infantry," Quinn said. "Got back home last April from the Rio Grande."

"What about your brothers?" Gabe asked.

"James stayed home. Adam was in the 28th U.S. Colored Infantry. He survived the Battle of Crater at Petersburg. A lot of his buddies was kilt there. His unit was transferred to Texas like me, but he come home last February." Quinn paused for a moment before asking Gabe about his brothers.

"I's sorry when I hear'd 'bout yer brothers. They was good boys."

Gabe just nodded. "What about your mam and pap?" Gabe asked, wanting to change the subject.

"Pap passed 'fore I come home, one year ago last Christmas. Mammy found him. He didn't come in for dinner one day, as he always did."

"He was always good to me," Gabe said, saddened to hear the news.

"He always thought a lot'a you, Gabe. He said you was a different kind'a white boy. 'It's his raisin', he would say. He would say you was taught to see the world as it should be, not what it is."

"I wish the world was a different kind of place," Gabe said somberly, then smiled and laid his hand on Quinn's shoulder. "I am glad both of us are home now."

The period following the War brought unsettling times to Southern Kentucky. Nearly one thousand former slaves from one hundred nineteen former slave owners in their county alone were emancipated. Many left farms and plantations for the towns and cities. Unfortunately, there was no one like Moses or Joshua of the Bible to lead them. John Wilkes Booth claimed the life of President Lincoln, and President Johnson started sympathizing with the Southern Democrats who sought to hinder the assimilation of former slaves into society. He sided with the Democrats when he vetoed the Civil Rights Act, but his veto was overturned by Congress. This Act created the Freedmen's Bureau, but the Bureau was not welcome in Kentucky by many white folks. U.S. General Fisk, who was in charge of establishing the Bureau in Kentucky and Tennessee, reportedly said, "… a more select number of vindictive, pro-slavery, rebellious legislators cannot be found than a majority of the Kentucky legislature." Kentuckians resented that, but it was true. Much of the debate centered on the constitutional authority of the U.S. Government to enforce the Freedmen's Bureau's jurisdiction over the southern states. Because of this, Kentucky began to sympathize more with the South.

The agents of the Bureau were federal agents. They worked to ensure fair treatment, protection, and assimilation of former slaves into becoming U.S. citizens. Former slaves now had the right to vote and testify against white people who violated the Freedmen's law. Many believed that the integration of former slaves should be managed by the states. However, as per Federal Law, any resistance or infringements were now considered federal crimes. The resentment this caused became a seedbed for rebellion and hatred for former slaves and their descendants. Eager former Confederate soldiers and pro-slavery activists began to intimidate and terrorize black people. In Pulaski, Tennessee, a new organization called the Ku Klux Klan had been organized.

A couple of weeks after Gabe and Quinn's reunion, Gabe traveled to town on his horse, Whirlwind. Whirlwind caught everyone's attention. He stood sixteen hands high, a beautiful stud, chestnut in color with a black muzzle and a streak of white from his forehead down the bridge of his nose. His mane and tail were black as coal. The two letters "U S" were branded on his left shoulder. He was formerly the property of the U.S. Army, stolen by outlaw Lane Shaw. He named his horse *Whirlwind* because of what the prophet Amos said about those who sow the wind. Lane Shaw reaped the whirlwind. Since the horse was stolen property, Gabe purchased the horse from the U.S. Army.

Whirlwind trotted with his head held high as if he were escorting the emperor. He would throw his head back like a Tennessee Walker when he passed another horse. Sitting astride Whirlwind and towering in the saddle, Gabe was no longer the lad familiar to the town but a man forced to mature by the trials of war and the guiding hand of Divine discipline. People watched as Gabe rode by, not recognizing who he was. His black flat-brimmed slouch hat sat level on his head and just above his eyebrows, shading his eyes. He wore black trousers and a navy-blue shirt. A Colt Navy revolver was strapped to his right leg. He possessed a meek spirit but could dispense justice if needed.

As he passed the burned-out courthouse, he noticed men were still salvaging what remained of the rubble that had not been burned during the War by Confederate marauders. Gabe's business in town that day was to visit an old friend, Sheriff Nathan Ritter. He was a few years older than Gabe, but he and Gabe attended the same one-room schoolhouse when they were boys. That brought to mind recollections of the Taylor brothers. They liked to bully anyone smaller or perceived as weaker. Nathan and Gabe's older brother, John, would stick up for him. One day, while Gabe was walking home alone, the Taylors jumped him. After Nathan and John saw how he had been bloodied and bruised, they ambushed the Taylors and left them bloodied and bruised. They thought twice about bullying Gabe after that.

Gabe tied Whirlwind to the hitching rail and entered the Sheriff's Office. Nathan glanced up, his eyes widening in surprise as if he had just witnessed Lazarus rise from the tomb.

"Well, look who decided to come home," Nathan exclaimed, rising from his desk chair. "Where in the world have you been since the War ended?"

"How in the world are you, Nathan?" Gabe replied as they exchanged firm handshakes.

"Sit down, sit down. Let me get you some coffee. Boy, it sure is good to see you, friend. Someone told me you were back home."

"Oh, who?" Gabe asked as he took the cup of coffee he was offered.

"Her," Nathan said, glancing at Gabe to see his reaction. Gabe knew precisely. It was Abigail Ray. Gabe didn't say anything at first.

"If you hadn't heard," Gabe replied, "I'm happily married now."

"I heard you married a girl from Missouri. Miss Abigail knew that, too."

Gabe changed the subject, and they caught up on each other's lives during and since the War.

"It's a new day, but I can't say it's a better day, Gabe. The government is making me work with Freedmen Bureau agents that come down from the North. They don't know how to deal with people down here. Their northern ways cause them to get crossways really fast. I wind up having to step in and settle offenses."

"Well, Nathan, you've always been the one to dive right into the middle of a conflict," Gabe said with a grin.

Nathan smiled back. "I know," he replied. "It's a curse, I reckon. You ought to work with me. I could get you signed up as an agent. The pay isn't great, but it's better than nothing."

As they continued to talk, the door flew open. It was one of the Henderson boys. He was nearly out of breath and panicked when he came in.

"Sheriff!" he cried. "There's trouble down at the livery stable."

"What trouble?" the sheriff asked, rising from his chair.

"There's been a killin'! Mr. Turner, Mr. Turner!"

When Gabe and Nathan made it to the livery, several people had gathered. "What's going on?" the sheriff asked as he and Gabe dismounted their horses.

"Mr. Turner's been shot. The ones who done it rode south," one bystander said.

"How many?"

"Two."

Nathan checked to see if Mr. Turner was living or dead. "He's alive, but he won't last long with that wound in his stomach. Get him to Doctor McKinney's. Gabe, come with me."

Gabe and Nathan mounted their horses and headed south toward Harlan Crossroads as hard as they could ride. Whirlwind had no problem keeping up with Nathan's black three-year-old gelding. Two miles further and riding between split-rail fences, there was no sign of the ones they were after. They reached Harlan Crossroads and stopped.

"They either have the fastest horses we've ever seen, or they veered off somewhere," Gabe remarked.

"Reckon we best make our way back to town," Nathan suggested. "Maybe we can get more information."

They headed straight for Doctor McKinney's office when they returned to town. When they entered, they saw Mrs. Turner and her daughter sobbing and consoling each other. Mrs. Turner looked up at the sheriff with tear-filled eyes.

"The doctor is workin' on him," she said, weeping and her voice breaking. "He don't look good, Nathan. Why would anybody do this?"

Gabe and Nathan stepped outside. "Let's go back to the livery and see what you can find out," Nathan said.

They arrived back at the livery stable and began looking around.

"Judging from where Mr. Turner was lying, the shot came from the back of the stables," Nathan observed.

They walked to the rear doors, which were still partly open. In the corral were six horses, but they noticed two that appeared out of place. It was obvious that they had been ridden hard and left in the corral. Sweat had dried white with salt on their shoulders, necks, and across their backs. They walked back into the stable and exited through the front. Gabe noticed blood on the ground as he glanced down, most likely from Mr. Turner, he figured. He continued to walk further away from the door, seeing a trail of blood leading away.

"Turner must have shot one of them," Nathan said. They looked around even more.

"There it is," Gabe said. Mr. Turner's revolver had fallen from his hand when he fell and lodged between the wall and sacks of feed.

Nathan checked the cylinder. "Not one, but two shots had been fired." The sulfuric smell of burned powder was still in the barrel. Suddenly, footsteps and a voice were heard from behind them.

"The one Mr. Turner shot was hit pretty bad." Gabe and Nathan turned to see an old black gentleman.

"You saw this?" Gabe asked.

"I's over yonder at the feed mill when I hear'd shots," he said. "A minute later, two men rode hard right by me there. One was slumped over."

"Did they ride south?" Nathan asked him.

"They did, but I seen 'em turn yonder way," the old man said as he pointed in the direction he was speaking. "Maybe toward Hestand," he told them.

"Hestand? They could be almost to Celina by now," Gabe said with frustration.

"Not with that wounded fella, they ain't. I wager they didn't make it to the Tennessee line."

"What's your name, sir?" Gabe asked.

"Rufus Owen," the man replied.

"We are much obliged, Mr. Owen."

Back at the doctor's office, Mr. Turner managed to survive the surgery. A significant blood loss meant that his chances of making it through the night remained uncertain.

"If he is still with us by morning, his odds will improve," Doctor McKinney told them. "Mrs. Turner," the Doc said, "we have a room here where you and your daughter can stay overnight."

Gabe and Nathan arrived and told the Doc and Mrs. Turner more about what happened. "If one of them was wounded that badly, chances are they're still in the county," Nathan remarked. "Gabe, I could use your assistance. I can deputize you to make it official."

"I'll need to send word back to my wife," Gabe informed Nathan, prompting them to ride back to the sheriff's office, where they could coordinate their efforts.

By this time, Frank Tate showed up. "Frank," Nathan said, "ride out to the MacCallans. Let them know what has happened and that I need Gabe's assistance, and then you remain here in town. Bill, you come with us," Nathan said to his other deputy.

While the sheriff and his deputies were preparing to ride out, the two bushwhackers did indeed ride toward Hestand. Jim Armstrong and William Burns were ex-Confederate soldiers. Both of them were from Sumner County, Tennessee. They had just robbed a stagecoach near Edmonton when they showed up at the livery stable. No one was seriously harmed during the robbery. However, they managed to steal three hundred dollars in cash that was bound for the National Bank in Glasgow. They needed fresh horses to ride into Tennessee because they had plans to go to Texas. However, Will was now gravely wounded. Turner had inflicted two gunshot wounds, one through Will's right shoulder, while the other bullet lodged in the right side of his chest. He was bleeding badly and struggling to breathe.

They rode up to a small cabin on the west side of Sulphur Creek. The man who lived there was a former slave. He never married and lived alone. His former master gave him forty acres of land, a mule, and a plow when he freed him from slavery. Old Asa was away tending his field when Armstrong and Burns rode to the cabin. He hid in the fence row when he spotted the two white strangers at his cabin. He could see that one of them was slumped in the saddle. The other dismounted his horse and helped his wounded friend into the cabin. Old Asa couldn't move very fast, but he made his way to the big house of his former master as quickly as he could on foot. Mr. and Mrs. Fraser saw Asa coming toward the house. They knew there was something wrong. Asa never came to the house unless he rode bareback on his mule. He was distraught when he told Mr. Fraser about the strangers.

"I will go for the sheriff," Mr. Fraser said to his wife. "You stay here, Asa. Mary will get you some cool water."

"Yes, sir, Mr. Fraser. That sho' would be kind. I'm dry as cotton from walkin' all the way up here," Asa replied graciously.

Fraser swiftly saddled his horse, mounted, and rode towards town. About a mile up the road, he encountered the sheriff and his deputies riding southward as hard as they could ride. Fraser signaled for them to stop and told them about Asa and the strangers.

"It looks like we just got lucky," Nathan said. "Bill, you ride to the entrance of Asa's place. Stay out of sight, but position yourself where you can see the cabin. Gabe, go with him. Tie your horse with his, but you work toward the rear of the cabin. I will make my way toward the front."

It took a few minutes, but each one got into position. There was complete silence, except for the rustling of fallen leaves in the breeze and the calling of blue jays. Gabe could see the rear of the cabin through the tall goldenrod, but there was no sight of the men. It was at that moment that he heard Nathan call the men out.

"You there inside the cabin, this is Sheriff Ritter. Come out and throw your weapons on the ground with your hands raised."

Still, there was not a sound from within the cabin. Suddenly, the breaking of glass was heard, and Armstrong spoke from inside.

"Ain't happenin', Sheriff." Armstrong could see his horse, but getting to it was the problem. He called to Will. "Will you still with me?" Will never responded. As Armstrong checked for signs of breathing, he came to the grim realization that Will was dead. "Dadburn it! I could have already been in Celina, Tennessee, by now."

Nathan called Armstrong once more. "What's your name?"

The sheriff wanted to buy Gabe a little time if he could approach them from behind.

"Armstrong!"

"I didn't shoot that man at the livery, Sheriff. That was my partner. Now, he's dead." That was all Gabe needed to hear. He ran from the weeds at the edge of the woods and crashed through the back door.

Before Armstrong could get his revolver turned and leveled on Gabe, Gabe fired three shots, hitting Armstrong in the shoulder and ribs. Armstrong doubled over in pain, cursed, and dropped his revolver.

"You can come in now, Nathan," Gabe yelled.

"Who's your partner, Mr. Armstrong?"

"Will Burns," Armstrong said, grasping his shoulder and painfully trying to get his breath.

Nathan, Gabe, and Bill loaded the two on horses. "Bill," Nathan said, "go to the Frasers. Let Old Asa know that he can come home. Tell him there's a broken window and a little to clean up, but the trouble is over. We'll meet you back in town."

When Gabe and Nathan arrived back in town with their prisoner and the body of Will Burns, Gabe was surprised to find Hannah at Doctor McKinney's office. She was tending to Mrs. Turner and her daughter.

"Are you angry with me?" Gabe asked.

"No, just glad you're alright. Mrs. Turner is a pitiful sight. I feel so sorry for her." Hannah replied.

"What about Mr. Turner?" Gabe asked her.

"He's still alive."

"We caught the men who did it, but one's dead," Gabe said.

"I came here to fetch Doc McKinney to patch up the wounded prisoner."

Gabe and Doc McKinney went to the jailhouse. Still strapped across the saddle was Will Burns' body.

"Looks like Turner sent one to his Maker unless that was by one of you," the Doc said.

"No, that one is Turner's doing."

"Gabe, it looks like you came home with a pretty little wife," the Doc commented.

"Yes, sir."

"She stepped right in, introduced herself, and went to work tending to Mrs. Turner while my Mrs. cared for Mr. Turner."

"Not surprised," Gabe responded proudly.

"Looks like you did real good," Doc complimented.

Doc and Gabe stepped inside the sheriff's office. "Doc McKinney, your patient is over here," Nathan said. While Doc McKinney went to work on Armstrong, Gabe and Nathan stepped into the office.

"I learned from Armstrong that these two robbed a stage this morning near Edmonton. That's where the three hundred dollars came from. I sent Wyatt to Glasgow to inform the sheriff about what's happened here. After a robbery and an attempted murder, if Armstrong doesn't die on us, the Doc is mending him to stay alive just long enough to hang."

"Gabe, I could sure use you around here. Talk it over with your wife and let me know."

"I will," Gabe replied, feeling he could do some good as a lawman.

Meanwhile, Hannah was getting acquainted with Mrs. McKinney at Doctor McKinney's office. "Hannah, we need someone like you to help around here," Mrs. McKinney said. "I can tell you don't shy away from getting your hands dirty. Would you be interested in working with us?" Hannah's face lit up with surprise and excitement at the offer.

"I always wanted to become an assistant to a doctor. I would love that," she replied. Mrs. McKinney smiled. "Then it's settled. Can you come tomorrow?"

"I will be here bright and early," Hannah replied with a big smile. Just then, Gabe came in. She was so excited, and Gabe wondered what had happened.

"I'm going to work as an assistant to Doctor and Mrs. McKinney. I start tomorrow," she eagerly told him.

Gabe couldn't have been prouder because it appeared as if Hannah had found her place now.

"I need to ride back to Old Asa's place," he explained. "I need to repair a door I damaged and help Asa clean up the cabin.

"I will be back home as soon as possible." She hugged his neck and kissed his cheek.

"You know that you rescued me," Gabe tenderly told her.

"The Lord did that," she replied, as she smiled. "I just caught you before you got away. Be home before dark," she said and kissed him again.

Hannah returned home on the buckboard while Gabe rode out to assist Old Asa clean up the mess they left behind.

Gabe had begun to re-establish himself in the county as a servant in the community. However, one of the deputies, Frank Tate, disapproved of Gabe becoming the center of attention, and Gabe's past returned.

15

Two years quickly went by. It was a Saturday in early summer of 1868. The planting was finished. Early summer always marked the beginning of another growing season when warmer weather was expected.

The dinner table at the MacCallans was filled with everything from fried potatoes, pinto beans, corn pone, and fresh turnip greens with country ham. After giving thanks to God for seeing them through another harsh winter, the conversation around the table flowed seamlessly from one topic to another.

"Glazebrooks Emporium is coming to town," Mama MacCallan announced.

"Samuel Marrs sold the whole east side of the town square to Glazebrooks. That's what I heard, anyway," Gabe added.

"I heard that it will have everything you can think of, just like a big store in the city," Mama MacCallan said excitedly."

"And entertainment of some kind, too," Gabe's sister, Mary, said.

"The town will be as big as Louisville in ten years. You watch," Aaron said. "I don't like it," he muttered.

"Mama, everything on the table is really good as always," Hannah complimented.

"You sure put the scold on the gravy this time, Mama," Gabe added.

"Save some room for dessert," Mama MacCallan said. "I found a recipe for Lafayette Gingerbread in the newspaper. I thought I would try it."

"Gabe, can you help me next week?" Aaron asked. "I have several things that need to be done before we plant sorghum cane."

"The York's bull broke through the fence yesterday morning," Gabe said. "Repairing the fence will have to be added to the list."

While Gabe and his father discussed what needed to be done on the farm, the women were interrupted by a baby's cry. Gabe and Hannah's son, Alec, was born a month earlier. Hannah left the table to change and feed their little one.

"Speaking of next week," Mama MacCallan interjected, "next Saturday is the political rally. Girls, we will be helping with the registration booth."

"Do we have to?" they asked.

"Everyone has to do their fair share," their mother replied. "The good Lord has given us a second chance in this country. We best not squander it."

Gabe decided not to sign up as a Freedmen's Bureau agent. It was a good thing he didn't. The Bureau didn't last long in Kentucky, not because of a lack of need but because of resistance that hindered them from doing their job. Instead, Gabe became a deputy sheriff, while Hannah thrived as Doctor McKinney's trusted assistant, earning the love and respect of the community for her unwavering dedication and reliability. Mr. Turner survived his injuries, although it took about a year before he was well enough to work at the livery again. Armstrong was tried, found guilty, and sent to prison.

Life seemed to be going well, but unfortunately, not for all. Former slaves were terrorized by Confederate Democrat loyalists and rebel outlaws who formed gangs. There were multiple reports, although scattered, of numerous incidents involving intimidation, beatings, and even murders. Threats and notices from a so-called "Judge Lynch" were sometimes left at night for black families to find the following day. The mistreatment of former slaves caused problems for the sheriff, Gabe, and his fellow deputies.

Two of the troublemakers were Tom and Travis Walbert. The Walberts grew up on Kettle Creek near the Tennessee line. This area, located in a remote part of the county, remained fiercely loyal to the Confederacy. The Walberts were ruffians, taking pleasure in taunting the sheriff and his deputies. However, their mockery took an unexpected turn when they encountered Gabe MacCallan.

The courthouse lawn was a regular gathering place for the county, even after the courthouse was burned during the War. 1868 marked the arrival of an election year, which brought out politicians vying for votes. A large crowd had gathered. Children were running and playing, families were mingling, and everyone enjoyed the music. Gabe was mounted on Whirlwind, keeping a watchful eye to prevent any potential disturbances because some had brought moonshine and whiskey. The Walbert brothers caught Gabe's attention when they rode up. They were always looking for an audience and had no trouble finding it there.

"Look who's here, Travis," Tom said.

"Why, would you lookie here. It's the new deputy, Deputy MacCallan," Travis replied mockingly. They spoke loud enough for everyone around to hear. Gabe dismounted Whirlwind and led him by his bridle to where the Walberts were making fun.

"Are you boys planning to run for office? You've got everyone's attention," Gabe snidely said.

"Wearin' that there badge makes ya think yer purdy smart, don't it, deputy," Tom replied.

"Not as smart as my horse." Gabe continued to mock as he stroked Whirlwind's forehead.

"So, yer dumber than yer horse." They had fun with that and laughed.

"That's what he thinks, don't you, Whirlwind?" Gabe smiled as if to set a snare for a couple of fools. Gabe had been working with Whirlwind and teaching him a few tricks. He taught him to shake his head whenever he asked questions. It drew laughter out of the crowd when Whirlwind shook his head as if to say he was more intelligent than Gabe. The Walberts didn't find it amusing.

"In fact," Gabe smiled and said loud enough for all to hear. "I'll bet Whirlwind is smarter than you boys. Whirlwind, what is ten minus five?" Gabe asked. Whirlwind stamped the ground five times. The crowd applauded with amazement and laughter, and the Walberts just looked at each other, not knowing what to say.

"It's your turn, boys. Do you want to compete with my horse?" They were silent while the crowd laughed again. The Walberts just stared at

Gabe while becoming angrier by the second.

Gabe added insult to their injured pride. "Whirlwind, do you think you're smarter than these boys?" When Whirlwind shook his head three times, the crowd laughed and applauded louder than before. The Walberts knew they had been made to look like the fools they were. Red-faced and insulted, they glanced around at the laughing crowd, mounted their horses, and left. After watching them ride away, Gabe resumed his visits with people in the crowd. Several children ran to Gabe and Whirlwind, asking him to do more tricks. Nathan was seated on the courthouse step, watching the whole thing as Gabe walked up, leading Whirlwind.

"That was the most fun I've had in a long time," Nathan said, still laughing about it.

Hannah witnessed everything, too, and shook her head in amazement at how skillfully Gabe interacted with people. She was working one of the political booths to register men to vote for the Republican party when a young lady walked up.

"Your husband knows how to steal the show," she said to Hannah.

Hannah glanced at her and smiled. "He enjoys showing off his horse. Sometimes, I think he has more affection for that horse than he has for me." She smiled and introduced herself. "I'm Hannah MacCallan."

"I'm Abigail Ray. It's a pleasure to meet you."

Abigail was a remarkably beautiful woman. Some said that she was the most beautiful woman in the county. Her family was wealthy. They owned over five hundred acres, most of which lay in rich river bottom. She inherited everything after her parents passed away. She was a former slave owner who owned forty slaves until the Emancipation Proclamation granted their freedom. After exchanging polite introductions with Hannah, Abigail joined the crowd and the festivities.

"I've been wondering when she would finally introduce herself," Gabe's sister remarked mockingly. Hannah looked at her with a curious glance.

"That's Gabe's old girlfriend," she said.

Hannah looked in Abigail's direction as she was gracefully walking away.

"We were worried that he would marry her," his sister added, hugging Hannah and kissing her cheek. "I'm thankful that God had someone else in mind. It was you." Hannah had not heard about Abigail, which was bothersome. Gabe had never mentioned her.

While the town was enjoying the celebration, the Walberts arrived back at their favorite waterhole after they had been humiliated. It was a small, ramshackle log cabin near Hestand, a favorite hangout for roughnecks and outlaws. They were still rubbing their wounded pride after being humiliated by Gabe's horse. They walked in, cussing and yelling before sitting down. Those who were there didn't pay them any mind. The Walberts were always fuming and trying to get even.

"That deputy just earned himself a place in my gun sights," Travis growled as he grabbed a jug of moonshine and turned it up. They entertained ways to ambush him and weren't afraid of being overheard.

"You talkin' about MacCallan?" a voice cut through their conversation from across the room. Travis turned to see a man in the corner, shuffling his cards.

"If you want to lure MacCallan," the man said as he sipped on his glass of whiskey and took a draw from his cigarette, "you'll have to do as I tell ya."

"How do you know MacCallan?" Tom asked him.

"I didn't say I knew him," the man replied, his voice calm and measured. "But I know someone who does, and he will pay good money to get him out of the way." The Walbert brothers slid their chairs over to his table to listen to what the man had to say.

16

Gabe noticed that Hannah had been unusually quiet the last few days since the courthouse yard political gathering, and it was beginning to annoy him. Settling things and moving on was his way, but that doesn't always work with a woman, as he soon learned. It was early in the morning, and they were heading to town. As usual, he was on Whirlwind, and Hannah was in the buckboard.

"Do you want to talk about it?" Gabe decided to ask.

At first, she didn't want to respond, but then she said, "Why didn't you tell me about her?"

"Who?" Gabe asked.

"You know *who*?" she replied sharply.

Gabe tried hard not to burst out laughing, which didn't suit Hannah very well. She pulled back on the reins to bring the horse to a halt.

"You think I'm being funny," she remarked in a raised voice.

"Is that what's been stickin' in your craw? I thought I had surely done something wrong."

"You did, Gabe," she snapped back. Now, she was getting more upset. "I'm mad because you kept her from me." It was hard for Gabe to hold back his amusement, knowing she would become even more angry at him.

"I reckon you met her the other day then?"

Hannah didn't respond, but the irritated look she gave him spoke volumes.

"It would have been nice if you had told me that you had an old girlfriend here. That's all."

"We courted for a while at church gatherings and such, but that was all."

"Did you kiss her?" Hannah asked.

"Right on the lips—twice," he replied with a smirk. Hannah sneered, shocked and appalled.

"The way you're smilin', you must have liked it," she replied.

"I did. Why would I not?"

She cut her eyes at him again with a scornful frown, snapped the reins, and left him behind. Gabe just smiled.

"She sure is cute when she's jealous," he said to himself. "Whirlwind, take my advice. Leave the fillies alone. You will never figure them out."

Gabe slapped Whirlwind's flank, and he jumped to a gallop. When he caught up with Hannah, he grabbed her horse's bridle.

"Whoa! Whoa!" he said, bringing the mare to a stop. "Hannah, it never crossed my mind to tell you about her. Why would I?"

Hannah kept her arms crossed and looked away, but was listening.

"I was eighteen. Abigail was sixteen. Of course, I liked her." He paused a moment. "But I don't think you are that jealous of a little romance between two teenagers. Am I right?" Hannah started to cool off as she wiped away her tears.

"No, I'm not jealous because she is some old girlfriend of yours. It's just that—it's just that she is so perfect. Her skin is as white as buttermilk, and her hair is a beautiful red. She's tall and has big green eyes; to top it all off, she is as sweet as molasses."

Gabe smiled again. "She might be all that," he said, "but she's not for me." Hannah heard what she wanted and needed to hear. Her sense of insecurity was getting the best of her, and she realized it.

"I'm sorry for being such a fool," she said. "Let's get to town. We both have things to do," she said, wiping more tears away.

Gabe tied Whirlwind to the rear of the buckboard and rode the rest of the way with Hannah. When they reached town, Hannah entered the doctor's office, and Gabe took the horses to the livery.

"Good morning, Hannah," Doctor McKinney said when she entered the door. He was seated at his desk reading mail that had arrived.

"Have a seat, my dear. I have something to ask you."

Hannah sat beside his desk as Doctor McKinney removed his glasses and rubbed his bushy gray mustache. He had her worried for a moment.

"How would you like to study to become a nurse?"

Hannah was stunned and speechless but honored that he thought enough of her potential to ask.

"You have shown me the skills that it takes. You never shy away from getting your hands dirty and are good with people. I think you would make a wonderful nurse." He then leaned forward to say, "When the field opens up for women to become doctors in this country, you will be ready, should you decide to do so."

"Doctor McKinney," she replied, with surprise in her voice. "I would love to become a nurse, but a doctor? Whoever heard of such a thing?"

"You leave that to me. Now, you will have to do a lot of studying." Then he rose from his chair, pulled three books from his shelf, and laid them on his desk before her. We will start with this book on human anatomy. You are officially back in school. Congratulations!" he said with excitement in his voice. Do you think Gabe will approve?"

"He will," Hannah said with a bit of hesitation. "I hope. Yes, I know he will."

"Good," he replied.

Hannah couldn't have been more excited. She couldn't wait to tell Gabe and write to her family back in Missouri about the good news.

When Gabe entered the sheriff's office, feeling much better after clearing the air with Hannah, Frank Tate, and Bill Wyatt were there. Tate was not a Kentuckian like everyone else. He was a Yankee, a sizable man, standing six feet tall, single, and in his early thirties. He was cocky and polished his badge a lot. His way with people was rough, as Yankees who came to the South usually were. He believed that throwing foul language around asserted his authority. Intimidation was his way of manipulation that kept him the top-dog deputy, at least in his mind. Bill was a smaller fella. He wasn't interested in being the top dog, so there wasn't any competition between them. Tate seemed to make sure of it.

Gabe was like a third wheel. He was good at sizing men up. He had Frank Tate pegged thirty minutes after he first met him. Tate tried his manipulative Yankee ways on Gabe, but it wasn't working. Gabe was always one step ahead of him, and Tate knew it. For that reason, and because Gabe was Nathan's friend, Tate was jealous and felt threatened.

When the time came, Tate wanted to be sheriff when Nathan was voted out or resigned. It wouldn't be this year, but he was willing to wait, that is, until Gabe came along.

"Good morning, gentlemen," Gabe said as he poured himself a cup of coffee. They replied with the same. Frank and Bill played cards and held the fort while Nathan was in Bowling Green. Nathan had to appear in Federal Court to testify about the murder of a black man near Beaumont and was scheduled to meet with the U.S. Marshal. There was a gradual increase in threats, terror, and murder of former slaves in the South. Black Kentuckians were falling victim to the Klan, making its way into southern Kentucky, and they were recruiting members. One night in Cumberland County, a group of hooded men dragged a man out of his house and hanged him in front of his family. They targeted him because he served in the U.S. Colored Soldiers Kentucky Unit during the War. For his service, he was given land by the government, which was often a death sentence in the South. The marshal gave the sheriff a list of suspects for this crime and others. As Nathan read through the list of names, he recognized a few. Among them were the Walbert brothers. They were listed as Klansmen. He wasn't surprised.

Back in Monroe County, the three deputies engaged in small talk, mainly between Bill and Gabe, until Tate abruptly left.

"Where is he going?" Gabe asked as they watched him go out the door without saying a word. Bill gathered the cards and started to play solitaire. Without looking up from his cards, he replied, "He said something about meeting someone this morning."

Gabe walked over to the window and sipped his coffee as he watched Tate ride away. "Did he say who or where?" he asked, turning to Bill, expecting a reply.

"I didn't ask. He didn't say," Bill replied while concentrating on his card game. Gabe glanced back out the window, pondering.

"Bill, if you don't mind, I think I'll also go out for a while."

Bill remained absorbed in his game, giving no response. Gabe adjusted his hat, lowering it over his brow, and left quietly. He waited a few minutes to ensure Tate had a head start before mounting Whirlwind and setting off southward.

Maintaining enough distance and staying out of sight, Gabe trailed

Tate through Hestand toward Martinsburg. Soon, Tate approached a cabin. Gabe halted about two hundred yards back, dismounted, and led Whirlwind into the cover of the woods, descending cautiously until he reached a ridge. There, he secured Whirlwind and proceeded on foot, silently closing the gap until he was just thirty yards from the cabin.

Horses were tied out front, but he couldn't tell how many. The area around the cabin looked unguarded. Even so, he moved closer with caution. His heart was racing. His senses were heightened. *There was something about this that didn't feel right*, he thought to himself. It was too quiet, which made Gabe more uneasy. Not a songbird, not the rustling of squirrels. Nothing was moving, not even a breeze. He watched the cabin for what seemed to be an hour. He was about to ease his way back to Whirlwind when two men walked out of the open door. One of them was Frank Tate. Who the other man was, he didn't know. They talked for a few minutes, then shook hands. Tate got on his horse and rode back toward town. *Who did he come to see, only to meet and leave?*

Gabe's curiosity piqued at this point. After Tate departed, the stranger returned indoors briefly before emerging again, mounting one of the horses, and riding in the same direction. Gabe made his way back to Whirlwind and followed him. Just before getting to Hestand, the stranger turned west. Gabe noticed as he turned down a familiar lane. "He's heading toward the Ray plantation," Gabe muttered to himself. He could see the farmhouse, so he dismounted and stood by Whirlwind out of view. The stranger rode up to the house, dismounted, and walked to the front door. It opened. There was Abigail Ray. She talked to him for a moment and let the stranger inside.

Uneasy about the situation but unwilling to linger, Gabe decided to retreat. It seemed clear Abigail knew the man, but Gabe's instincts nagged at him. He carefully made his way back to the road and headed back to town, his mind grappling with what he had witnessed. Despite his attempts to dismiss it as an innocent visit, a persistent feeling in his gut told him there was more to this. He needed additional information to make sense of it all.

There was a small store at Hestand's crossroads, so he decided to stop for a visit. Across the road, there was a feed mill and a cotton mill. Herbert Atwell, who owned the store, lived on the opposite side of the road. Seated there on the porch were Mr. Atwell and two older gentlemen. It was a favored place to pass the time. Wood shavings covered the porch deck, where they whittled on red cedar sticks, traded knives, and gossiped. Mr. Atwell was cleaning the dirt out from under his fingernails with his pocket knife when he glanced up to see Gabe dismounting his horse. Gabe tied Whirlwind in front and stepped up to the porch.

"Mornin' gentlemen," Gabe said. "Do you have any cheese and crackers, Mr. Atwell?"

"What the rats ain't got into," he said with a toothless grin. "Come on inside, young feller."

Gabe followed Mr. Atwell into the store after politely tipping his hat to the two seated on the porch. The store was old, dark, and smelled of cat urine. At that point, Gabe was beginning to regret asking for cheese and crackers.

"The cracker barrel is over yonder. I'll cut ya a slice of cheese. You want one or two?" Mr. Atwell asked.

"One is fine," Gabe replied.

Atwell shooed the cat away with a flick of his hand. "Scat! Pss! Get out of here!" With the counter cleared, he placed a chunk of cheese down and sliced off a thick piece with his pocket knife. Gabe grabbed a handful of crackers but made sure to reach deep below the surface. At least he felt it would be less likely to have cat hair and who knows what else.

"Three cents, deputy. What else can I do ya for?"

"Maybe you can help me," Gabe replied. "There's a cabin just down the road from here. Who owns it? Do you know?" Gabe asked as he laid a copper three-cent nickel on the counter.

"You mean that waterhole? Abigail Ray owns it, I reckon. Since land got so cheap, she's been buying land with that old money she inherited."

"Why do you call it a waterhole?" Gabe was curious to know, even though he suspected the reason why. He was keeping the conversation going.

"Nothin' but scoundrels. That's all that's down there. It makes me wonder why Miss Ray would put up with it. Several of the neighbors are startin' to fuss about it." He continued. "It can get a little rowdy down there at times, shootin' and shoutin' and carryin' on."

Gabe took a small bite of cheese and stale crackers. "Have you seen anyone new around?"

Atwell thought for a moment. "You know, come to think of it, there's a feller I have been seein' from time to time. He stopped in a few days ago. Ain't seen him since, though."

"Did you get his name? What did he look like?"

"I don't recall a name, but I do recall that he looked like he just walked out'a Washington."

"What do you mean?" Gabe asked, finding that to be an odd description.

"He looked like a Washington politician and talked like one, too. He weren't from here, that's fer shore. I wondered what the likes'a him was doin' 'round here, but I figured he was one of them there Bureau men."

"Mr. Atwell," Gabe nodded appreciatively. "You take care now… and… if you don't mind, don't mention to anyone that I came by askin' 'bout this fella you mentioned."

"Yes, sir, young feller. Yer welcome anytime, deputy."

Gabe's gut feeling was becoming confirmed, but how was Abigail involved, and in what? What role did Tate have? These questions needed answers, Gabe thought to himself. He made his way back to town, but after going a short distance, he tossed the cheese and crackers to a stray dog.

By now, it was noon. Gabe rode back into town to Doctor McKinney's office. He wanted to see how Hannah was doing. When he entered, Hannah was excited to see him. She eagerly shared her plans to study nursing, and Gabe couldn't help but smile. "Well, that suits you," he remarked. "You'll be the best one around."

"Good afternoon, Gabe," Doc McKinney said as he came from the back room. "Hannah, Mrs. Goodman needs your assistance. I have to make a call at the Harlow place. One of the children has been feverish."

"Yes, doctor," Hannah told Gabe that she would see him tonight and hurriedly went to help Mrs. Goodman.

"She is an asset and will make a good doctor one day, Gabe. I'm proud that you went to Missouri and brought her back." The Doc smiled, slapped Gabe's arm a couple of times, and grabbed his medical bag.

"She has my support, Doc," Gabe said as he beamed with pride and followed him out the door. Doc tipped his hat, and he rode to the Harlow's place.

As the Doc rode away, Gabe noticed Frank Tate heading toward the sheriff's office, so he walked over. However, as Gabe was on his way to confront Tate, someone else caught his attention. It was the mysterious stranger he had seen at Abigail's. He was walking toward the bank. Gabe quickly made his way there. Kora Lawson was seated outside the bank and waiting for her husband, who was inside. Mrs. Lawson looked up and saw Gabe.

"Why, hello, Gabe," she greeted.

"Hello, Miss Kora," Gabe replied with a smile.

"How are you and your new wife and the baby?" she asked.

"We are doing fine, Miss Kora. Hannah and the baby have settled just fine."

"She seems like a sweet girl," Miss Kora added.

"Yes, ma'am, thank you."

"Miss Kora, the man who just went into the bank, would you know who he is?

"Oh, you must mean Miss Ray's foreman, Mr. Davis. He runs her farms now."

"Davis?"

"Yes, Russell Davis," she replied.

"He arrived in town sometime before you came home. He met Miss Ray and was soon hired as her foreman. I was surprised that a fella like him would settle here."

"Miss Kora, you have been most helpful. Thank you. Give my greetings to your husband."

"I surely will. You say hello to your sweet wife for me, you hear," Miss Kora replied.

"Yes, ma'am."

Gabe left before Davis came out of the office and walked to the shop next door, taking a seat on the porch bench. The townspeople spoke as they walked by. He watched as construction on the new courthouse was nearing completion, and children were running and playing along the street. After a few minutes, Davis exited the bank. He didn't look Gabe's way but walked to the County Clerk's office. It was clear that he was here doing business for Abigail. *Why would a man who looked like he could do better for himself be a foreman for a plantation owner?* These were questions that troubled Gabe. Eager to find out, Gabe followed Davis to the Clerk's Office. There were two other men there, Sam Pearson and Ell Crews.

"Well, what'da ya say there, Deputy MacCallan?" Ell Crews couldn't hear thunder, so when he spoke in his deep voice, he was so loud that everyone in the county could hear him.

"Hello, Mr. Crews. How are you doin'?" Gabe replied.

When Davis heard Gabe's name, he turned. Davis didn't mind looking like a city slicker from his hat down to his polished black boots. Standing about six-one, Davis was wearing a stiff flat-brimmed hat that had silver buckles as a band, not your average fancy hat that one would find in Monroe County. It fitted level over his eyebrows. He was clean-shaven and clean-cut. His white shirt was buttoned at the top. Around his collar, he wore a black bola tie of braided leather with a turquoise and silver clasp. What caught Gabe's attention was the belt and guns strapped to his waist, black leather holsters with two slick bone-handled .46 caliber Remington revolvers.

"Deputy MacCallan, my name is Russell Davis. I am Abigail Ray's foreman."

Gabe shook hands with him. You can tell a lot about a man when you shake hands. To be a foreman, Gabe thought it was odd that he didn't have the calluses of a working man.

"Very pleased to meet you, Mr. Davis. I can tell that you aren't from around here. Do you mind if I ask where you are from and what brought you to southern Kentucky?"

"I'll tell you what, Deputy, I'm about to go for dinner. Why don't you join me at the hotel, and we can get to know one another. I can take care of my business later."

"I don't want to interrupt your business," Gabe replied.

"I insist," Davis said with a smile.

After a short walk to the hotel together, they were served coffee, and Davis decided to begin the conversation to answer Gabe's question. "I'm from the northeast, originally Pennsylvania. Years ago, I traveled as far west as Arizona. I lived there during the War but never could get used to the desert and heat, so I moved back East. I intended to travel to Cincinnati, but I stopped here on the way from Nashville. I liked it and decided to stay."

"So then, you prefer a hot, humid climate, I take it," Gabe asked in good humor.

Davis laughed. "Maybe."

"Family?" Gabe asked as he took a sip of his coffee.

"No family. You might say I'm looking to settle down."

"Here?"

"Who knows," Davis replied. "If the scenery is nice enough."

Their food arrived at the table: country ham, hominy, fried potatoes, pinto beans, and cornbread. "I must admit," Davis remarked, "I have never eaten anywhere as well as I have here."

"You can't beat good southern cooking. I'll grant you that," Gabe replied. "Mr. Davis –," Gabe continued but was interrupted.

"Please call me Russ. That's what my friends call me."

"Mr. Davis," Gabe politely declined his request, "you said you are Miss Ray's foreman. That must be a big responsibility. She has, what, about five hundred acres?"

"Five hundred twenty, to be exact, and adding more. This is why I am in town today." Davis responded. "Since the Civil Rights Act, managing the plantation has been a problem. It is my job to do what's needed to run things. I am also assisting her with her investments." Davis grinned as he wiped his mouth. "What about you, Gabe?"

"MacCallan … Deputy MacCallan," Gabe responded, which drew a line in their acquaintance.

"I served in the War, like most, along with my two brothers, who did not survive. After the War, I went to Missouri, met my future wife, married, and returned home."

"You sound like a man who knows what he wants and goes after it. Would I be right?" Davis asked. Gabe finished his coffee and replied, "I was just thinking the same thing about you."

Davis laughed and sat back in his chair. "Yes. You and I are not so different, deputy."

After about thirty minutes, Davis tossed his napkin onto his plate and laid two silver dollars on the table.

"This is on me," Davis said.

"Keep your money, Mr. Davis. I took care of it when we came in."

Davis looked at Gabe and smiled. "You also like to stay one step ahead, I see. Thank you, deputy. It has been a real pleasure," Davis said as they both rose from the table. Davis took his hat and set it squarely on his head. Both men looked each other straight in the eyes and shook hands, each understanding the other.

"Yes, a pleasure," Gabe replied, and Davis left the hotel.

Just as Gabe and Davis were parting ways, Hannah was busy at Doc McKinney's office, straightening the office, cleaning, and tending to minor ailments. She finally had a minute to study from one of her medical books when someone stepped inside. Hannah recognized her immediately. It was Abigail Ray. Hannah rose from her chair, surprised to see her.

"Good morning," Hannah greeted coolly, but trying to be cordial.

"Good morning, Mrs. MacCallan," Abigail replied, also coolly.

"Is Doctor McKinney in?"

"No, he is out at the moment. Can I help you?"

Abigail strolled leisurely towards the desk where Hannah stood. Her heels clicked against the hardwood floor with the rustle of her dress. Abigail was dressed to the hilt, while Hannah was dressed to work and with a bandana to pull back her hair. Hannah couldn't help but notice Abigail's scrutinizing gaze. She felt intimidated and asked again. "Can I help you?"

"Do you remember me?"

"I know who you are," Hannah replied. "We have already met at the political rally, if you recall."

"I suppose Gabe told you about our history," Abigail said as she glanced from the corner of her eye to see Hannah's reaction.

"More of a short story from what I was told," Hannah replied as she stepped away from the desk. "Miss Ray, why have you come?"

"I really didn't come to see the doctor. I came to see you."

"Me? Why me?" Hannah asked.

Abigail turned to Hannah. "You might be Gabe's wife, but I still care about him. I am concerned for his safety."

"What on earth do you mean?" Hannah was now beginning to be annoyed, but Abigail's whole demeanor changed at that moment. Hannah could tell that she was genuinely concerned as she walked closer to Hannah.

"I overheard a conversation a few days ago between one of the other deputies and my foreman. I am afraid they are plotting the hurt Gabe or worse."

"Why are you telling me this? Why not go to Gabe and Sheriff Ritter?"

"I can't. If my foreman were to find out about this, it would spell trouble for me. I'm frightened," Abigail confessed with tears now welling up in her eyes.

"Why would they want to hurt my husband?" Hannah asked with concern in her voice.

"I'm not sure. Please tell Gabe to be careful." Abigail turned to leave but paused before going out the door and glancing back at Hannah. "Hannah, you don't need to fret about me interfering in your marriage." Then she stepped out and departed. For the first time since meeting Abigail, Hannah realized how mistaken she may have been in her judgment toward Abigail. She felt as concerned for Abigail as she did for Gabe. It sounds like she made a wrong business arrangement with this foreman and is now afraid of him for some reason. *Which one of the deputies was she talking about,* she wondered to herself.

"It has to be Frank Tate," she said out loud. Hurriedly, she loosened her nurse's apron and set it aside, determined to find Gabe. She finally found him at the hotel. "Where have you been?" she asked Gabe, her voice filled with urgency. "I've searched for you all over town."

With a curious expression, Gabe responded, "I just had an

interesting encounter with Abigail Ray's foreman, Russell Davis."

"Well, I just had a visit from Abigail," Hannah replied. "Gabe, she's frightened."

"What is she afraid about?" Gabe asked.

"Her foreman," Hannah replied. "And that isn't all. She is concerned about you."

"Me? Why me?" Gabe asked in a tone of surprise.

"Abigail said she recently overheard a conversation between one of the deputies and her foreman. They were talking about you. She is worried that they might be planning something against you."

"She must be referring to Tate," Gabe replied.

Hannah nodded in agreement. "Abigail didn't say, but that's what I thought, too," she confirmed, her concern deepening.

"I followed Tate out of town this morning to where he met with Davis. Afterward, Davis went to her house."

"Do you think he is after Abigail?" Hannah asked with concern.

"Maybe. He certainly has the charm. I believe he could charm a rattlesnake." Gabe took his bandana and wiped his forehead. "Davis is overseeing her investments. I think he wants something more."

"If Davis is after her wealth, what role would Tate play?" Hannah questioned, still not understanding the connection.

"I don't think Tate is interested in what Davis is up to," Gabe replied. "I think Tate wants to be sheriff someday, so he is seeking help from Davis. Tate thinks I will stand in his way, and he's right. I will. He's a corrupt man. I'm convinced now that both of them are corrupt."

"Gabe, this makes me nervous," Hannah said, expressing her concern even more.

"Don't worry. I'll keep a close watch on Tate and Davis from now on," Gabe assured.

"Should we warn Abigail?" Hannah asked since Abigail could be harmed.

"Not yet. Let me think about this. I trust Nathan. I'll speak with him."

17

I t was Sunday in the fall of the year. Church members were leaving the meeting house after morning worship.

"Good sermon, Brother Gabe. I hope your father is better soon. Say hello to your Mama for me."

"Thank you, sister. I certainly will," Gabe replied kindly.

Hannah held little Alec in her arms and greeted the church members as they left. They loved Hannah but loved little Alec even more. Hannah's attention was directed to someone standing by the road. It was Abigail. Hannah hadn't noticed her during the service. Without wasting a moment, Hannah made her way to her.

"Abigail, what a pleasant surprise. I'm sorry that I failed to see you during worship."

Abigail smiled. "You didn't fail to see me. I didn't come inside. I stayed out here. I could hear Gabe's message. It was a good sermon."

"Why not stay for dinner?" Hannah suggested warmly, reaching out to take Abigail's hand, noticing her downcast expression.

"People don't have the best opinions of me," Abigail replied, hesitating.

"Oh, nonsense. Join us for dinner," Hannah insisted, introducing Alec to Abigail. "Would you like to hold him?"

"I don't…" Abigail hesitated, clearly unsure.

"Of course you do. Here," Hannah interjected, gently placing Alec in Abigail's arms. It was a wise and heartfelt gesture. As the members saw Abigail cradling Alec, the ice began to melt.

That afternoon, Hannah and Abigail were inseparable and became good friends.

As Gabe and Hannah made their way back home, the late afternoon sun was beginning to set behind the tree line. Alec was fast asleep. Gabe and Hannah heard the rhythm of horses' hooves pounding against the dirt road and coming quickly from behind them. They wondered who was in such a hurry. Someone was riding toward them at full gallop.

"Gabe! Gabe!" the panicked rider was heard shouting.

Gabe pulled back on the reins and set the brake on the buckboard. It was Quinn's brother, Adam. He dismounted his mule before it could stop, and he ran to them. He was crying so much that he was hard to understand.

"Gabe, Miss Hannah, you got to come home wit me. It's bad. They shot Quinn. They dun kilt him, Gabe. They dun kilt him. Laudy, Laudy. What we go'na do now?" Adam cried, being beside himself with emotion.

"Who, Adam? Who did this?"

"Please come wit me! Please come wit me!" Adam cried.

They rode to Freetown as quickly as possible. By that time, a crowd had gathered at Quinn's home. Cries of pain and sorrow filled the air. Quinn's wife, Maggie, was sitting on the step of the front porch, rocking back and forth, stunned and in shock. Hannah immediately ran to her side. Gabe made his way through the crowd and entered the house. Everyone knew Gabe. There, on the table, was Quinn's body. He had been shot through the heart. Gabe had seen wounds during the War. He could tell he was shot at close range, and it appeared to be from a .44 caliber.

"I need to know everything," Gabe said as he turned to the crowd. "Any eyewitnesses?"

"They be two men that did it," Adam spoke up and said. "Quinn was splittin' wood when they rode up. I was stackin' wood in the shed. I seen 'em ride up. They's faces was covered. I hear'd one say, 'Are you the one they call Quinn?' He said, 'Yes.' I don't know why he didn't run when they rode up. And then one pulled his gun and shot him. They just shot him like he was a mad dog, Gabe." Adam broke down, weeping bitterly.

"They didn't see you?" Gabe asked him.

"No," Adam replied, sobbing as he spoke. "I was hid in the shed. I knew they would kill me, too."

"Did you recognize who they were?"

"No. Laudy, Laudy, have mercy, oh Laud," he said and then broke down and sobbed. Everyone wept in anguish. Gabe walked out of the house and into the yard. Adam followed.

"Which way did they go, Adam. Tell me?"

"They rode that'a way," Adam replied, pointing south.

Gabe walked back to Maggie and Hannah, still seated on the front porch step. He kneeled before Maggie as the family gathered around her. Gabe led them in a prayer.

"Father, lay thy merciful hand of comfort upon Maggie and her people. We ask, dear Lord, that thou may awaken thy vindication and use me to bring these men to justice with thy almighty hand."

Everyone responded, "Amen," and then there was only the sound of sobs.

"Maggie," Gabe said softly, "I will find them."

She gazed into his eyes, her own pain too deep for words, and nodded. Hannah needed to get Alec home. So, Gabe and Hannah made their way back in the darkness, Hannah silently wiping away her tears. Gabe's mind raced with questions—who would target Quinn, and why? Then, he happened to think of Davis and Tate, but the thought was so outrageous that he wanted to dismiss his suspicions.

Sleep eluded them that night. At the earliest possible hour the next day, Gabe met Nathan at his office, where the sheriff had already heard the news.

"I'll get Tate and Wyatt to Freetown with me and start lookin' around."

"No!" Gabe said sharply, which Nathan thought was an odd reaction. "Nathan, I can't prove anything yet or tell exactly why, but we need to look into this—just you and me."

"Why?" Nathan asked, his curiosity piqued. Gabe removed his hat, an expression of deep concern etched on his face.

"Have a seat," Gabe insisted. As Nathan settled into his chair, Gabe expressed his suspicions about Tate and Davis. Nathan rubbed his chin, not understanding where Gabe was going with his theory, spat into the spittoon, and leaned forward in his chair.

"Tell me if I understand you right," Nathan said. "Tate wants my job, and you believe that him and Davis are somehow connected to this murder?"

"I know how this sounds, Nathan," Gabe admitted. "But you and I need to go to Freetown, not Tate."

"What has this to do with Quinn?" Nathan asked.

Gabe lowered his head. He couldn't answer except to say, "I don't know."

"Listen," Nathan said, trying not to seem impatient. "I think you are distraught right now. Nothing that you are suggesting makes any sense, Gabe. Come along with us and tend to Quinn's family. The other two deputies and I will take care of this."

Gabe understood Nathan's skepticism; none of it made much sense to him either. Realizing Nathan wouldn't be much help, he followed instructions and rode to Quinn's place ahead of the others. When he arrived, Hannah was already there, preparing Quinn's body for burial. Gabe found Adam sitting by the woodshed near the bloodstained ground where his brother had died.

Gabe walked over and sat on a wood block beside him. For the first five minutes, neither of them spoke a word. Finally, Gabe stood up and decided to look around, hoping to find something that might provide a clue to this senseless tragedy.

"Adam, where were the horsemen when they rode up?"

"Over yond'a," Adam pointed.

Gabe circled the area. There were hoof prints all over. "Can you describe the horses?"

"One was brown. The other was pale," Adam told him.

"Pale?" That caused Gabe to think about the day the Walberts rode up to the town square and Gabe humiliated them in front of the whole town. He remembered that one of them rode a pale-colored horse. As Gabe paced the area, he noticed something different among the hoof prints.

"One of the horses has thrown a shoe, Adam."

Gabe knew that he would be disobeying orders, but he grabbed Whirlwind's reins, slid his boot into the stirrup. Whirlwind threw his head back, rearing to go. "Ya!" Gabe yelled to Whirlwind. He raised his front hooves and jumped into a gallop toward Fountain Run Road. Gabe knew where he might find the Walberts.

At the sheriff's office, Nathan gathered deputies Frank Tate and Bill Wyatt. "There's been a murder in Freetown," he told them.

"Where's MacCallan?" Tate asked, curious about his absence.

"Don't worry about him," Nathan said.

"Who was killed?" Bill asked. Nathan glanced at Tate to answer Bill's question.

"Quinn Howard," Nathan finally said. Tate was visibly disturbed by the news. "Tate, I need you to stay here while Wyatt and I go to Freetown."

Tate stared coldly at Nathan but held his tongue as Nathan and Wyatt exited, leaving Tate behind. Once they left, Tate walked out onto the porch and sank into a chair. Across the street, Davis was leaving the County Clerk's office. He noticed Tate and made his way over.

"Good morning, Frank."

Tate rolled his cigarette, ignoring Davis' greeting.

"I just heard there was a killing in Freetown," Davis added, watching Tate strike a match across the heel of his boot. He waited for a response, but when none came, he started to walk away. As Davis was about to leave, Tate extinguished the match after letting it burn down to his fingertips and finally spoke.

"Wyatt and the sheriff are headed to Freetown," Tate said, looking up at Davis with a cold stare. "Why him, Russ? Why this one?"

Davis removed his hat, brushed the brim, straightened the silver-buckled band, and placed it back on his head. "You want to be sheriff, don't you?" he asked, then walked away. Tate took a long draw from his cigarette, watching a ring of smoke rise above his head.

"Not like this, I don't," Tate muttered.

Davis continued to walk away as if he didn't hear Tate's remark.

Nathan and Wyatt arrived at Freetown. After paying their respects to the family, they went to work gathering information, all of which Gabe already had.

Hannah approached Nathan. "Morning, Nathan. Thank you for coming," she said.

"Hannah, I expected Gabe to be here with the family. Where is he?"

"He was here, but he left," Hannah replied.

"Where to?" Nathan asked.

"He left in a hurry. I don't know. Is there something I should know?" Hannah was now very concerned.

"He went toward Fountain Run Road, Adam told them. About an hour ago."

"Adam, tell me what Gabe said before he left," Nathan said. Adam told the sheriff what he knew about the pale horse and the tracks of one horse without a shoe. Nathan turned to Wyatt and was careful not to say what he was thinking in front of Hannah.

"Let's head down that way. Hannah, if Gabe returns, let him know we were here and for him to stay here."

"I will, but you know how stubborn he can be," she replied as they left.

They left the same way Gabe had gone. Nathan's instinct was to head toward Hestand because of what Gabe had told him earlier. "Gabe knows who did this," he said to Wyatt. "I hope we find Gabe before he finds them." Gabe knew now who killed Quinn.

Around midday, Gabe reached Hestand. He noticed Mr. Atwell and a few familiar faces gathered on the front porch of Atwell's store. Coming to a halt at the crossroads, he was studying what to do next. He was reluctant to proceed down the road leading to the cabin called the Waterhole, fearing that the Walberts, if they spotted him, would manage to elude capture or set up an ambush.

"Deputy!" Mr. Atwell called out from the porch, prompting Gabe to approach the store.

"Morning, Mr. Atwell."

"Get down and visit a spell. I'll fix some more cheese and crackers," Mr. Atwell offered kindly.

"Thank you, Mr. Atwell, but I'm in somewhat of a hurry," Gabe replied. "Perhaps another time. Mr. Atwell, how can I get to that cabin you called a Waterhole without riding down this road?"

Sitting on the porch was an older fellow chewing tobacco and whittling on a stick. "I own the farm on the other side of the road from it," he said without looking up.

"May I have your permission to ride onto your place, Mr. –."

"The name's Huffman. Sure. I don't mind."

"Which way is your farm?" Gabe asked.

Mr. Huffman pointed down Vernon Road. "That way. I'll take you there."

In about fifteen minutes, they were at Huffman's farm. On the way, Gabe explained that he needed to position himself in clear view of the cabin.

"I have a barn down yonder. You should be able to hunker down inside there if you have a mind to."

Gabe thanked Mr. Huffman and made his way to the barn. As he carefully walked to the barn leading Whirlwind, he flushed a covey of bobwhites, causing his heart to skip a beat. Whirlwind was also startled. "Whoa, boy," Gabe said softly. "It's only quail," he said, trying to calm his own nerves.

The fall breeze created a shower of leaves, filling the air with the distinct aroma of autumn in Kentucky. Gabe reached the barn and walked inside the gangway with Whirlwind. It was an old stock barn with a loft. The north and west side logs were chinked to block the harsh winter winds. As Gabe entered, a startled groundhog whistled and darted to its hole under the log wall. Pigeons roosting in the rafters fluttered to escape the barn. Gabe took a moment to catch his breath and look around.

After tying Whirlwind near some leftover hay for him to nibble on, Gabe grabbed a tier pole overhead and pulled himself up to the hay loft. More pigeons flew from the opening at the top of the barn roof gable. Gabe was careful not to step on any weak boards. The last thing he needed was a broken leg from a nasty fall. Sweat poured down his face. His shirt was soaked. He crept slowly along the outside wall facing the road and peered through the gaps between the weathered plank boards toward the cabin. The area was eerily quiet, save for the chirping of crickets and the high-pitched hum of locusts in the overgrown field of goldenrod between the barn and the road. The midday sun blazed down, and he could hear the distant calls of bobwhites. The shade from the trees around the cabin obscured the five horses tied at its side, making their colors hard to see. The cabin door was open, and a man was leaning back in a chair against the wall, seemingly asleep.

Twenty minutes passed without any change until a man stepped outside. He kicked the chair out from under the sleeping man, causing him to tumble to the porch deck. The man cursed and yelled as he picked himself up from the porch while the other mounted one of the horses and rode south, laughing as he went. Gabe stayed hidden, remaining vigilant.

Another thirty minutes dragged by, and just as Gabe was about to abandon his post, he heard the distant pounding of hooves coming from the south. Three riders came into view, one on a pale-colored horse. They dismounted, tied their horses near the water trough, and entered the cabin. Gabe's heart raced. Now's my chance, he thought. He was about to climb down from the loft when more horses approached, this time from the northwest. Gabe squinted, trying to identify the two riders, and then he recognized that it was Nathan and Wyatt. *They must have stopped at Atwell's store and found out where I was,* he realized. *This could be providential,* he thought to himself as he made his way down.

The man on the porch stood from his chair and walked to the porch's edge when Nathan and Wyatt approached the front of the cabin. Gabe could hear their voices but couldn't understand what they were saying. He led Whirlwind through the trees along the edge of the field to the road without anyone noticing.

While Nathan kept the man on the porch distracted, Wyatt, remaining on his horse, circled around to inspect the horses. He noticed a pale-colored horse fitting the description that Adam gave them. Wyatt also remembered what Adam had said about one horse that had only three shoes. He dismounted to check the pale horse for a missing shoe. It had all four shoes and was evenly worn. Wyatt continued to check the other horses while Nathan continued to keep the man on the porch busy. Just then, another man came out of the cabin onto the porch.

"What's the problem, Sheriff?" It was Samuel Stuart.

"Hello, Sam," Nathan greeted cordially but coolly. "Mind if I come in?"

"Help yourself, Sheriff."

Nathan dismounted, tied his gelding, and entered the cabin. The place was dank, dimly lit, and smelled of mildew and whiskey. There were five tables. Nathan knew there were seven horses outside. He made a quick head count. Nathan counted six men. In the corner, facing away from him, was someone he would recognize anywhere. He always wore a derby hat tilted to one side. Nathan found it curious that he was seated alone.

"Travis Walbert!" the sheriff called out; his senses heightened as he prepared for a confrontation. Walbert pivoted to face the sheriff with a steely gaze.

"Where might your brother be, Travis?" Nathan asked.

"He ain't here," Travis snapped back with a tone of defiance and turned away.

"Are you in the habit of riding two horses at once, son?" Nathan questioned.

Travis, his eyes filled with a smoldering hatred, responded, "Where's MacCallan?"

By this time, Gabe had arrived to see Wyatt inspecting one of the other horses' hooves. This one was missing a shoe.

"Is this the one we are looking for?" Gabe asked as he approached Wyatt.

"Looks that way," Wyatt replied. "Nathan is inside. I'll head towards the rear and keep an eye on the back entrance. You go around and position yourself on the front porch to back up Nathan," Wyatt advised.

Nathan's back was to the front door, which made him uneasy despite Wyatt being outside.

"Travis, come outside with me," Nathan demanded.

"Sheriff, I ain't movin' from this here chair," Travis bristled, glaring defiantly.

"You still haven't answered my question. Where's your brother?" Nathan continued, knowing he was around somewhere. The other men in the room just sat and watched, not wanting to get involved.

"Where were you and your brother yesterday afternoon, Travis?"

"Celina," he replied with a sneer.

"At a Klan gathering, I presume?" Nathan prodded.

Travis cast a scornful look up at him.

"That's right," Nathan said in response to his insolence. "I know that you and your brother are Klan members. The marshal in Bowling Green has his eye on you. But you weren't in Celina, were you, Travis? Now, let's go outside peacefully."

As Wyatt moved to his position, he heard something from the corner of the cabin. Without warning, Tom Walbert suddenly appeared from around the far corner, brandishing his revolver. Seeing Tom's action, Wyatt shouted, "Gabe!"

As soon as he shouted his name, a sharp crack of gunfire echoed through the air as Tom fired two shots. Chaos erupted. Hearing the gunshots, Travis went for his gun, but not fast enough. Nathan drew and fired, striking Travis in the stomach. He doubled over in searing pain and fell to the floor. Nathan quickly turned his gun to the others in the cabin, who sat with their hands raised.

"You!" he ordered. "All of your weapons… right here… now!" He disarmed Travis while keeping his gun on the others as they laid their weapons on a table before him. None were eager to suffer the same fate as Travis Walbert, who lay bleeding out. Nathan gathered their guns, backed out of the cabin, and threw them toward the road.

"Wyatt!" Nathan called out as he replaced the spent cartridge in his cylinder.

"Wyatt is down," a voice to his right was heard to say. Nathan looked to his right, startled but glad to see it was Gabe.

"Tom!" Nathan yelled in frustration. "Give yourself up. You're not going to get far on foot."

Nathan turned to Gabe. "I will stay here while you take the other side. See if you can get to Wyatt."

"You keep talking," Gabe said, "while I work my way around."

"Tom! This is Sheriff Ritter. Your brother is dying. We need to get him to Doc McKinney. Do you want your brother to die? Step out. Give yourself up. We know that you and Travis murdered Quinn Howard in

Freetown yesterday. Now, you have shot an officer of the law. You aren't making matters any better by resisting arrest."

While Nathan tried to distract Tom, Gabe made his way slowly around the rears of the horses. A watering trough was at the corner of the cabin, which provided low cover. Peering around the end of the watering trough, he could see Wyatt lying on the ground, but there was no movement. Then he caught a glimpse of Tom's shoulder behind a poplar tree about twenty yards into the edge of the woods.

"Sheriff!" Tom finally replied. "I weren't the one who shot that buck in Freetown."

"It don't matter now, Tom."

"Send out MacCallan," Tom hollered. "I'll surrender to him."

"Tom, there's only one way this will end if you refuse to lay down your weapon," Nathan replied. "Give yourself up."

With Tom's back to Gabe, Gabe eased himself quietly toward him until he closed the distance to approximately ten yards between them. Gabe rose slowly, careful not to draw Tom's attention. He positioned himself steadily, firmly gripping his revolver that was leveled at Tom's position.

"Where's MacCallan?" Tom yelled in his anger.

"Tom! Gabe yelled, his voice startling him. Tom swiftly turned when Gabe shouted, "Don't do it, Tom!" Gabe fired his gun first, and then Tom fired his. The echo from the discharge of both guns reverberated throughout the woods like claps of thunder. For a split second, and what seemed like a moment out of time, Gabe's mind returned to a skirmish in Eastern Tennessee when he was forced to kill a Yankee soldier to save the life of one of his fellow soldiers. The Yankee soldier was just a kid. Gabe tried to prevent him from making the same tragic mistake, but he had no choice. Since that ill-fated day, the image of the young man's face just before Gabe pulled the trigger has haunted his memory. He never knew the boy's name.

The smell of spent powder filled the air as the lingering smoke slowly drifted away in the breeze. Gabe came to himself when he heard Nathan calling for him.

"Gabe! Gabe! Gabe!"

Gabe was shaken by what transpired. Nathan had come from the front of the cabin and was kneeling over Wyatt. Gabe walked toward Tom with his gun drawn. Tom was lying on his back with a wound to his chest. Gabe kneeled and gently pried the gun from Tom's grasp. His eyes focused on Gabe struggling to speak.

"Deputy, you have an enemy. Watch…your…back." He then exhaled, and his eyes became a vacant stare. Gabe was puzzled by his warning, but in his gut, he knew who it was.

Nathan was tending to Wyatt. He was hit in the side and bleeding badly. The five men in the cabin began to file out one by one, offering to help. Travis Walbert had also died.

"Abigail Ray's is just up the road a piece," Nathan said to Gabe. "I'll get Wyatt to her place with the help of a couple of these men. You go for Doc McKinney."

Gabe grabbed the reins of Whirlwind's bridle, mounted the saddle with intense urgency, and hurried to town.

18

By the time Gabe arrived at Doctor McKinney's office, Hannah had come back from Freetown, where she had been helping to prepare Quinn's body for burial. She could tell Gabe was on a mission when he stormed through the door.

"Hannah!" Gabe said with his voice raised and shirt drenched with sweat. "Where's the Doc?" The intensity in his eyes told her that something was seriously wrong.

"What's wrong?" she asked. Hannah's heart skipped a beat as she sensed the gravity of the situation and dreaded his reply.

"Wyatt has been shot. Nathan has taken him to Abigail's."

Doctor McKinney came from the back room.

"Doc! Wyatt has been shot. It's pretty bad. We have taken him to Abigail Ray's."

"Where is the wound?" the Doc asked.

"His left side."

"You'll need to be more specific than that, deputy."

Gabe pointed at his left ribcage at about elbow level. "Right here."

"Hopefully, it missed his lung and didn't shatter his spleen. Hannah, I'll need my dark green pouch, bandages, and a second set of hands. You're coming with me," Doc McKinney insisted.

"I'll meet you there," Gabe said, bolting out the door.

Tate was standing outside the sheriff's office. He noticed the commotion down the street and watched as Gabe quickly rode by him. Gabe caught a glimpse of Tate with the corner of his eye, and for a brief moment, he and Gabe locked cold gazes with one another. A shiver ran down Tate's spine as Doc and Hannah raced by him in a buckboard, causing him to realize that something tragic had happened.

Onlookers in the town courtyard noticed the commotion, too. Some approached Tate, curious about what was happening, but he remained silent, his gaze fixed on the road and a cloud of dust. Then Tate retreated into the sheriff's office. His mind was consumed by unsettling thoughts. Anxiety and restlessness crept over him. He pondered the worst-case scenarios, wrestling with his fears. Beads of sweat rolled down his forehead.

Just then, the door opened, and Russell Davis entered. "You don't look well, deputy, a little pale," he remarked.

"What do you want, Alan?" Tate asked as he splashed cool water from the wash basin on his face.

"Alan? I thought we agreed never to use our real names," Davis reminded him. It's not what I want right now, but I will want it later," Davis responded as he sat down, propped his feet onto the desk, and rolled a cigarette.

"MacCallan just high-tailed it out of town in a hurry after leaving Doc McKinney's office," Tate told him. "There's trouble brewing, and it ain't good."

"And?" Davis asked, tossing his hat onto the desk. "Whatever it is, it'll be taken care of," Davis tried to assure him. Tate paced the floor, making his way to the window, and then turned to Davis with a look of irritation.

"Why Quinn Howard? Why him?" he demanded in frustration.

"He was the bait, plain and simple," Davis replied coolly. "We needed to draw MacCallan out, make him slip up, do something foolish."

Tate erupted in anger, slamming his fist down on the desk. "Who did it?"

"The Walbert brothers," Davis replied coolly, stoking Tate's anger even more.

"Are you out of your mind? Tate exploded. "The Walbert brothers? Those idiots won't keep their mouths shut. Alan, I'm warning you…"

Davis sprang to his feet, cutting off Tate's rebuke.

"I'm going to remind you only once more. Never use my real name. Then he took a draw from his cigarette and looked into Tate's eyes with a sinister smile. "You know, Tate, you should learn to speak more respectfully to the man who will make you sheriff. It might do you some good." Davis fixed his hat squarely on his head and walked to the door. "MacCallan won't be around to find out, and Ritter won't know the difference. Have a pleasant day, deputy. Try to relax," Davis said dismissively before walking out the door.

At Abigail Ray's, Abigail had the sheriff take Wyatt to a downstairs bedroom.

"What in the world happened, Nathan?" she asked, her voice filled with fear and concern.

"We were ambushed at that cabin of yours down the road," Nathan replied.

"Oh, my word," she gasped. "I was afraid something like this would happen," Abigail said angrily. "That does it. I'm burning it down."

"What about Gabe? Where's Gabe?" she asked, realizing he was not with them.

"He's gone after Doc McKinney." She was relieved to hear that he was safe.

"Was my foreman, Russell Davis, involved in this?" Nathan glanced at her with a furrow in his brow, studying her question, wondering why she asked.

"No, he wasn't anywhere around," Nathan replied. Wyatt was beginning to regain consciousness and was in a lot of pain.

"I'll start boiling water and get fresh towels," Abigail said as she hurried into the kitchen.

Gabe arrived at the house and was soon followed by Doc McKinney and Hannah. Doc and Hannah went to work treating Wyatt's wound while Abigail assisted them. Nathan and Gabe went outside and were finally able to talk about what had just happened. "What does the law say about conspiracy, Nathan? What is needed to prove a conspiracy?" Gabe asked strangely.

"Conspiracy? Other than two or more parties agreeing to commit a crime, there must be intent and acting on that intent. Why?" Nathan asked curiously.

"I still have suspicions about what I told you but haven't put the pieces together," Gabe responded. After half an hour working on Wyatt, the doctor came out of the house, wiping his hands on a bloody towel.

"Deputy Wyatt is a mighty fortunate man. He'll live," Doc was glad to say. "The bullet grazed his spleen, but he will be okay. Anyone else needin' patchin' up while I'm here?"

"Thankfully, no," Gabe replied. "The other two won't need anything anymore, except the mercy of the Lord."

"What two?" Doc asked.

"The Walbert brothers," Nathan replied.

He shook his head. "I can't say I'm surprised," Doc said. "God help their souls."

"Well, my job is done here. Abigail said Wyatt could stay here overnight. I'll visit his wife to let her know what's happened. I'm sure she will come right on over."

Just then, Hannah and Abigail came out of the house. As Hannah made her way towards the buckboard, Gabe approached her.

"Tomorrow is Quinn's funeral," she said. "Your mama, your sisters, and I are taking food to Maggie's in the morning. I told Doctor McKinney that I wouldn't be at the office."

"The Walbert brothers killed Quinn," Gabe told her. She was shocked but not surprised.

"Nathan said they were in the Klan, but I can't help but feel there was more to this than a couple of vindictive Klansmen. I'll see you at home as soon as I can," Gabe said. Before leaving, she hugged and kissed his neck and said, "Thank God you are safe. The thought that it could have been you terrifies me."

"I'll be fine. Don't worry," he reassured her.

Gabe and Nathan went back into the house. Abigail carefully gathered the heavy, damp towels, which were soaked in blood. Wyatt was resting.

"Miss Abigail," Nathan said, "your kindness is appreciated for offering to let Wyatt stay here tonight. His wife should be here shortly."

"She can stay as well, as long as needed. I have plenty of room," she said. "Besides, I feel some responsibility, that dreadful cabin belonging to me and all. I'm having it burned down first thing tomorrow. You can count on that. I never did like what was going on there, but what can a woman do about such things?"

"What about your foreman, Mr. Davis?" Gabe asked, finding an opening to bring him into the conversation.

Abigail gathered the stained towels in a pan and washed her hands in another. "Honestly, he's part of the problem, Gabe. I made a rash and foolish business deal when I hired him. I don't trust him anymore. I don't know how I ever did. Now, I'm afraid of what he might do."

"Abigail, I share your suspicions about him," Gabe replied. "Davis is up to something."

"Gabe, will you find out for me, please?" Abigail asked in a pleading tone. "If you uncover anything, will you let me know?"

"I promise," Gabe assured her.

On their way back to town, Gabe and Nathan started piecing together a few things. Russell Davis had become a person of interest.

The following day, Abigail Ray ordered Davis to burn the cabin to the ground. As he watched it burn, chewing on a straw, he searched his malicious mind, pondering his next move and what to do about MacCallan. Davis noticed that Abigail's demeanor towards him had changed, which made him curious. When he questioned her decision to burn the cabin, she snapped at him, saying, "Need I remind you, Mr. Davis, that our business arrangement is not a partnership and that you are my employee?" He replied, "Yes, ma'am, but we have an agreement."

"Yes, but not one that cannot be terminated," she responded with a look in her eyes that he had not seen before.

While smoke could be seen for miles around as the cabin burned to the ground, Nathan, Gabe, and Hannah were attending Quinn's funeral. It was a cloudy Tuesday, October 20, 1868. There was a large crowd from the community. Gabe had a few words to say from his memories as a childhood friend and from scripture. Six men carried the coffin to where Quinn was to be buried. Gabe was one of the six pallbearers. The crowd sang hymns and spiritual songs as they walked to the gravesite. Maggie walked behind her husband's coffin with her head bowed low in grief.

Well before dawn the following morning, Tate was at his home. He couldn't sleep most of the night and decided to rise early. He lit a lamp on the kitchen table. As the lamp's glow illuminated the room, he took a piece of paper and began penning a note. He dressed, placed the note in his pocket, and left just before dawn. He made his way to Freetown, the place where Quinn had been laid to rest the day before. Without dismounting, he gazed down at the fresh earth mound covering the grave. "What have I done?" he asked himself. Songbirds began to welcome the new day, but no sound was cheerful enough to ease his troubled mind. He glanced up to see lamp light through a nearby cabin window. In eerie irony, a rooster crowed a third time. Tate thought of the apostle Peter when he betrayed Jesus. A sick feeling settled in the pit of his stomach. He pulled the reins of his horse and left. Maggie stepped out of the cabin to toss some water and noticed the silhouette of a horseman slowly leaving the cemetery. She wondered who it could be at that hour of the morning. *Surely that ain't Gabe*, she thought to herself.

Gabe and Nathan met later that morning at the office. "Nathan, do you remember me asking about what makes a conspiracy?"

"I do."

"I think Russell Davis is up to his chin in one," Gabe said.

"I think so, too, now that I have had time to think about it," Nathan responded.

"Do you want to know who else I think is in on it?" Gabe asked.

"Frank Tate?" Nathan replied.

"Yes."

"Why him?" Nathan was afraid to ask.

"I believe he wants me out of the way and has found someone willing to do his bidding," Gabe responded.

"Davis?"

"That's my theory," Gabe remarked.

"Tell me again, what did Tom say before he died?" Nathan asked.

"Tom's last words to me before he died were, 'You have an enemy. Watch your back.' I believe Quinn's murder was intended to draw me into a fight with the Walberts, hoping I would be killed," Gabe replied.

Gabe and Nathan sat absorbed in thought for a moment.

"Where could Tate be?" Nathan pondered aloud, gazing out the window and peering into the street.

19

A few hours later, Gabe was seated outside the sheriff's office, with the sun's warm rays on a crisp fall morning against his face. He had leaned back in his chair with his feet propped up on the hitching rail when Tate rode up. Gabe was peeling an apple with his Barlow knife and didn't look up. Tate was about to enter the office door when Gabe asked, "Where have you been, Tate?"

Tate stopped momentarily, didn't respond, and entered the office to find Nathan at his desk.

"Tate, I was wondering where you were," Nathan said. "Have a seat."

"I'll stand if you don't mind, Nathan." He reached into his shirt pocket, took out his badge, and laid it on the desk with the note he had written.

"I'm done here, Nathan," Tate said, observing the mixture of surprise and confusion on Nathan's face. "I'm goin' to catch the next train to Louisville. I'm goin' back north of the Ohio River."

"Are you sure about this, Tate?"

"I'm sure," he replied.

"What brought this on?" Nathan continued to ask.

"I've made a lot of mistakes in my life, Nathan, that I regret. I don't deserve to clip that badge on my shirt another day."

"I believe there's more to this than you're telling me," Nathan suggested, his eyes fixed on Tate's expression of remorse.

"If you're wondering whether I had any involvement in what occurred in Freetown, I can assure you I did not," Tate replied defensively.

"Tate, tell me the truth. Did the Walberts act alone? Was Davis involved?"

"Keep an eye on Davis. That's all I'm going to say," Tate replied.

"Alright, Tate, I accept your resignation, but reluctantly, I must say."
Tate turned to the door as Nathan picked up the note.

"Follow the note," Tate said. "There is your answer."

He then walked out the door, closing it behind him. Gabe was still leaning back in his chair, eating his apple. Tate stood silently, facing the street with his hat in hand. He didn't spare a glance in Gabe's direction. With a quiver in his voice, Tate said, "Gabe, please offer my condolences to Quinn's wife. It should never have happened." He mounted his horse and rode up the street, leaving Gabe to wonder about his odd behavior. Moments later, Nathan emerged from the office, holding Tate's badge and a note.

"Tate just resigned."

Gabe dropped his boots from the rail and sat up straight in his chair. "What?" he asked with shock in his voice.

"I think your suspicions are turning out to be true, Gabe." Nathan walked back into the office, and Gabe followed. "Tate said he was heading back north to Ohio. I asked him if he knew whether the Walberts acted alone. Was Davis involved?"

"What did he say?" Gabe asked anxiously.

"He gave me this note," Nathan explained, showing it to Gabe. "He wrote just three words, 'Clifton Vernon knows.' He also said, "Keep an eye on Davis."

Tate returned to his house and started packing his belongings. Afterward, he informed his landlord about his departure and settled his affairs. Before leaving, he glanced at his pocket watch to check the time. Knowing it was approximately a half-day ride to Glasgow Junction, and the morning was already getting late. He figured he might as well wait until early tomorrow morning before leaving.

Tate was the kind of man who didn't have many friends. His ways often rubbed southern folks the wrong way, and his ambition led him to take risks. He didn't know much about religion, but he recalled preachers saying pride goes before destruction and the wicked are snared by the works of their hands. Now, Tate found himself as living proof of those words. He sat alone at his kitchen table, lost in his thoughts and regrets. The house was quiet except for a mouse scurrying along the wall towards a small hole it had chewed in the baseboard.

He just sat there until he noticed something unusual at the open window. A mourning dove had landed on the windowsill. Tate rose from his chair and walked slowly to the window, but the bird didn't fly away, as if it wasn't afraid. He came within just a few feet of it and watched it for five minutes before it flew to a nearby tree. He remembered from some local superstitions that birds can be omens. If a bird flies into a house, it's an omen of death to someone in the family. However, if a dove lands on the windowsill, it can be an omen of peace. Tate didn't believe in God or what he called hillbilly superstitions, but he was ready to reconsider.

Peace, he thought to himself. Let's hope this superstition is right. He dipped his hand in a water basin and washed his face as if he had awakened from sleep. *There won't be any peace as long as he is around,* he thought to himself. *I have something to do before I leave,* and he left again for town.

At the Sheriff's Office, Gabe and Nathan discussed their next steps.

"I think I'll ride out to Quinn's place to check on Maggie and then see if I can find Tate at home. Maybe I can talk to him," Gabe suggested. "He may be willin' to talk to me now."

"I'll track down Clifton Vernon," Nathan responded, "and see what his involvement is in all this."

They left the office and went their separate ways.

When Gabe arrived, Maggie was seated on the porch with her sister from Coe Ridge. She met him in the yard as he approached the house. "Gabe," she greeted, happy to see him.

"How's Miss Hannah and the little one?"

"Mornin', Miss Maggie. Hannah and Alec are doing just fine. I wanted to come by to see how you were doin'."

"The Laud is wit me. My sister, Abby, is here. I'm doin' as well as one can expect," she said tearfully. "It hurts real bad, Gabe. I just don't know what I'm goin' a do now. But the Laud knows. I trust him."

Gabe stepped onto the porch and sat after greeting her sister.

"Gabe, this mornin', someone was at the cemetery 'bout daybreak. Was that you?"

"No. It wasn't me. Did you get a good look?"

"All I could see was a man on a horse. I wonder who it could've been if it wasn't you?" Maggie asked.

Gabe pondered for a moment. "I think it might have been Frank Tate. This morning, he asked me to offer his condolences," Gabe replied, his suspicion growing.

The thought of Tate coming to the cemetery before daybreak was as troubling as it was mysterious to Gabe. After spending about an hour visiting Maggie and her sister, ensuring she would be alright, he departed. The lingering question about Tate's behavior that morning weighed heavily on his mind. Now, more than ever, he hoped to catch Tate at home. Maybe then, he could finally get some answers.

Tate lived on the east side of the York farm, renting a small house from them. When Gabe arrived, he found the place empty. He didn't even dismount, noticing nothing looked out of place. "I bet he's already left for Glasgow Junction," he thought regretfully. "I should have come here first."

Not far from Tate's house was the main York residence. Gabe decided to visit them. He knocked on the door, and Mrs. York opened it.

"Why, Gabe MacCallan, what a surprise! Come right in and sit down. How's your mama and papa? And that wife and baby of yours? Hannah is the sweetest thing."

"Everyone is doing just fine, Mrs. York. Thank you for asking," Gabe replied as he removed his hat.

"Let me get you something, maybe something to drink. I have some fresh homemade grape juice from the vineyard. I aim to take a pint to church next Sunday for the Lord's Supper, but there's plenty."

"No, ma'am. Thank you. I'm sure it's fine grape juice, and the Lord will be pleased. I really need to see Mr. York if he is around."

"Well, I am so sorry. Mr. York had to go to Summer Shade this morning. He bought a sow and pigs from Mr. Witty. Hog killin' ain't too far off, and we are down to just two hogs. He figured he should get some fresh stock for next year and should be back late this afternoon."

"Mrs. York, I just came from Frank Tate's house, hoping to catch him at home. I was just wondering, have you ever noticed anyone peculiar coming and going other than Frank, I mean?"

She thought for a minute. "Well, yes. Of course, I didn't think anything of it. Frank Tate, being a Yankee and all, has always been very polite, as far as we were concerned. But there was one fella that would come over yonder that I don't care for."

"You have seen someone coming and going there, then?" Gabe asked.

"It was that fancy fella, always very well dressed. He works for Abigail Ray, I reckon."

"Does he come here very often?" Gabe asked.

"Not much. One afternoon, we heard a lot of shootin'. Mr. York went over there to see what it was all about. He said they were shootin' their pistols. Mr. York said that the new fella was the fastest with a gun that he had ever seen. He could shoot with both hands. They wasn't hurtin' nothin', just shootin.'"

"Mrs. York, thank you for your hospitality. I should be getting back to town."

She walked him to the door. "Be sure to tell your people and that pretty wife of yours that I said hello."

"I will, Mrs. York, thank you." Gabe returned to town with nothing more than what he had when he came, except for one added note of interest. Davis appears to be good with those slick bone-handled .46 caliber Remingtons that Gabe noticed when they first met.

As Gabe rode back to town, Tate had already arrived. At this hour, the man he was searching for was likely in the hotel dining room, finishing his breakfast. Tate tied his horse to the hitching rail and walked inside, his boots heavy on the wooden floor. Standing at the entrance of the hotel, Miss Ina, the owner's wife, approached him with a warm smile that quickly faded when she saw his haggard appearance.

"Deputy, do you want your usual?" she asked, her voice tinged with concern. Tate's face was rough with stubble, and his eyes were shadowed from a sleepless night.

"No, ma'am," he replied, his voice low and resolute. "I'm looking for Mr. Davis."

"He's right over yonder," she said as she stared at him strangely. "Are you well, deputy?" She asked in a concerned way.

Without a word, Tate walked over to the table where Davis was seated, his back to the entrance, enjoying breakfast. A large mirror on the buffet wall in front of Davis reflected Tate's approach.

"Deputy Frank Tate, have a seat," Davis said, catching Tate's image in the mirror and not bothering to turn around. Tate moved around the table and sat opposite him. Davis glanced up, taking in Tate's disheveled appearance.

"You really should clean up a bit, Deputy. It's a poor reflection for a public servant," Davis remarked.

Tate didn't respond but instead opened his vest to reveal he wasn't wearing his badge. Davis finished his biscuits and gravy and took a sip of his coffee.

"Are you trying to tell me something, Tate?" Davis asked, his tone icy. "I thought we had a mutual agreement. I help you become sheriff, and you don't ask questions. But from the looks of it, you've had a change of heart."

"I only wanted MacCallan out of the way," Tate replied, his voice strained with rising anger. "Not like this!" He tried to keep his voice down, but the tension was noticeable. "I don't recall that you specified any particular way, Tate," Davis replied, lighting a cigarette with a casual flick of the match. "It will still work out. You'll see."

"No, Russell. I'm out."

"Out?" Davis chuckled, extinguishing the match with a deliberate flick. "You're as guilty as I am, Tate, and you know it. As far as the law is concerned, there's no proof—just one man's word against another. Thank whatever god you believe in that the Walberts are dead and can't testify to anything."

"An innocent man is dead, who didn't deserve to die," Tate replied, his voice low but taut with suppressed anger.

"Are we getting overly sentimental all of a sudden?" Davis asked with a condescending tone.

"Call it what you want. There's a widow in Freetown now," Tate said, leaning back in his chair and fixing eyes on Davis with a stern gaze. "I don't care about our arrangement anymore," he declared. "I don't care."

Davis leaned forward, his eyes narrowing. "You don't care? If you cross me, Tate, I assure you that you will care."

Tate smiled a poker player's smile, rising from his chair and leaning across the table, his face inches from Davis's. "Hope you enjoyed your last meal as a free man. I'm leaving tomorrow morning, but not before setting everything straight."

He strode out onto the street. The air was cool, damp, and overcast, signaling an impending cold rain. Yet, Tate felt only his determination and the sweat trickling down his furrowed brow. As he walked toward the Sheriff's Office, he heard Davis call his name.

"Tate!"

Tate stopped and turned his ear toward Davis, but his back was still toward him. Davis stepped off the hotel porch, his voice carrying an air of arrogance.

"Where are you headed, Tate?"

Tate remained silent.

"Don't be a fool, Tate. You have no proof. It's my word against yours," Davis taunted as he walked closer.

"I forgot to mention, Russ, I have a witness who will corroborate my testimony." Tate referred to the man in the cabin the day Davis conspired with the Walbert brothers against Gabe.

"You didn't seem too concerned about being overheard that day."

"You're lying. It's too late for lies, Tate," Davis retorted, his confidence faltering.

"Lies, Russ? Or should I call you by your true name, Alan? Are you ready to call my bluff?" Tate challenged, turning to face him. Their confrontation began to attract attention, drawing a crowd.

At that moment, Gabe approached the town from one direction while Nathan rode in from the other. Sensing something was happening, they both headed toward the hotel in the center of town. As they drew closer, they saw Tate on the right and Davis on the left, about thirty paces apart.

"Gentlemen, may I inquire as to what's transpiring here?" Nathan's voice cut through the tension.

"Nothing of consequence, Sheriff," Davis replied smoothly. "Just a misunderstanding between Tate and me, easily resolved. Isn't that right, Tate?"

Nathan's gaze shifted to Tate. "I need both of you in my office," he stated firmly.

"I'm afraid I have pressing matters for Miss Ray, Sheriff. Perhaps another time," Davis interjected confidently.

Unexpectedly, Abigail emerged from the crowd. "That's quite all right, Mr. Davis. You should accompany the sheriff. My affairs can wait," she said calmly, catching Davis off guard with her presence.

"What is the meaning of this, Sheriff?" Davis inquired, clearly now unsettled.

"Very well," Nathan replied sternly. "I possess a signed statement implicating you in a conspiracy against a lawman, which includes the murder of Quinn Howard," Nathan announced, his words creating a stir in the gathering crowd and spreading like wildfire.

"Tate, you too," Nathan added. "Let's go."

Davis knew at that moment that he had played his last card. "I'm not going to jail, Sheriff."

"That will be for a jury to decide, Davis." Davis glanced at Tate and then shifted his gaze to Abigail.

"Well then, Sheriff, you leave me with no choice," he sneered.

"Davis!" Nathan cautioned.

Nathan could see that he was about to do something foolish. He and Gabe eased out of their saddles and stepped away from each other. Davis positioned himself at an angle where he could see all three men.

"Davis, you are about to make a big mistake. Drop your weapons," Gabe demanded.

"You!" Davis scolded Gabe. "Did you know that Tate wanted you out of the way?" Davis continued, trying to provoke Gabe. "That's right. He had hoped you would be taken out of the way. He saw you as an obstacle to his glorious ambitions in this backward little nothing of a county. Unfortunately, the Walbert brothers were foolish enough to shoot the wrong deputy, and not even a good shot at that," he mocked, laughing.

"What a fool I was," Davis remarked.

Tate remained silent, having turned to face Davis with his gaze unwavering.

"What's wrong, Tate? You look like a man who wants to pull from that leather strapped to your leg. I've seen you use it. Pull it!"

Davis lit a cigarette as he taunted him. Tate clenched his fist to resist the impulse. Davis fixed his eyes on him, ready to draw his weapon if Tate was foolish enough.

"What's it going to be, Tate?" Davis prodded as he took another draw from his cigarette and exhaled a cloud of smoke.

"This is madness, Davis!" Nathan's voice boomed.

"Not if he pulls first, Sheriff," Davis retorted, his eyes still on Tate.

"The real question is, which of you is willing to take that risk. Gabe, I bet you're itching to do the same. You want to know who else was in my sights?"

"Shut your mouth, Davis," Nathan interjected sharply, having gleaned the information from Vernon's interview. Gabe struggled to contain his fury, suspecting Davis was alluding to Hannah.

"Don't let him get under your skin, Gabe," Nathan advised sternly.

The crowd had quieted and was watching intently, but well out of the line of fire. Most had moved inside the stores and hotel, peering out windows, eager to see what would happen next. But Abigail was still standing outside as it was starting to rain. Hannah, however, was at the doctor's office and noticed something was going on around the corner toward the hotel. She stepped out to investigate and approached a passerby, asking, "What's happening over yonder?"

"The sheriff and his deputies have a fella cornered. There's liable to be a fight," the man replied as he hurried to watch.

Upon hearing this, she ran toward the hotel, saw what was happening, and quickly ran to the Sheriff's Office.

"You have thirty seconds, Davis," Nathan called out.

Davis refused to be taken to jail and was determined not to go down alone. He assessed his odds with two men on the right and one in front. Tate was thirty paces out. Nathan and Gabe were about forty paces and three paces apart. He calculated his speed and the angle of each shot.

Davis weighed the odds that could secure his escape, a sinister grin spreading across his face as he glanced at Tate. Then, with lightning speed, he drew his revolvers quicker than anyone could follow. His left hand aimed at Tate, but before he could fire, a shot struck Davis squarely in the chest. The impact caused him to wildly discharge the revolver in his right hand. Nathan and Gabe, however, hadn't fired a single shot and remained motionless.

In the blink of an eye, Davis lay sprawled in the cold mud of the street. Tate was also on the ground, grimacing in pain, clutching his wounded shoulder. Nathan and Gabe approached Davis, lying face down, dead, and still clutching his Remingtons. Gabe reverently placed Davis' black, silver-buckled hat over the exit wound on his back.

Turning to Tate, they saw that he couldn't have fired the fatal shot because his gun was still in its holster. Gabe and Nathan exchanged puzzled glances, wondering who had made the deadly shot.

In that instant, Gabe caught sight of Hannah making her way toward them, firmly gripping Gabe's .44 caliber Henry rifle. She was the one who killed Davis. When Davis made his move for his revolvers, Hannah pulled the trigger. Her timing had to be perfect, and she had only one shot. Because when she fired the rifle, the recoil knocked her to the ground. Hannah hurried toward Gabe to make certain that he was okay.

"Are you hurt?" she asked as he wrapped his arms around her.

"No, thanks to you, it seems. I owe your father for teaching you how to use a rifle," Gabe replied with relief.

Hannah handed the rifle to Gabe, then noticed Abigail standing on the porch, and she went to her.

"Are you okay, Abigail?"

"I'm just shaken," Abigail replied. She and Hannah turned their attention back to the street as the crowd emerged.

Abigail Ray discovered later that Davis had embezzled money by manipulating the books. Though she managed to recover some of her losses, she became much more cautious about hiring in the future.

Davis was laid to rest. As Gabe and Nathan stood over his grave, Gabe recalled Psalm 7:15. "He made a pit, and digged it, and is fallen into the ditch which he made."

Abigail and Hannah grew close, developing a sister-like bond. Abigail underwent a remarkable transformation, becoming known for her generosity and kindness, setting a positive example, and influencing the community for the better.

Part Three

Reaping the Whirlwind

"For they have sown the wind, and they shall reap the whirlwind."
Hosea 8:7

20

Nearly three years passed after the death of Russell Davis in the fall of 1868. It was late spring of 1871. Nathan Ritter was re-elected as sheriff. Bill Wyatt recovered and remained a deputy. The grand jury did not charge Frank Tate because of a lack of sufficient evidence in the murder of Quinn Howard, and he returned to Ohio. Gabe remained a deputy and the one everybody favored to take Nathan's place someday. He was in the office reorganizing files and paperwork when Hannah entered the office with her three-year-old son, Alec, in her arms.

"Here's your father. Alec's been wearing me out, asking for you all morning," she said to Gabe, catching her breath.

"There's my little man." Gabe scooped Alec up and swung him in the air.

"Gabe, don't do that. It frightens me every time."

"He likes it. Don't ya, Alec?" Alec laughed and giggled, wanting his father to swing him again.

"Your mother and father are in town," Hannah said. "I'm going to have them take Alec back home with them. I need to work at the doctor's office, so let me know before you head home."

Hannah finished her studies to become a nurse and was as good as any doctor in that part of the country. She set broken bones, stitched lacerations, and delivered most of the babies in the county over the past two years.

"Wave goodbye to your father," Hannah playfully encouraged little Alec. "I'll see you this afternoon," she told Gabe.

"Have a good day, Nathan and Bill."

"Take care, Miss Hannah," Nathan replied as Bill waved and returned to playing solitaire.

A couple of hours later, there was a knock at the door. "The door is open," Gabe called out.

A man in an officer's uniform entered. "Sheriff Ritter?" the man asked.

"That's me," Nathan replied. "Can I help you?"

"Sheriff, I'm Lieutenant John Carson, U.S. Army. I have a warrant for a citizen in your county."

"A warrant? Who for?"

"Alan Kilpatrick," the lieutenant responded.

"Sorry, lieutenant, I don't know anyone by that name, and I know everyone in this county."

"He also goes by the name Davis," the lieutenant replied.

"Davis?" Gabe asked. "Do you mean Russell Davis? I'm afraid you are three years too late, lieutenant. Davis was killed in a gunfight back in '68."

The lieutenant removed his hat with a word or two of disgust and disappointment. "If that don't beat all," he muttered. I have tracked him from Arizona, where he and a business partner were involved in embezzlement."

"Why is the U.S. Army involved?" Gabe asked, being curious.

The lieutenant removed a folded piece of paper and handed it to Gabe. He opened it to see that it was a Wanted Poster he had not seen before.

Wanted—Alan William Kilpatrick

For Embezzlement Against the U.S. Government

Reward: $2,000

"That's him, alright," Gabe observed.

"I just found out recently that he had a partner," the lieutenant continued. "They embezzled several thousand dollars as government contractors in Tuscan back in '65. I also learned that 'Davis' is not his only alias."

"Well, once again, Lieutenant, the man you refer to as Kilpatrick is not your problem anymore," Gabe replied as he handed back the Wanted Poster.

"Perhaps, but I have reason to believe that his partner is also in the area," the lieutenant added.

"His name is James Fergusson."

"Never heard of him either," Nathan commented.

"He, too, has more than one alias. It was assumed that they went in different directions. The trail was cold until now. Newspapers can be a good source of information, sometimes offering valuable details without even realizing it," the lieutenant explained as he handed Nathan an old newspaper. "Take a look and tell me if this rings a bell," he continued, as Nathan scanned the page.

"This article is about the grand jury decision regarding Frank Tate."

He handed the paper to Gabe, who glanced up at the lieutenant with a puzzled expression.

"Frank Tate? Is this the other man you're after?" Gabe inquired.

"It was by chance that we noticed the name 'Frank Tate' from your local newspaper involving a murder in '68. It seemed too much of a coincidence for both names to be in the same county," the lieutenant remarked.

"Until three years ago, he was a deputy sheriff here," Gabe noted. "Tate said he was going back to Ohio."

"He isn't from Ohio. He's from Missouri," the lieutenant corrected. Gabe glanced at Nathan, who had a look of surprise.

"Where in Missouri, Lieutenant?" Gabe asked.

"Kansas City."

Gabe turned to Nathan with a curious look in his eyes. "I reckon what we mistook for Yankee arrogance was just his plain sorry personality," Gabe remarked, clarifying his thoughts for the lieutenant. "Folks from outside these parts tend to rub us the wrong way. We call it the Yankee way of dealing with folks around here."

"Lieutenant, I'd appreciate it if we could verify if Tate really headed north," Gabe requested.

"What's your plan, deputy?"

"If it's alright with you, let's meet up in Glasgow tomorrow morning. We'll check the L&N passenger list for December 9, 1868, at Glasgow Junction."

"Very well," the lieutenant agreed. "I happen to be staying at the

Kentucky Inn on North Race Street in Glasgow. "I'll see you two in the morning."

The lieutenant left them eager to find out more. Several things were going through Gabe's mind, tracing back through the summer and fall of '68 and the incident ending with Davis in the town cemetery.

Gabe and Nathan rode into Glasgow early the following day while Deputy Wyatt stayed behind to hold down the fort. Glasgow was a bustling little town, and like most county seats, the courthouse was situated in the center of the square, surrounded by stores and other merchants.

They rode through town, the streets still muddy from the spring rains. As they turned onto Main Street, someone was heard calling to them.

"Sheriff Ritter! Deputy MacCallan!" They stopped and turned in their saddles to see that it was Sheriff Bill Freeman.

"What brings you two to Glasgow?" Sheriff Freeman asked, glad to see them. Freeman and his deputies did a good job keeping the peace and appreciated Nathan and his deputies helping keep their county the same. Trouble has a way of spilling over from one county to another.

"We're here on business," Gabe replied, and they spent a few minutes catching up.

"I figured as much. Your business wouldn't have anything to do with an Army Lieutenant staying at the Kentucky Inn, would it?"

"Actually, yes. We're here to meet with him," Nathan replied.

"The lieutenant told me ya'll was comin'. You boys had to get started before the rooster crowed to get here this early," Freeman remarked. "This must be purdy important."

"I see you've already gotten acquainted with the lieutenant?" Gabe asked.

"I wouldn't be doin' my job if I didn't. Would I be stickin' my nose in y'all's business if I tagged along?"

"I've never known of a sheriff being nosey," Nathan said with a hint of humor. Freeman laughed at that, and the three rode to the Kentucky Inn. As expected, the lieutenant was waiting on the front porch, smoking his cigar while enjoying the scenery. When he saw them, he arose and walked into the yard where his horse was saddled and ready to go.

"Mornin', Lieutenant," Sheriff Nathan greeted.

"Mornin', gentlemen, and Sheriff Freeman."

"We had ourselves a right fine visit last evening over a bottle of bourbon," Freeman said. "Swapped a few war stories, and it turns out he knows one of my army buddies from Indiana." Then he turned to Lieutenant Carson. "Nathan and Gabe told me where ya'll are headed. May I ride along?"

"The more, the merrier, Sheriff," the lieutenant responded as he put the cigar stub into the side of his mouth and grabbed the reins of his horse. "Let's ride."

Glasgow Junction was several miles southwest of Glasgow toward Mammoth Cave. The L&N railroad that connected Louisville and Nashville, built the depot in 1863. It was named Glasgow Junction. On their way to the depot, Gabe and Nathan learned more about the trail left by Tate and Davis, but the lieutenant had a question for Sheriff Ritter. "How did Fergusson become a deputy so quickly after arriving in your town?"

"It seems I was fooled by his slick-talkin' ways," the sheriff admitted embarrassingly in Freeman's presence. "Which is not an easy thing to do," trying to salvage a bit of his pride.

"He fooled a lot of other people too," the lieutenant noted regretfully.

After less than an hour, they arrived at the depot. There were a few people around, mostly people passing through. Bell's Tavern was located on the east side of the tracks, and the depot office was on the west side. The clerk, busy outside giving instructions for a hemp shipment headed north, didn't notice the lawmen's arrival. It wasn't until he rounded the corner to his office that he spotted them waiting.

"Good morning, fellas," the clerk greeted cheerfully.

"How can I help you?"

The lieutenant introduced the four of them and stated their business.

"Well, you are welcome to look through the ledger book," the clerk greeted with a smile. He pulled the volume from the bookcase and laid it on the counter. He opened it and flipped through the pages to December 9, 1868. As they skimmed the list of passengers that day, they did not find the name they had hoped to find.

"If you don't mind me askin', who exactly are you lookin' for?" the clerk inquired.

"The name of the man we are looking for may have traveled using the alias *Frank Tate*, or his real name *James Fergusson*, with a double 's' in *Fergusson*," Nathan replied.

"Are you sure about the date you are lookin' for?" he asked.

"December 9, 1868," Gabe replied.

The clerk licked his finger and turned the page. "Try the 10th."

They searched through the list. There was a passenger named Tate listed, and the first name was *Franklin*.

"Where did he travel?" the lieutenant asked.

"Nashville. He went to Nashville," Gabe replied with surprise in his voice. Gabe glanced up at Lieutenant Carson. "Do you think he's gone back to Missouri?" Gabe asked.

"There is one way to find out," the lieutenant responded. The lieutenant asked the clerk, "Sir, can you get a telegram to the Missouri Pacific Railroad Depot in St. Louis?"

"I'll need to take it to the telegraph office, but yes, I can do that for you," the clerk assured them.

The lieutenant wrote a request on L&N stationery to the Missouri Pacific Railroad Depot in St. Louis, asking them to search their ledgers for these names: Franklin or Frank Tate and James Fergusson, with the estimated dates he may have traveled. He signed the note:

Please expedite your reply. I am your servant, with kind regards, Lieutenant John Carson, U.S. Army

"I will have it sent this afternoon," the clerk promised.

"I think we have done all we can, gentlemen," Nathan said. "Now, we wait."

Gabe and Nathan returned home while the lieutenant agreed to extend his stay in Glasgow, hoping for a prompt reply to the telegram sent to the Missouri Pacific Railroad Depot in St. Louis.

"Let me know what you find out," Sheriff Freeman requested.

Several days went by without any word from the lieutenant, leading Gabe and Nathan to believe the trail had gone cold once more. However, three weeks later, the lieutenant rode back into town.

"Lieutenant, come in. Have a seat," Gabe greeted him warmly. "I'll pour you a cup of coffee. We were starting to wonder if we'd see you again."

"Thank you, Deputy. Honestly, I wasn't so sure myself," he replied, easing himself into the padded chair and gratefully accepting the coffee. "I'm gettin' too old for this. Can't ride long like I used to."

"What have you learned, Lieutenant?" Nathan asked eagerly, both he and Gabe leaning forward in anticipation.

"I think you'll find this interesting, gentlemen," the lieutenant said, placing a telegram from the St. Louis depot on Nathan's desk. Nathan read it aloud:

To Lieutenant John Carson, U.S. Army:
Per your request,
A passenger by the name of Franklin Tate traveled to Kansas City, Missouri, on Monday, December 28, 1868, from St. Louis, Missouri.

"Well, I'll be," Gabe said in disbelief. "It looks as if he went back home to Missouri."

"But that was three years ago," Nathan interjected firmly. "Tate, or Fergusson as you called him, could be anywhere by now."

The lieutenant took a sip from his coffee and then nodded in agreement. "Yes, sir. He could have been in California by now, but he isn't."

"How do you know that?" Gabe asked.

"I sent telegrams to the U.S. Marshal in the Western District in Kansas City. The marshal was a bit stubborn, but he had one of his deputies do a little investigating in Wyandotte City, just across the river in Kansas. He was willing because the name *Fergusson* caught his interest. He finally responded. After Fergusson's arrival date, a Deputy Marshal looked into county records for new business transactions. This is what he found."

The lieutenant presented another telegram from his shirt pocket.

The telegram said that on March 10, 1869, a partnership deal was recorded at the County Clerk's office in Wyandotte City, Kansas, with a certain Mr. J.T. Fergusson.

"This person could be a brother or cousin. Who knows? The last name is spelled the same, which makes it more than a coincidence," Carson explained.

"What's the nature of the business?" Nathan asked.

"Cattle," the lieutenant replied. "As you may know, beef is in big demand. Kansas City is perfectly situated as a hub between the east and the west. There's a lot of money being made."

"If the marshal has found him, have him arrest him," Gabe said.

"Therein lies the problem," the lieutenant explained as he struck a match to light his cigar. "That's not an option. If he arrests him, it will disrupt an investigation involving a cattle-marketing scheme he's been workin' on. He thinks this J.T. Fergusson is in the middle of it."

Nathan and Gabe exchanged a knowing glance as the lieutenant hesitated before making a request.

"I need one of you to track him down. You know him well enough to recognize him," he said. Nathan turned to Gabe and said, "I can't go, and you have in-laws in Missouri."

"I'll let my wife know," Gabe said. "I reckon she'll welcome a visit back home."

"Good," the lieutenant replied. "I will travel ahead of you and meet you in St. Louis."

"Lieutenant," Gabe spoke up. "Instead of meeting us in St. Louis, travel on to Warrensburg. It's located on the rail. That's my wife's hometown." Gabe instructed him where to go, who to see, and where to stay. Gabe also instructed him to let her folks know they were on the way.

"Deputy," the lieutenant replied as they shook hands. "I will see you in Warrensburg."

After the meeting with Lieutenant Carson, Gabe went to the doctor's office. Hannah was there tending to a young mother with a sick newborn while Doc McKinney was doctoring a horse out back with a shoulder injury. Doc McKinney was as good a veterinarian as he was a physician. Hannah had become so good at her practice by now that many of the county's people were asking for her. She was noted for saving a family that contracted cholera. She traced the source to a contaminated well that was receiving water from an underground spring. Spring water ran through a family cemetery to the well about fifty yards away. She realized the problem during the burial of a family member. Water filled the bottom of the grave as fast as they could bail it out. She had difficulty getting them to close the well, but eventually convinced the family and arranged for a new water source. As a result, the spread of cholera ended for that family. Doc McKinney suggested that Hannah write a report detailing what she had discovered and send it to the medical school in Louisville. It was well received and helped save many more lives.

Gabe walked into the doctor's office with a smirk, which Hannah immediately noticed.

"You look like the cat that swallowed the canary," she remarked, sensing he was up to something. "What's got into you?" she asked, her voice and smile reflecting suspicion.

"Pack your bags," Gabe told her, grinning ear-to-ear.

"Pack my bags? What on earth for? That's certainly not what I expected to hear," she responded, clearly surprised.

"We're going to visit your folks."

"What?" Her eyes widened with excitement. "What did you say?" she asked, making sure she heard him correctly.

"I said, pack your bags. We're leaving to visit your folks in Missouri," he repeated with a big smile.

"What made you decide such a thing?" she asked, her voice brimming even more.

"Well, do you want to go or not?" Gabe asked, already knowing her answer.

Before she could respond, Doc McKinney, who had just finished treating a horse, overheard Gabe and joined the conversation, curious about the sudden trip.

"That's what I'd like to know. What's the occasion?" the doctor asked.

Gabe explained that he had received an assignment that required him to go to Kansas City, and he thought it would be a good opportunity for Hannah to visit her family. The news was not what Doc McKinney wanted to hear, but he was glad that Hannah would have an opportunity to go home for a visit. Hannah was so excited that she wrapped her arms around Gabe's neck and couldn't wait to start packing.

"When are we leaving?" she asked.

"In three days."

"Three days? I have to go. There's so much to do. Doctor McKinney…"

"You'd better run along, my dear," Doc said. "Just promise me you will return as soon as possible."

"We will. We will. Thank you," Hannah responded, turning to Gabe and saying, "I'll see you at home."

"Break the news gently to my parents," Gabe told her as she hurried out the door.

"Thank you, Doc. I'll have her back here, hopefully soon. Lord willing," Gabe said gratefully.

"What's the assignment, Gabe, if you don't mind me asking?"

"I have accepted an assignment from the U.S. Army to apprehend Frank Tate."

"Frank Tate? I thought we had heard the last of him," Doc McKinney said in surprise.

"So did I."

"Be careful, son." Doc McKinney warned. "I think he could be dangerous if cornered."

In preparation for their departure, Gabe and Hannah spent the next couple of days getting everything in order. Gabe's parents and sisters understood, but they knew Alec needed to know his other grandparents and Hannah's family. The word spread quickly. People came and went to say goodbye. Among them was Hannah's close friend, Abigail Ray. She was saddened to see them leave, but looked forward to when they returned.

The evening before their departure, Hannah was busy packing the last things and too excited to consider what Gabe might face. Gabe needed some time alone, so he walked to the family cemetery. As Gabe stood there, a whippoorwill's call echoed through the nearby woods, a lonesome call he had heard many times before. Against a moonlit sky, a bat darted back and forth, reminding Gabe of his childhood, growing up with his brothers. They would tease bats by tossing up small pebbles to watch them dive after them.

He felt a deep gratitude for God's providence that had brought him home, blessed with a wonderful wife and a son. Hannah was a pioneer wife in every sense of the word, and he cherished her. However, unease crept into his mind as he considered the days ahead. Doc McKinney's warning about potential danger lingered in his thoughts. Gabe had faced danger many times before, but now he had a family to think about. His thoughts wandered as he stood there, contemplating the uncertain future.

He recalled the wise words of Miss Alice Adair in Warrensburg when he had expressed his frustration about trouble following him. Her response had been a source of comfort and inspiration to him. "Does trouble follow you?" he could hear her gentle voice asking, "or has it something to do with your calling? I believe there is a purpose we are meant to fulfill. We are lights. Whenever light enters a dark room, the darkness flees. It flees and struggles to return. As long as light is present, darkness has to remain in places that light has not reached. As lights, we are called to expose what is in the darkness. The trouble you speak of is the struggle that darkness causes when you expose what lies within it."

As Gabe thought about her words of wisdom once again, he wondered how they might apply to this new challenge. It was then that Gabe heard Hannah calling him, which brought him back to the moment, and he walked back to the house. Before retiring for the night, he and Hannah prayed and read the scriptures together.

No one in the house slept for more than a few hours. The following morning, the buckboard was loaded with two trunks. Gabe didn't want to leave Whirlwind behind, but he had no choice. He would have to make arrangements for a horse when he arrived at Warrensburg. The family went with them to Glasgow Junction, where they bid tearful farewells.

Their expenses were paid, thanks to the U.S. Army, so they boarded the train from Glasgow Junction and traveled to Nashville. From there, they went to Memphis and, finally, aboard a steam freighter on the Mississippi to St. Louis. They were back in Missouri within a few days of leaving Gabe's home in Kentucky. Disembarking from the freighter with their luggage, they found themselves at a bustling river wharf filled with people and boats waiting to load and unload. Their journey had been uneventful, for which they were grateful, but tiring. However, the last train to Warrensburg had already departed, and they had no choice but to spend the night in St. Louis.

The next day, Gabe sent a telegram to the Warrensburg Depot addressed to Hannah's father, Silas Clayton, and they began their journey to Warrensburg, Missouri.

21

Their arrival in Warrensburg was on Saturday, May 20, 1871. As the train approached the station, Hannah excitedly held Alec to the window to show him his first glimpses of her hometown. She was so excited to be back. The recent rain cleared the air, and the sun shone through the parting clouds. Stepping off the train onto the platform, she took a deep breath, savoring the familiar sights and scents.

"I didn't realize until now how much I missed my home," she exclaimed, smiling at Gabe, who was happy for her. The two of them stood embracing one another with Alec in her arms when they heard someone calling over the noise of the steam engine.

"Hannah! Hannah!"

Her brother, Eli, had transformed from the little boy she had left five years ago into a young man with a deeper voice and much taller stature.

"Eli?" Hannah exclaimed in surprise. "Is that really you? Oh, my gracious! You have grown up!"

Behind Eli, but moving a bit more slowly, were her parents. After years of separation, they were finally reunited. Emotions overflowed as they embraced each other tightly, tears of joy streaming down their faces. Three-year-old Alec, a little overwhelmed by the excitement, clung tightly to his mother. Despite his shyness, he quickly became the center of attention. Gabe warmly wrapped his arm around his brother-in-law's neck and gave his father-in-law a firm handshake.

"How's Whirlwind?" Eli asked with a big grin.

"He's just fine," replied Gabe. "I wish I could have brought him with me. You look like you're doing fine yourself. You're a man now. How tall are you, five-eleven?"

"Almost," Eli said as he straightened his posture. "I can handle a gun as good as you now," Eli boasted.

"Well, let's hope you never have to use one," Gabe replied.

With smiles on their faces and tears of joy, they prepared to make their way back to Hannah's cherished homeplace.

Before leaving the depot, Gabe asked if there were any messages for him. There was a message from Lieutenant Carson indicating that he was staying at the Adair House. He wanted to meet Gabe at the sheriff's office after his arrival. The lieutenant always reported to the nearest law enforcement office as a gesture of courtesy. Since it was Saturday, Gabe replied by sending a message to the lieutenant announcing his arrival and inviting him to worship at the Tabernacle in the morning.

Hannah's mother had already started supper. When they arrived, they shared a good meal, caught up on the news, and then moved to the front porch, where it was cooler. Sitting on the same porch swing where they once courted, Gabe and Hannah recounted their long and tiring journey from Kentucky to Warrensburg. Alec was starting to warm up to the grandparents he had not met until now, and they all thanked God for their safe arrival. The night was peaceful, and they rested.

The next day dawned with a glorious Sunday morning. After completing their morning chores, everyone prepared for worship at the Tabernacle. The sunlight filtered through the treetops, illuminating the fresh green leaves with a golden glow. When they arrived at the Tabernacle, a welcoming crowd had gathered. Among them were Sam and Emma, eager to see them. Gabe's eyes were drawn to someone he had been looking forward to seeing—Lizzie Adair, accompanied by Lieutenant Carson.

"Mr. Gabe, it is so good to see you and Miss Hannah," she said happily. "Welcome home! It looks like you brought someone else back with you. You are a proud father, I see."

"Hello, Miss Lizzie. It is so good to see you too. "Yes, ma'am. We are proud parents now. How I wish Miss Alice was still with us," he said. "She made a strong impression upon me. I loved her dearly."

"She made a strong impression on us both, Mr. Gabe. Yes, sir. I think of her every day."

Gabe turned his attention to the lieutenant and shook his hand. "It looks as if you made it here just fine. I'm sure you have been well cared for," Gabe said.

"Indeed, I have," the lieutenant replied, smiling. "In fact, Miss Lizzie seems to think I'm too thin. She's been trying to fatten me up." They all laughed, agreeing that Lizzie's good cooking could easily be a good man's undoing.

Their worship that morning was uplifting, deeply meaningful, and Christ-centered. Gabe and Hannah enjoyed hearing Sam Clayton preach the Word and with the passion he puts into it. As always, dinner on the grounds was a perfect way to end their day of worship. The community was excited to see Hannah and their little one.

This gave Gabe and Lieutenant Carson a moment to discuss business. The lieutenant informed Gabe that he had already met with the sheriff, who was not pleased about Gabe being assigned to work with him instead of one of his deputies. However, the sheriff was willing to help if necessary.

"Since you are out of your jurisdiction," the lieutenant continued, "the marshal will deputize you when we get to Kansas City. He understands you will be a federal officer assigned to me but under his authority."

Gabe listened carefully to Lieutenant Carson's plans, feeling slightly overwhelmed, but was ready to take on the job. They agreed to meet at the sheriff's office in the morning.

Gabe took some time to catch up with Sam and Emma Clayton. They still ran the merchandise store in town and hinted that Gabe could have his old job back if he wanted it. "We passed the 17th Amendment last year, giving our black citizens the right to vote," Sam mentioned. "I was part of the delegation that pushed it through, but unfortunately, it's caused trouble for some of our black folk."

Sam continued, "Do you recall the Loyalty Oath law?"

"I remember it well," replied Gabe. "It prevented people like me from serving publicly, teaching, or preaching."

"Well, it was ruled unconstitutional a few years ago. Things are slowly getting better," Sam said with a sense of relief.

Gabe then asked, "What about Gray Horse? Do you ever see him?" Gabe had already planned to visit him.

"I see him about once a year, usually at random times. He's kind of a loner, as you know. You should visit him before you leave. He'd like to see you," Sam suggested.

"I will," Gabe promised.

Gabe and Hannah spent the rest of the afternoon catching up with everyone's news. There's nothing quite like returning home after being away for a while, reconnecting with old friends and hearing familiar stories.

Gabe saddled up a horse borrowed from his father-in-law and rode into town the next morning. As he crossed the railroad tracks and headed toward the old town of Warrensburg, memories washed over him. This place had changed the course of his life in such a short time. Even the familiar scents of burning coal and wood smoke from kitchen stoves gave him a comforting sense of home.

Arriving at the Sheriff's Office, he noticed four horses hitched to the rail, recognizing one as the lieutenant's striking roan-colored gelding, whose imposing demeanor matched its owner's. Gabe stepped into the familiar office to find a group of men gathered around the sheriff's desk, drinking coffee and swapping stories.

Removing his slouch hat, Gabe greeted them with a nod. "Mornin', gentlemen."

The lieutenant nodded and introduced Gabe to Sheriff Anderson, a man Gabe hadn't met before.

"Tom Wells was sheriff when I left," Gabe remarked.

"He's retired now," Sheriff Anderson replied. "Bill Wyatt's retired too. Pleasure meetin' you, Deputy MacCallan. Heard a lot about how you helped Sheriff Wells clean up a few messes around here. I also heard you married Silas Clayton's daughter."

"That I did," Gabe said with a proud smile. "And we've got ourselves a little boy now."

"Well, congratulations! Looks like you're part of the family here in Warrensburg now," the sheriff said.

"Thank you. It sure does feel like home," Gabe replied warmly. He then noticed another man in the room whom he hadn't met. The sheriff made the introduction.

"This here's Deputy Robert Miles." Gabe shook hands with him. "Deputy Miles is originally from Amarillo, Texas, but hails from West Plains."

"A West Plains man, huh? What brought you to Missouri?" Gabe asked.

"I was driftin' and, like you, met a young lady here and decided to settle down," Miles replied with a grin. "These Missouri gals sure know how to lasso a fella."

Gabe laughed and turned to the lieutenant. "Hear that, lieutenant? There's hope for you yet here in Warrensburg."

"Alright, gentlemen, let's get down to business," the lieutenant replied dismissively, changing the subject, to which they all laughed.

"Deputy MacCallan knows the man we're after personally. As I mentioned, he worked with him for a spell as a fellow deputy in Kentucky. That's why I've tapped him for this job. His main task will be to identify and locate the man. The U.S. Marshal and I will handle the arrest," the lieutenant explained, pausing to rub his chin thoughtfully.

"Since arriving and talking with Sheriff Anderson, I've got one more thing to add," the lieutenant continued. "Sheriff, if you can spare Deputy Miles, he can assist MacCallan. It must be understood that MacCallan will be under my direction, and both of them will be under the authority of the U.S. Marshal."

Sheriff Anderson glanced at Miles for his reaction. "I'm willing," Miles said without hesitation.

The sheriff nodded. "Alright, Lieutenant, we're grateful for the chance to serve."

"Good. We'll leave Wednesday at 0700 hours," the lieutenant informed them.

As the lieutenant and Gabe stepped out, the lieutenant motioned to Gabe. "Come with me. I've got something for you." Gabe walked over to where his horse was tied and noticed another horse hitched beside it.

"You'll need a good horse," the lieutenant said, handing over the reins of a stunning black stallion. The horse was a beauty, tall as Whirlwind and sleek as a mole, solid black with white ankles.

"This is Midnight, and he's yours," the lieutenant declared. "He's part of your compensation. I made sure you got a horse and saddle I'd be proud to own." Gabe was left speechless, taken aback by the generous surprise, and expressed his heartfelt thanks.

"No need for thanks," the lieutenant replied. "He's not a gift. You'll have to earn him."

Gabe put his left boot in the stirrup and settled into the saddle. The buckles on the straps gleamed with polished brass, and the pleasant scent of freshly tanned leather filled the air. It was the finest saddle Gabe had ever seen, as if it had been custom-fitted just for him. He took the reins of his father-in-law's mare to lead her home.

"I'll see you in a couple of days at 0700, Deputy," the lieutenant said, tipping his hat. Gabe returned the gesture and rode off toward the farm, feeling the thrill of adventure and responsibility ahead.

Silas was busy working a plowed field with his mule, preparing to plant corn. The chickens were scattered about, paying no mind to the cat that paid no mind to them. Eli was helping his father when he saw Gabe ride down the lane on a different horse and leading his father's mare. Excitedly, he jumped off the drag being pulled behind the mule and ran to Gabe.

"Wow! He is a beauty," Eli exclaimed, his eyes as wide as silver half-dollars. "What's his name?"

"Midnight," Gabe replied, dismounting and admiring everything about him.

"His name suits him," Eli replied, stroking Midnight's face. The rest of the family came out of the house, and Silas emerged from the field, admiring Gabe's new horse.

"You didn't buy this horse?" Hannah asked in a slightly testy tone.

Gabe had a habit of spending money without Hannah's consent.

"The lieutenant gave him to me as part of my compensation," Gabe explained to calm her concerns.

"I reckon he must'a been afraid you'd back out on him. Now, you're beholdin' to him," Silas chuckled.

Gabe smiled. "I hadn't thought of it that way, but I reckon so. We will be leaving for Kansas City Wednesday morning," Gabe said. "I was thinking that since I have some time today, I'd like to visit Gray Horse."

"Oh, Gabe," his mother-in-law responded, expressing concern. "Be careful around him. He's a strange one."

"I'll be fine. We are friends. Eli, would you like to go with me?"

His mother forbade it when Silas interrupted and gave him permission. "Let him go. He can go," he said.

"But, Silas –," she protested.

"Let the boy go," Silas replied. "It's time for him to venture out. Besides, I can't think of him bein' with anyone better," referring to Gabe. Eli jumped with excitement onto the mare's saddle.

"We'll be back before dark," Gabe promised.

"Come on," Eli shouted. "I'll race ya." Gabe looked at Silas and grinned.

"I hope you know what you've got yourself into, son," Silas warned, smiling back at Gabe.

Gabe tapped his sides, and Midnight leaped into a run that quickly caught up with the mare and passed her up.

"Hey!" Eli protested. "That ain't fair!" Gabe just laughed as he raced down the road.

As they passed through town and rode north of the stone quarries toward the Black Water River Valley, Eli asked, "They call him the Black Water Ghost, don't they?"

"Gray Horse?" Gabe asked. "That's right."

"Is he really a ghost?" Eli asked with a bit of concern. Eli was starting to be a little nervous about who he was about to meet.

"No, he's a man like you and me, just half Osage Indian. He can hide in plain sight; you would never know he was there. He can move through the woods and not be heard."

"How do we find him?" Eli asked.

"Don't worry. Gray Horse will find us."

They rode deeper into the thickly wooded valley and property owned by Gray Horse. The canopy of the trees almost completely blocked the sun's light, and the temperature in the air was noticeably cooler. As they rode by a cave opening about a hundred feet to their right, the cold dampness from the cave made their hair rise. Black Water River was on their left. Eli was beginning to wish he hadn't come along.

"Stop!" a voice commanded, but they couldn't tell whether it came from the front of them or behind.

"Gray Horse!" Gabe called out. "It's me, Gabe MacCallan."

Gray Horse stepped out of the thick brush. When he saw that it was really Gabe, he smiled, and with three long steps, he was standing by Gabe's horse, clasping his hand. Gray Horse was thrilled to see him again.

"It is so good to see you, my friend," Gray Horse said. "It has been too long. Who is this with you?"

Eli was shivering, both with fear and from the cold. "This is my young brother-in-law," Gabe introduced proudly. Gray Horse approached Eli, who was too afraid to move from his saddle. Gray Horse was so tall that he could almost look Eli in the eye from the saddle. "You are always welcome," he said kindly. "Come, I have meat."

Gray Horse's mother taught him the ways of the Osage people, and his father made sure he also learned to read and write. Eli began to warm up to Gray Horse as they entered the log cabin. He kept a small fire in the center of the cabin. Eli was amazed to see the hides covering the walls and that the smoke from the small fire in the center of the cabin went straight up and out of an opening in the center of the roof.

"Please, sit," Gray Horse insisted. Eli looked around to find a chair, but there was none. Gabe grinned at him and gestured for him to sit on the floor covered with hides around the fire. Gray Horse served them the meat he had previously prepared. Eli stared at the meat mixture, not wanting to eat it. Gray Horse noticed his hesitation.

"Warm by the fire. Eat. It is good," Gray Horse told him.

Eli did as he was told. He placed the clay vessel by the fire to warm his meal. With no utensils, Eli used his fingers to eat. To his surprise, it was delicious.

"Groundhog," Gray Horse explained. "It is groundhog, wild onion, and potatoes."

Gabe and Gray Horse talked for two hours while Eli listened until Gray Horse told Eli, "If you will visit me, I will teach you the ways of the Osage." That excited Eli, but he wasn't sure his parents would approve.

Gabe, sensing his thoughts said, "Perhaps, Gray Horse, you can come to church so that his mother and father can get to know you better."

"I would not be welcome," he replied.

"Eli's family will make you welcome because they are my family," Gabe replied. "If you are not welcome, I am not welcome."

Their visit was extended until late in the afternoon. As they prepared to mount their horses, Gray Horse clasped Gabe's hand firmly. "It was good to see you, dear friend," Gray Horse said with a big smile. "Please say hello to your wife for me. You are my family. Now, young Eli is my family."

Gray Horse gave him a knife with a handle made from deer antlers fitting snugly in its buckskin sheath. "This is my gift. This is a token of our new friendship. I will look for you to come back."

"Thank you, and thank you for the groundhog, sir," Eli replied, the most he had said since their arrival. Gray Horse smiled and patted his shoulder.

On their way back, Eli would not stop talking about his experience and the new friend he had made. They made it home before nightfall. Upon reaching home, he excitedly recounted the whole experience and proudly showed them his new knife. However, Gabe cautioned him not to mention Gray Horse's invitation until he could get his mother to warm up to the idea. Eli agreed to his good advice.

22

I t was a quiet Wednesday morning on May 24, 1871, with the sun slowly rising in a red sky. Hannah's father and Eli were almost finished milking and feeding the animals at the barn. Hannah and her mother had prepared breakfast and set the table. Despite the busy morning, Hannah's thoughts were preoccupied with Gabe and his departure. Gabe was saddling Midnight and loading what gear he would need. One of the items he made sure to take with him was his father's worn-out Bible that had been entrusted to him since the end of the War.

Hannah's father approached Gabe and asked, "Do you have everything you need, Gabe?"

Gabe glanced up and replied, "Maybe another day to wish I didn't have to leave," he said with a smile. In his heart, however, he was serious. A few weeks ago, he was eager for the job. Suddenly, he was having second thoughts.

"You'll be back home in a few days," Silas said, trying to lighten the mood.

Just then, Eli came from the barn. "That dadburn calf still won't let me catch it." He then noticed that

Gabe was getting ready to leave. "When are you coming back?" Eli asked.

"As soon as I can." Gabe looked toward the house to see Hannah, who was calling them to breakfast.

They sat down at the table, prayed, and ate with a little less conversation than in the past couple of days. Little Alec had awakened, sleepy-eyed and hungry. After breakfast, Gabe bid farewell, hugged and kissed his wife and son, and headed out the door. As much as he wished he didn't have to leave, something deep down was driving him to go.

"Let us go with you to the depot," Hannah urged him.

"It's better if you stay here," Gabe replied tenderly.

With tears in her eyes, she said, "Please come back safely. You know how I worry since what happened with Davis."

"I promise not to be away very long," Gabe reassured her.

The farm was close to the depot, and Lieutenant Carson was already there when Gabe arrived. Deputy Miles joined them as they prepared to load the horses. "Gentlemen, I hate to tell you, but I can't go," the deputy informed them. Both Gabe and the lieutenant looked surprised. The lieutenant took a draw from his cigar and asked, "Why not?"

"My wife is expecting a baby, but she wasn't due until next month. She might be going into labor already."

"Don't worry about it, Deputy. You've got more important things to tend to," the lieutenant assured him.

Gabe spoke up. "Head over to my in-laws' place and ask for my wife, Hannah. She's a nurse and has a lot of experience with birthin' babies. I'm sure she'll be glad to help."

"I sure am sorry, fellas," the deputy said, tipping his hat. He wished them good luck and headed to the Clayton farm to find Hannah.

As the deputy left, the lieutenant turned to Gabe. "That might have worked out for the best."

"May I ask you a question, Lieutenant?"

"Ask away, Deputy."

"Do you fear God, Lieutenant?" The lieutenant paused, curious about a question that seemed to come out of nowhere.

"I've heard that to fear the Lord is the beginning of wisdom. I suppose I do. Why?"

"Because I sense that the Almighty might have a bigger purpose in our assignment," Gabe said somberly as a train whistle was heard in the distance.

"I hear the train coming. Let's get our tickets," the lieutenant said, wondering what Gabe was implying as they walked toward the depot clerk's window.

The two men quickly loaded their horses onto a livestock rail car and settled into their seats. The lieutenant began discussing his plan. "We'll head straight to Marshal Northrop's office. He'll deputize you as a Deputy Marshal since you'll be out of your jurisdiction. You'll still be under my oversight, but we'll be operating under the Marshal's authority."

Gabe was eager to get started. The sooner they began, the sooner he could be back home.

The train made stops at Holden and Kingsville before rolling into Kansas City. The city was bustling, with buildings stretching as far as the eye could see and streets crowded with people. As the train pulled into Union Depot, a massive four-rail hub, the lieutenant and Gabe made their way to the platform. They stepped off the train and headed to the rear car to claim their horses.

"Now, we need to find the marshal's office," the lieutenant said.

They approached a Baggage Master and asked for directions. "You'll find the federal offices on Independence and Troost Avenues, sir," he replied kindly.

With that, they mounted their horses and rode off through the bustling streets of Kansas City, ready to take on whatever lay ahead.

The noise, the smell of a big city, and the clamor of people were slightly overwhelming to Gabe. Kansas City, Missouri, was a booming city. After riding through dusty streets and past the shops and businesses, they spotted the Federal Building that housed the Marshal's Office. They tied their horses at the front and stepped inside.

"Excuse me, sir," Gabe asked a young man who appeared to work there. "We are looking for the U.S. Marshal's Office."

"Second floor," he responded.

They reached the second floor at the top of the winding staircase and walked down a long hallway filled with various offices. At last, they came to the office door with a sign that read, "Jameson R. Northrop, U.S. Marshal, Western Missouri District." The door was open.

The lieutenant shifted his cigar from one side of his mouth to the other. "I hope he's in," he said as they stepped inside.

"May I help you, gentlemen?" asked the young lady at the front desk.

"Marshal Northrop is expecting us," the lieutenant told her, and he gave her their names.

"Please take a seat. I will let him know you are here."

Portraits of George Washington, Abraham Lincoln, and Ulysses Grant hung on the walls. Two American flags draped across each other hung on another wall. There was also a copy of the Declaration of Independence and the Bill of Rights. Gabe was impressed with the size of the office compared to the tiny one he had run back in Kentucky. The walls were lined with walnut wood panels and large windows overlooking the busy street below.

Just then, Marshal Northrop entered the room. His high boots and long guns caught their attention, and his badge was prominently displayed on his black vest. He was middle-aged, but the lines on his face and white hair made him appear older.

"There you are, Marshal," the young receptionist said. "These two men are here to see you. They said you were expecting them?"

He glanced in their direction as they both stood up. "What can I do for you, gentlemen?"

"Marshal, I am Lieutenant John Carson, U.S. Army. This is Deputy Gabe MacCallan from Kentucky."

"Kentucky, huh? I went through Kentucky back in '67, Lexington, I think the town was. Nice place. Fast horses and good bourbon," he recollected with a chuckle. "Come on into my office."

He hung up his hat and unbelted his guns. He was about to hang them up when Gabe said, "I couldn't help but notice your Colt Navy revolvers."

The marshal took one of the pistols from its holster. "Yes indeed. One of the finest revolvers ever made, but I've heard that Colt is about to issue a new one this year. I changed the cylinders in these to use cartridges," he said. He pulled one click back on the hammer, spun the cylinder, set the hammer back on an empty slot, and placed it back in its holster.

"I have one just like it," Gabe said as he took his gun from his holster.

"It looks like we have the same taste in firearms." The marshal smiled and then asked, "How can I help you?"

The lieutenant reminded him about his previous communication with the local sheriff.

"Oh, yes, yes," the marshal remembered. "I've been expecting you. I don't know why that didn't occur to me when you mentioned Kentucky."

He rose from his desk and went to the door to close it, but he called to his deputy before he did. "Jim, come in here." The marshal pointed to a couple of chairs. "Gentlemen, have a seat." His deputy walked into the office. "This is Deputy Jim Bower," the marshal introduced. "Jim, these are the two I told you about who were coming from Kentucky, and the reason I sent you a while back to look up the name of one of them, Fergussons."

They exchanged greetings, and then the lieutenant handed the marshal a folder from his canvas pouch. "Marshal Northrop, Deputy Bower, this is why we are here."

The marshal opened the folder and thumbed through the papers. "This fella has been busy—embezzlement, falsifying identity, and a few other things," the marshal observed. "I take it that you are here to apprehend him?"

"We have information about an illegal cattle-marketing scheme that he is allegedly part of," Gabe remarked.

"I am aware of what you are referring to, and we are investigating," the marshal said in his deep voice. "Therefore, I'm hesitant to allow you to come in and potentially disrupt an ongoing investigation."

Deputy Bower spoke up. "What if we let these two shake a few bushes and see what they can scare out?"

The marshal shook his head in disagreement. "No, it could set us back for months if something happened. The last thing I need is that dadburn Marshal Yates gettin' his panties in a wad."

"This investigation has hit a brick wall in the last couple of months, Jameson." Bower insisted again.

The marshal sat with his hands folded together, glancing at Gabe and then Lieutenant Carson. He rose from his chair and walked to the window, his hands clasped behind his back. After a few minutes of pondering, he returned to his chair. He paused again, then looked sternly at Gabe and the lieutenant.

"How do you plan to identify this man?" the marshal asked.

"I know him personally," Gabe replied. "He managed to hide his true identity and serve as a deputy sheriff in my county."

The marshal leaned back in his chair. "Knowing him could be a double-edged sword. He must be a slick one, which means he could spot you first. I have reservations about this," he said to Bower.

"Do we have your consent?" Gabe pressed, wanting to either wrap up the conversation or get approval.

The marshal paused before reluctantly saying, "If you find your man, you report back to me. Understood?"

"Yes, sir," they agreed in unison.

"Very well. Don't ask a lot of questions. Keep your ears open, and most importantly, stay clear of J.T. Fergusson," the marshal warned. "These men are killers. Some of the roughest in the country. You'll be under my authority," he added. The lieutenant glanced at Gabe.

"Deputy, you're the lead man," the lieutenant said.

"Give me the badge. I'll bring him to justice," Gabe replied confidently.

"You find him," the marshal said, correcting him sharply. "I'll bring Fergusson to justice." After discussing their plan and strategy, the marshal deputized Gabe as U.S. Deputy Marshal MacCallan, Western District of Missouri.

23

They awoke to a rainy morning. Gabe and Lieutenant Carson sat down for breakfast at the Broadway Hotel before dawn. They quickly got down to business. Carson was dressed in civilian clothes, which piqued Gabe's curiosity.

"If we are going to be cattle buyers, we'd best look the part," the lieutenant explained and handed Gabe a piece of paper. "Your new identity is Randall McCowen, a buyer for Rutherford Cattle Company."

"Where did you get this?" Gabe asked.

Carson chuckled. "While you were preparing to leave Warrensburg, I did a little research from the depot advertisement wall. This flyer was posted on the board advertising the Rutherford Cattle Company. We'll get some cash sometime later today. That's really the only credentials we will need."

"The marshal said the big dog here is J.T. Fergusson. He owns the Double J Ranch. Apparently, he deals with some cattlemen from Texas and Colorado. His operation is across the river near the Colorado Cattle Yards. As Marshal Northrop warned, we want to stay clear of him. He is not our concern. Your first task is to just learn the lay of the land. Get acquainted with a few people first. Find a lead within Fergusson's circle that will get us near James Fergusson."

"Got it," Gabe nodded.

"Good. I will see you later today. From now on, I will be Mr. Carson and see what I can learn from my end."

They left the hotel together and went their separate ways. Gabe headed to the livery to retrieve his horse and rode across the river to Wyandotte City. He had a strong aversion to the city with its noise and filth, not to mention the rats darting between buildings and the unpleasant odor that hung in the air, becoming a lingering stench after the rain. Gabe felt like he had stepped into a foreign country.

He was dressed like a businessman and now sporting a dark and full beard. He was sitting astride a horse that complemented his image. He rode slowly down Sixth Street, tipping his hat to those he passed. The clouds were beginning to part now, and only a sprinkling of rain was hitting his black flat-brimmed hat. As he rode down the street, heads turned to see this stranger, even though strangers in town were common.

He spent time exploring, eventually making his way to the cattle yards. Colorado Cattle Yards were vast, covering several acres with hundreds of cattle in various lots. Gabe had never seen so many cattle in one place. A cattle yard that size has a smell like no other, and the constant bawling of cattle made it hard to hear anything else.

"Out of the way!" Someone yelled, startling Gabe. "Out of the way!" It was a rough old codger leading a mule pulling a dead steer.

The stench was so unbearable that Gabe had to cover his face with his bandana. He maneuvered Midnight around and began searching for a local livery stable. He found one a few blocks down from the Lucky Kansan Saloon. Gabe paid the livery owner to stall and feed Midnight for a few hours.

"Where you from, mister?" the livery owner asked as he scooped feed out of a burlap sack.

"Not from around here," Gabe answered, flipping an additional silver dollar to him.

"Only the best for my partner?" Gabe requested.

The old gentleman caught the silver dollar and smiled. "He'll eat like a king. I promise," he said. "I have some fresh Timothy hay, too, that he will like."

Gabe stepped onto the muddy street and took the pocket watch from his vest to check the time. It was nearly 9:00 A.M.

"It's still a bit early, but I think I'll walk toward the saloon," he said.

He crossed the increasingly busy street, scraping the muck off his boots on the boardwalk. As he walked, he came upon a small bakery, the aroma of fresh bread wafting out the door. Unable to resist, he pushed open the door, the bell above jingling with his entrance. Closing the door behind him, he took in the warm, inviting surroundings. The shop owner emerged from the back with a tray of fresh bread. She noticed Gabe, whose back was turned, examining the display of country hams hanging by the window.

"I didn't think you could get country hams in cattle country," he murmured. As the lady set the tray on the counter, he turned to face her.

"Beef is king around here," she remarked in her southern drawl. "My shop is one of a few that stock country hams in town for those who still yearn for good ole country ham. I have them delivered straight from Tennessee," she explained. He could tell by her accent that she was not from Kansas.

"What can I do for you, stranger?" she asked, her eyes expressing curiosity.

"The scent of fresh bread drew me in," he replied with a smile.

"Try a buttered biscuit. I just made these." She handed him a warm biscuit, and he thanked her, accepting the offer. As he took a bite, it melted in his mouth, rich and full of flavor.

"Ma'am, if I wasn't already married, I might propose to you right here. This is the best biscuit I've ever had."

She chuckled warmly. "I've lost count of how many proposals I've turned down. I'm Sadie Fergusson." The last name made Gabe pause and take notice.

"Ga… I mean, Rand McCowen, ma'am," Gabe replied, almost slipping his real name.

"Very nice to meet you, Mr. McCowen," she responded warmly.

"Are you visiting or planning to stay? I assume you're new in town since most folks here already know me."

"I'm here on business," he said. "May I ask you a question?"

"Of course," she said while placing hot, fresh bread in the glass case.

"I get the feeling you're not originally from here. Where are you from?"

"I'm from Arkansas, near Memphis. I came here five years ago after the War, married a wonderful man, and settled down."

"Who is your husband, if you don't mind me asking?"

"Jared Fergusson."

"I don't think I've had the pleasure of meeting him," Gabe replied.

"What kind of business brings you to town, Mr. McCowen?" she asked.

"I'm a cattle buyer."

She nodded, studying him from the corners of her eyes, which were dark and steady. "You look like a cattle buyer. Who do you work for?" she continued, clearly sizing him up.

"The Rutherford Cattle Company back east," he replied.

"I've heard of it, but you have a Southern drawl like mine," she noted.

"Yes, ma'am. I'm originally from Kentucky."

As customers began to trickle in, a young lady emerged from the back with more baked goods, giving him a convenient excuse to end the conversation. Gabe felt satisfied with what he had learned.

"Mrs. Fergusson, thank you for the finest biscuit I've ever had." He placed a fifty-cent piece on the counter.

"You're very generous, Mr. McCowen. I hope to see you again," she said with a smile.

Gabe tipped his hat and left the shop, grateful for their providential acquaintance. He went to the nearest tavern to see who might be hanging around.

As Gabe approached the Lucky Kansan Saloon, its wide-open doors seemed to beckon him inside. The bartender was outside, sweeping the front porch as Gabe took in his surroundings. He found a table, pulled out a chair, and sat down, making sure to face the entrance as he surveyed the room. To his left, two men were deep in conversation, while to his right, a lone man sat quietly at another table. Near the door, three men and a woman were gathered around a table. The aroma of sizzling steak drifted from the kitchen, making his mouth water. Suddenly, a young lady emerged, balancing three plates on her left arm and holding another in her right hand.

"I'll be with you in a minute, sir," she said when she noticed Gabe. Gabe laid his hat on the table, watching her with amazement at how she balanced those plates of food.

"Now," she said while catching her breath.

"What will you have?"

"Just coffee."

"Anything else?"

"A newspaper, if you have one."

She returned with his coffee and yesterday's paper a few minutes later.

As Gabe skimmed the newspaper, he quickly familiarized himself with the workings of the cattle market: the sellers, the buyers, and all the pertinent details. "$4.00 to $5.00 per hundred pounds?" he muttered. "I might be in the wrong business."

Just as he was pondering this, a dirty hat was abruptly dropped onto the table, interrupting his reading. He looked up, his eyes narrowing as he met the intruder's gaze. The man standing before him had a rugged look, his face expressing displeasure at Gabe's presence. Gabe folded his newspaper slowly, keeping his expression neutral as he prepared for whatever might come next.

"Son, you are sittin' at my table," the man drawled in a sharp and dismissive tone. He was middle-aged, well-dressed, a heavyset fella, flanked by two men who looked like they rode for him.

"I beg your pardon," Gabe replied politely. "Didn't see anyone here. You're welcome to join me." The man's eyes narrowed at this unexpected invitation. "You're inviting me to sit at my own table?" he asked sarcastically.

"It's your table. I reckon you can do what you want," Gabe responded, returning his attention to the newspaper.

The man was taken aback by Gabe's calm demeanor, hesitating before signaling his men to sit. He pulled out three chairs. "Rita!" he bellowed. "Bring us the usual! And be quick about it!"

There was a tense silence as Gabe continued reading while the trio stared at him. Finally, Gabe looked up and decided to break the ice. "Name's McCowen, Rand McCowen. I'm here to buy cattle. I'm looking for the one who sells for Fergusson."

"Why Fergusson?" the older man asked gruffly.

"Is there someone else I should know about?" Gabe replied, finishing his coffee. Rita brought the men their steaks and topped off their cups. The steaks were so large they hung over the edges of the plates, each topped with a pair of sunny-side-up eggs.

"I know where you can get a better deal on cattle than Fergusson," the man said, speaking through a mouthful of medium-rare steak and runny egg yolk.

"Where?" Gabe asked, wanting to keep the conversation flowing.

The man placed his elbow on the table and pointed his knife at Gabe. "Tell you what, young fella," he said, grease running down his chin, "after I finish this here steak, I'll take you to him."

"Who? Mister, a –" Gabe began to ask.

"Smitherton. Name's Ed Smitherton," he replied, laying his steak knife down and extending his hand to Gabe.

Gabe returned the courtesy, but said, "I'm sorry, Mr. Smitherton, I don't typically do business with people I don't know much about," Gabe said firmly. "Who is this person you are referring to?"

"His name is Red Kinsley."

"Who did you say?" Gabe replied with surprise in his voice.

"He owns the RK Brand. Red Kinsley. These boys ride for him. I'm his broker," Smitherton replied. Gabe could hardly believe his ears.

"I know, Kinsley," Gabe said. "Very well, take me to him." All at once, he remembered that he wasn't there as Gabe MacCallan.

"On the other hand," Gabe said quickly. "I need to meet him privately. Is that possible?"

Smitherton, chewing on a jaw full of steak, eyed Gabe warily for a moment. Despite his unease by his request, he replied, "Fine. Meet us at the corner of Sixth and Ninth."

Gabe laid six silver dollars on the table to pay for their meal, which Smitherton eyed suspiciously before nodding curtly, muttering, "That's mighty kind'a you, McCowen."

"Just get me to Kinsley. I'll see you in fifteen minutes," Gabe replied with a smile and tipped his hat.

He then made his way quickly back to the livery for his horse.

"That was quick," the owner of the stable remarked.

"I'll get your horse. The saddle is over yonder," he gestured. "I owe you some money since you paid me a little extra for the day."

"No need," Gabe waved off the offer. "I'm sure I'll be back." In no time, he secured his saddle onto his mount.

"By the way, I never got your name, sir," Gabe mentioned.

"Henry Eubank."

"Mr. Eubank," Gabe replied. "Do you know a man by the name of Ed Smitherton?"

"That's Red Kinsley's right-hand man," Mr. Eubank confirmed.

"What kind of man is he?" Gabe inquired.

"Decent sort, once you get past his rough edges."

"Thank you, Mr. Eubank."

Within a few minutes, Gabe was at the location to meet Smitherton as planned and followed him and his crew.

"Where are we headed?" Gabe wanted to know.

"Normally, Kinsley is at his five-hundred-acre ranch west of Rena, but he's in town today. We ain't going far."

As they rode through the streets, Gabe carefully noted the landmarks to remember his way back. He was looking forward to this unexpected meeting with Kinsley. The last time Gabe and Kinsley had been together was at Gabe's wedding in September 1866 in Warrensburg, where Kinsley had served as his best man.

After trailing behind Smitherton and his two cowhands, they finally arrived at a ranch-style house on the outskirts of town.

"This is Mr. Kinsley's home away from home when he needs to conduct business. I'll inform him that you're here and request a private meeting," Smitherton said before heading inside. The two cowhands departed, which was fine with Gabe. He remained on his horse, waiting patiently.

After a few minutes, Smitherton returned with Kinsley, who stepped out onto the porch. Gabe instantly recognized his old friend, still sporting a head full of red hair and a thick mustache, now streaked with white. However, Kinsley didn't recognize Gabe, who had put on weight and now wore a full black beard. He was also riding a different horse than Kinsley might otherwise remember.

"Mr. McCowen," Kinsley called out. "Hop down and come on in."

Gabe dismounted, tying Midnight to the hitching rail. With his hat shadowing his face, he walked up to the porch. Smitherton excused himself, and Gabe thanked him as he passed by. When Gabe approached

Kinsley, he lifted his head, revealing his face.

When Kinsley recognized Gabe, he hollered, "Well, if it ain't you, you ole hillbilly sodbuster!" He was both stunned and thrilled to see his old friend. They clasped hands, exchanging hearty slaps on the shoulders.

"What's this about, and why the different name?" Kinsley asked.

"Let's head inside, and I'll explain everything," Gabe replied.

Gabe and Kinsley spent the next three hours catching up on the last five years. As they talked, Kinsley's housekeeper stepped into the room. Mary made her way west from Tennessee with a wave of freed slaves heading west to carve out new lives.

"Gabe, this here's Mary." Gabe stood and nodded respectfully.

"Pleasure to meet you, ma'am."

"The pleasure's mine, sir. Will you stay for dinner? We've got plenty," she invited.

"Of course, he'll stay. We still have a heap to talk about," Kinsley said with a grin. "I was the best man at his wedding."

"Well then," Mary replied, smiling. "You're family, then. I'll get started."

Kinsley had done well in Kansas since the cattle boom, and he eagerly shared his stories with Gabe, detailing the ruthless world of cattle barons and the cut-throat nature of the business.

"Charlatans are always lookin' to take advantage," Kinsley complained. "When Smitherton mentioned someone wanted to meet with me, I figured you might be one. That Fergusson fellow you mentioned is likely kin to J.T. Fergusson. I've crossed paths with J.T. and had a few sour dealings with him. He's a slick one. And that Jared Fergusson you spoke of—he might be part of the family business, but he's not a top dog. Jared doesn't like to share much. Regardless, the Fergussons stick together. It's in their Scottish blood to be a clan. Cross one, and you'll face 'em all."

Gabe listened closely, realizing this task was gonna be tougher than he'd thought.

"If you can get me close to him," Gabe said, "all I need to do is identify the one I'm looking for. The deputy marshals will handle the rest."

"Alright," Kinsley agreed, "but I can't be seen as involved, Gabe. It would ruin my business here."

"Understood," Gabe replied. "You won't have to worry about that. No one will know anything."

After their meeting and a meal fit for a king, Gabe returned to the Broadway Hotel. Entering the lobby, he found the lieutenant seated by the fireplace, savoring his brandy and cigars.

"Take a seat, Mr. McCowen. Join me for a glass of brandy?" the lieutenant invited. Gabe, who never indulged, politely declined but took a seat on the sofa.

"You don't know what you're missing," the lieutenant remarked, gesturing with his bourbon.

"I appreciate it, just the same," Gabe replied. He then shared everything he had learned about the Fergussons.

"Well done for the first day," Carson complimented. "We'll lay out a plan in the morning."

As the night wore on, the lieutenant consumed more brandy, and his speech became slurred. Gabe suggested they retire for the night, and they agreed to continue their discussion in the morning.

24

Gabe and Lieutenant Carson had just finished breakfast when an attractive young woman entered the hotel lobby. It was Jared Fergusson's wife delivering her baked goods to the kitchen. She approached the desk manager, asking if a Mr. McCowen was staying at the hotel. As the attendant checked the guestbook, she noticed Gabe signaling from the dining room to get her attention.

"That's him," she informed the attendant upon seeing Gabe.

"Good morning, Mrs. Fergusson," Gabe greeted her as he and Carson stood up.

"Good morning, Mr. McCowen. Please excuse my appearance; I deliver baked goods on Wednesday mornings," she explained.

"No apologies needed. Carson," Gabe remarked, "she makes the best biscuits in town," prompting a smile from her.

"This is my business associate, Mr. Carson," Gabe introduced.

"Please, just call me Sadie," she said as they exchanged greetings.

"Please, sit with us," Gabe invited, pulling out a chair for her. Sensing an opportunity, he continued, "We're interested in purchasing some cattle from your husband. How might we find him?"

"His office is on the west side of the river," Sadie replied, giving them the directions, which Carson jotted down. After a few more pleasantries, she mentioned she needed to get back to work, so Gabe and Carson accompanied her to the lobby before parting ways.

"Excuse me, Miss Sadie, before you go," Carson asked, "Do you happen to know where I can find a bank?"

"The First National Bank is located on Main and Fifth Streets. Head north to Fifth Street and turn east. It's easy to find and not too far," she replied.

"Thank you, Miss Sadie. It has been a pleasure meeting you. You have been most accommodating."

"Indeed, Miss Sadie," Gabe added. "It was a pleasure seeing you again."

"The pleasure is all mine, gentlemen," she replied in her southern way and smiled politely before departing.

Carson turned to Gabe. "Before we pay a visit to Mr. Fergusson, we need to go to the bank for some cash," Carson said.

Following Sadie's directions, Gabe and Carson rode up to the First National Bank. Just as they were about to step inside, Gabe spotted Deputy Bower talking with a local. Catching sight of them, Bower strolled over and greeted them warmly. "Howdy, gents. How's it going?"

"Going well. We needed to visit the bank before meeting someone today," Carson replied.

"The First National Bank?" Bower asked with a note of concern in his voice.

"Yeah, Jared Fergusson's wife recommended it," Carson answered, noticing Bower's apprehension.

"The Fergusson family owns stock in that bank," Bower informed them. "If you make a transaction here, you might draw unwanted attention. Follow me," he suggested, leading the way.

Relieved by Bower's timely intervention, Gabe and Carson fell in behind him. Bower led them two streets over, turned north on Main Street, and brought them to Watson Bank.

"Ask for Mr. Rowe, the bank's president. Tell him I sent you. When the marshal needs confidential help, he deals through Rowe, and I reckon you should do the same." Gabe and Carson thanked Bower, who wished them well before heading off. After introducing themselves to Rowe and getting acquainted, Gabe and Carson secured the cash they needed.

Leaving the bank, Gabe and Carson headed west. They soon reached the western edge of Wyandotte City, crossing the Kansas River and riding south on Bluff Street. To the east, the Missouri Pacific Railway ran parallel to the road, with vagrant camps scattered along the wood line below and beyond the tracks. A foul odor lay heavy in the air from the camps, and the sound of children crying tugged at Gabe's heart as he imagined the bleakness of their lives. The men and women were former slaves. Despite emancipation occurring six years earlier, many former slaves were still struggling under harsh conditions. The Freedmen's Bureau was overwhelmed and unable to provide assistance to everyone in need.

When Gabe and Carson arrived at Jared Fergusson's place, they noticed cowhands preoccupied preparing for a cattle drive, not noticing Gabe and Carson. Mules were being harnessed and loaded with supplies. The two rode up to a building that appeared to be an office and dismounted. Gabe, wary of encountering James Fergusson—whom he knew as Frank Tate—kept his hat pulled low to conceal his face as he scanned the area. Carson approached the door, which was guarded by the largest man on the property. The man stood an impressive six and a half feet tall and weighed no less than three hundred pounds. His upper arms were as thick as stovepipes, and his hands looked capable of crushing a man's skull like a walnut. Carson stood before him, pulled a cigar from his vest pocket, bit off the tip, and struck a match on the doorpost to light it. Smoke swirled around the giant's head as he frowned and snarled.

"We're here to see Mr. Fergusson," Carson informed him. The massive guard glared at them sternly before finally opening the door. Inside, Jared Fergusson sat behind a desk, giving instructions to a cowhand, likely his foreman, who soon left. Jared then turned his attention to the visitors who had entered unannounced.

"What brings you here, gentlemen?" he asked.

Gabe stepped forward. "Mornin', Mr. Fergusson. Name's McCowen, and this is my business associate, Mr. Carson."

"Thank you, Ennis," he said to the big fella, who resumed his post outside the door. "Alright. You know who I am. Have a seat, gentlemen. State your business. I don't have much time." Jared requested straightforwardly.

"We're interested in buying a few steers," Carson said. "We heard that you could help us."

"What company do you work for, or are you buying for yourselves?" Fergusson asked. Gabe took the piece of paper from his vest and handed it to him.

"Rutherford Cattle Company, huh? I knew a stock buyer from that company a few years ago. His name is Jacobson. Do you know him?" Jared asked.

Gabe glanced at Carson. "He's no longer with us," Carson replied, implying that Jacobson was no longer associated with the company. Carson had no idea and was only pretending to know him.

"Yes, come to think of it," Jared responded. "He passed away, as I recall, now. He was a good fella."

"How many head are lookin' to buy?" Jared asked, now that Gabe and Carson seemed to be legitimate buyers.

"We are looking to buy a hundred head, depending on the price," Carson replied.

"My crew is gettin' ready to head out. They'll travel west of Topeka, loadin' and bringin' back a herd next week. If you want, I can take your down payment and reserve a hundred head. If you like what you see, fine. If not, I'll find what you want."

"What's your price?" Carson asked.

As Gabe and Carson haggled over the price of cattle, a knock sounded at the door, and it swung open. Gabe and Carson sat with their backs to the entrance.

"I've done everything you asked, Jared," a man said, his voice immediately catching Gabe's attention. It was the man they were seeking—James Fergusson, known to Gabe as Frank Tate. Fortunately, he didn't notice Gabe.

"Good," Jared replied. "Tell Leland he can head out whenever he's ready."

"I'll see you next week," James said, closing the door behind him.

This was a stroke of luck, or perhaps providence, Gabe thought as he exchanged a subtle glance with Carson. Carson, unfamiliar with James, didn't catch the significance of Gabe's expression.

While Carson continued to negotiate cattle prices, Gabe began formulating a plan. After about fifteen minutes, Jared asked, "Do we have a deal, gentlemen?" He extended his hand.

Gabe rose from his seat, shook Jared's hand, and said, "We have a deal. Just out of curiosity, are these cattle coming from one brand or several? We want to know what we're getting."

"They're coming from a quality ranch, the Double J," Jared said with a smile. "J.T. Fergusson. J.T. is my brother. I can personally vouch for the quality of these cattle," Jared added, still smiling.

"Mr. Fergusson, it's a pleasure doing business," Carson said as they shook hands and exchanged the down payment for a cash receipt. Jared had his money, and Gabe had his information. As they walked out the door, Gabe kept his head down, careful not to reveal his face despite the effective cover his thick, dark beard provided.

Before getting into his saddle, Carson called out to the burly fella standing guard at the door. "Ennis! Have a cigar." The big fella actually cracked a smile. As they rode out, they left the same way they came in without arousing any suspicions. When they returned to the street and headed back, Gabe said, "Well, you will be glad to know that we got more than just our feet in the door and a hundred head'a cattle."

"How so?" Carson replied curiously.

"The man who stepped in to speak to Jared is our man. That was James Fergusson, the one I know as Frank Tate."

Carson was taken aback. "In the flesh?" he asked, amazed at the chance encounter.

"Indeed," Gabe confirmed with a grin.

"We're lucky he didn't recognize you," Carson replied.

"I know," Gabe agreed. "Looks like our next stop is Topeka. It seems James will be taking the train ahead of the cowhands today."

"We should inform Northrop," Carson suggested.

As they rode eastward across the river, Gabe pondered, "What are we going to do with all that beef we bought?"

Carson chuckled.

"And another thing," Gabe continued, "How were you able to get that amount of cash from the bank, anyway?"

"It's government money," Carson said with a grin. "I'll have to pay it back one way or another. If I don't, you'll be addressing me as 'Private Carson.'"

"I hope you didn't spend it all, Private Carson," Gabe remarked.

"Watch it now, Deputy. You'll be glad to know," Carson added, "I used your salary as part of that down payment."

Gabe shook his head, smirking. "In other words, the government and I are partners in a cattle deal?"

"You might say that," Carson replied, still grinning.

"In that case, let's turn back. We need to visit an old friend before we report to Marshal Northrop," Gabe said. "I think I know how to get my money back and keep your rear end from being demoted. But I need you to trust what I'm about to do."

Carson laughed and glanced at Gabe, wondering what he had up his sleeve. Gabe and Carson turned around and made their way to see Red Kinsley.

"By the way, that was quick thinking when Fergusson asked about that Jacobson fella," Gabe remarked.

"I got lucky," Carson replied.

In the meantime, James Fergusson was purchasing tickets to Topeka on the Union Pacific Railway. Gabe's instinct was right.

"Topeka, Mr. Fergusson?" The depot clerk asked.

"Two tickets, Mr. Morgan," James replied.

After paying for the tickets, he walked toward a man standing on the platform and waiting by the rail.

"Jake, here's your ticket."

The man was Jake Kilpatrick, the twin brother of Alan Kilpatrick. Alan, also known as Russell Davis, had been killed by Hannah MacCallan with a .44 Henry rifle, saving her husband's life. Jake and Alan were nearly identical in appearance, style, and voice, but their personalities differed significantly. Alan was a manipulative and cold-hearted killer, while Jake was a schemer who would swindle you out of your shirt and then sell it back to you. However, he lacked the killer instinct his brother had. Fergusson had informed Jake that Alan died in a gunfight with a sheriff and his deputy in Kentucky. Jake had solemnly vowed to one day avenge his brother's death.

"All aboard for Topeka!" shouted the porter. Jake and James boarded a passenger car, were seated, and James discussed their plan regarding the next cattle shipment.

"The crew won't arrive until tomorrow," James informed. "I'll handle the paperwork at the ranch and meet you at the weigh house," he added.

Despite being one of the Fergussons, James' only allegiance lay with his love of money. He had a habit of falsifying the numbers on every shipment of cattle to divert a portion of the cash to himself and his partner, transferring the stolen funds to an assumed name to avoid suspicion. Though the amounts were small, the money accumulated over time, allowing the duo to pocket a few thousand dollars.

Gabe and Carson rode into Wyandotte City and headed straight for Red Kinsley's house to discuss their recent venture and Gabe's proposal.

"Come in, gentlemen," Kinsley welcomed them when they arrived. "I had a feeling I would see you again. Mary, bring these gentlemen some hot coffee, please."

"Don't bother, Miss Mary," Gabe told her kindly. "We can't stay very long. Red, this is Lieutenant John Carson."

They seated themselves on the front porch, and Gabe got straight to the point. He explained how they ended up purchasing a hundred head of cattle as a way to get inside Fergusson's circle.

"Carson was a pretty good negotiator," Gabe informed him, "and managed to get the cattle down to $4.75 per hundredweight."

"$4.75?" Kinsley reacted, pushing his hat back on his head. "I need you to work for me, lieutenant. I just bought a herd for $4.95. The market price is expected to rise as high as $6.75 this year. What do you have in mind?"

Gabe explained, "We paid fifty percent as a down payment, and we just want to recover our money when the cattle arrive."

"I tell you what," Kinsley interrupted.

"I'll do you one better than that. As an old friend, I'll give you $4.75 for your investment and $4.95 for the remaining half."

"Gabe, you stand to make a small profit," Carson said, grinning.
Gabe laughed. "I suppose you want a commission?"

Kinsley chuckled. "There is one catch, though," as he leaned forward in his chair. "I'll need to wait until the dust settles before giving you the money. That means the cattle must be in the stockyard, and you'll have to close the deal. The question is, how do you plan to apprehend Fergusson without getting caught like a fox in a hen house?"

Carson spoke up, "That's where the marshal comes in. We aim to find him, not apprehend him. No one will know we are involved."

Then Kinsley took on a stern look, "Be wary, boys. You're dealin' with a tough and ruthless bunch. They have eyes everywhere."

With firm handshakes to seal their deal, they walked out onto the front lawn. Kinsley wished them luck, and they made their way to report to Marshal Northrop.

As the noonday sun shone through a partly cloudy sky, they hurried to the Marshal's Office, catching him just as he was leaving for a court appearance.

"Lieutenant," the marshal said, "I almost didn't recognize you without your uniform."

"Marshal, we have a solid lead," Gabe interjected. The marshal signaled to one of his deputies. "Inform Judge Bryant that I'll be a bit late. Come in, gentlemen," the marshal said. "Jim, you too," he added, closing the door behind them. "Make it quick, if you don't mind, Deputy."

"James Fergusson is on his way to Topeka and the Double J Ranch. He's organizing a shipment due back in Wyandotte City next week. We're leaving for Topeka tomorrow," Gabe quickly summarized.

"Are you sure? You know this for certain, that he is headed to Topeka?" Northrop asked.

"Yes, sir," Gabe replied.

Carson chimed in. "Gabe identified him while we were in a meeting with Jared when Jared gave him orders to go to Topeka."

The marshal leaned back in his chair, rubbing his rough chin thoughtfully.

"Jim," Northrop commanded, "gather five deputies. The six of you will join MacCallan and Carson."

"Yes, sir," Deputy Bower responded, promptly leaving the room.

Marshal Northrop followed him to the door.

"Miss Ellen, do you have a train schedule to Topeka?"

"Yes, sir, I do."

"When's the next train?" Northrop asked.

She checked the schedule. "The last train today leaves at three this afternoon. Otherwise, there's one tomorrow morning at seven," she replied.

The marshal returned to his chair and sat down.

"You know how a predator culls its prey from the herd?" the marshal posed.

"Is that what you want us to do with Fergusson?" Gabe asked.

"That's right. If you can separate him from the others, you stand a better chance of apprehending him without a ruckus," the marshal advised. "Let me be clear: do not, I repeat, do not go to the ranch for any reason. If there's any suspicion that you are around, there will be a fight, which I want to avoid. Understood?"

"Yes, sir," Gabe and Carson replied.

Deputy Bower re-entered the room.

"Jim," the marshal instructed, "go to Judge Yager for a warrant for James Fergusson."

"Yes, sir."

"I expect to see you back soon—alive. You hear that, Deputy MacCallan?" he said, pointing directly at Gabe.

"Yes, sir," Gabe responded, feeling the weight of the operation settle on his shoulders.

"Good," Northrop said. "That's an order. Now, if you gentlemen will excuse me, I have an angry judge waiting on me." With that, he left the room.

Since they had extra time, Carson suggested, "Let's pay Miss Sadie a visit. Maybe we can ask her a few subtle questions. At least, if we don't learn anything, maybe she will have some leftover biscuits you were boastin' about." They crossed the river to Wyandotte City again and arrived to find Miss Sadie clearing unsold items from her shelves to be given to homeless people.

"Mr. McCowen! Mr. Carson! What a pleasant surprise."

"Good afternoon, Miss Sadie," Gabe replied. "We had a few minutes before returnin' to the hotel, so we thought we'd drop in to thank you for directin' us to your husband. Your husband is a fine man."

She smiled and said, "Why, thank you. It was my pleasure. I'm glad it was a productive visit."

"Yes, ma'am. You wouldn't have any of those biscuits left, would you?" Gabe asked.

"No, but I always bake a small batch of fried apple pies with a fresh pot of coffee," she replied. The smell of fresh coffee had already caught their senses.

"Would you like that, instead?"

"That sounds real good, Miss Sadie," Carson replied.

"Have a seat over yonder. I'll bring 'em right out."

They sat at a small table by the window, and Miss Sadie promptly served them their pies and coffee. For a few minutes, not a word was spoken. The pies were so good they almost forgot their purpose until Miss Sadie returned to refresh their coffee.

"Can I offer you another piece of pie?"

"Yes, ma'am, thank you. I never turn down seconds," Carson responded.

As she served them, Gabe said, "We'll be heading to Topeka tomorrow morning."

"I just love Topeka," she replied. "Have you ever been there?"

"This will be my first time," Gabe said as she sat down with them.

"Well, if you have time, let me tell you what you must see while you're there." For the next few minutes, she shared details about places, attractions, and what to avoid.

"My brother-in-law has a ranch northwest of Topeka," she added.

"I think your husband mentioned that," Carson remarked.

"Yes," she continued. "It's a beautiful place. The main house sits right in the middle of the ranch."

"We're meeting someone in town," Carson said. "Can you recommend a good place to stay?"

She paused to think for a moment, then replied with a warm smile, "Yes, I can. When you get off the train at the Kansas Pacific passenger depot, take Kansas Avenue across the river. The Papendick Hotel is right at the corner of Kansas and Sixth Street. That'll put you right in the heart of downtown."

Their conversation flowed naturally for a couple of hours, laughter and stories filling the time until Gabe suddenly realized how late it had gotten.

"Miss Sadie, we hate to part ways, but we have to be goin'. We are much obliged for your good company, but especially for those fried pies and coffee. We might have spoiled our supper, but I can't think of a better way," Gabe said with genuine appreciation.

Carson nodded in agreement, adding, "We'll definitely take your advice when we get to Topeka tomorrow. You've been very helpful."

Miss Sadie smiled as she replied, "I hope to see you again when you return. Safe travels, gentlemen."

As they rode across the river towards their hotel, Gabe and Carson discussed the day's events. Once at the hotel, they each retired to their rooms as the exhaustion of the day settled in.

Gabe, however, had a nightly ritual before turning in. He sat at a small table by the window, the moonlight casting a soft glow over his father's Bible. He opened it with care, feeling a connection to his past. A gentle breeze drifted through the open window, rustling the pages until they settled on one of many passages his father had underlined in pencil.

"And when her days to be delivered were fulfilled, behold, there were twins in her womb. And the first came out red, all over like a hairy garment, and they called his name Esau. And after that came his brother out, and his hand took hold on Esau's heel; and his name was called Jacob."

Gabe's eyes became heavier with sleep. He turned to the Book of Isaiah, which he had been reading the night before, where he read, "For the day of the LORD of hosts shall be upon every one that is proud and lofty, and upon every one that is lifted up; and he shall be brought low ..."

"The proud and lofty will be brought low," he murmured, those words echoing in his mind. He pondered how the events of the next few days would unfold as he drifted off to sleep.

25

It was Friday morning, May 27th. A high plains storm was brewing in the southwest, kicking up dust as seven lawmen and one U.S. Army Lieutenant stepped off the train at the K.P.R.R. Depot in Topeka, just north of the river. Their horses, skittish from the journey, were quickly unloaded. Gabe, the only one who knew James Fergusson by sight, was appointed their lead man. As they rode into town, they formed an impressive posse, four in the front and four in the rear, riding tall and resolute.

The six deputies from Kansas City were renowned for their skills, and their reputation preceded them, so much so that they seldom had to use their weapons. Next to Gabe rode Deputy Jim Bower. To his left was Deputy Will Brewer, the quiet one of the bunch. Brewer rarely spoke, but when he did, everyone listened. His wisdom was respected as being a straight shooter when it came to the truth, whether it was welcome or not. His stone-faced expression and coal-black eyes could make anyone's blood run cold, giving him the appearance of a cold-blooded, empty soul of a man. In reality, he was a steadfast servant of justice, showing no partiality.

To Brewer's left rode Deputy Emery Ladd, known to everyone as Preacher. He always quoted scripture and held the law in the highest regard. Preacher would often cite the apostle Paul's words, saying, "The law is not made for the righteous but for the lawless and disobedient," and adding, "There's no grace when it comes to the law." He knew the law as well as any judge and held everyone accountable without compromise.

Behind Preacher rode two half-Pawnee brothers, skilled trackers renowned for their abilities. Will, known as White Owl, and Sam, known as Gray Wolf, were legends in their own right. They once tracked a fugitive for a hundred miles, claiming it was through a dust storm. While that might have been an exaggeration, there was no doubt that you might as well surrender if these two were on your trail. They were also skillful negotiators with the local Indian tribes, which made them a critical part of the team.

Riding between them was Deputy Farrell Lewis. Lewis was a good friend of "Wild Bill" Hickok, the new marshal in Abilene. He taught Lewis how to use a gun and was nearly as fast as Hickok. However, Hickok could never beat him at poker. Lewis had a sharp eye and could spot anything out of place or unusual. He had a gift for knowing when someone was lying or telling the truth.

Bringing up the rear was Lieutenant Carson, the senior officer among them all, lending an air of authority to the posse.

The storm clouds loomed ominously, but the posse moved with a determined stride, ready for whatever challenges lay ahead.

After locating the Papendick Hotel, they set out to find a livery stable. They needed to quickly get their horses sheltered and return to the hotel as soon as possible. The scent of rain was in the air, carried by fierce gusts of wind that whipped up dust from the open plains.

"I will take care of the rooms," Carson told them, "while you all take care of the horses."

They found a livery on Jackson Street, not far from the hotel, the Huntoon Livery and Sale Stable, owned by a well-known doctor for his service as a Captain in the U.S. Army during the War. Through a sudden torrential downpour of rain, they quickly made their way to the hotel after stabling the horses.

As the state capital of Kansas, Topeka was a bustling hub of activity, offering everything from lively dance halls and rowdy taverns to upscale hotels where politicians cut their secretive deals. The markets brimmed with all sorts of goods, fresh produce, and prime beef. Being on the frontier's edge, it was common to see cowhands blowing off steam after a long cattle drive. Buffalo hunters were flooding into the territory through Topeka, leaving skinned carcasses numbering in the thousands to rot on the plains. The meat was worthless compared to the valuable hides, which were tanned, baled, and shipped to Europe. J.N. DuBois, a hide dealer out of Kansas City, was paying top dollar for hides, making it a booming market.

The storm blew through that evening with a vengeance, but that didn't keep the town from coming alive as night fell. The lawmen from Kansas City gathered in the quiet of Gabe's room for a meeting to go over plans and scenarios.

"Gentlemen," Gabe began with a voice carrying an air of authority, "I haven't had the chance to properly thank you for your help in apprehending James Fergusson, the man I knew as Frank Tate. He'll be at the Double J Ranch, getting a herd ready to ship to the Colorado Stockyards in Wyandotte City. Tomorrow, Carson and Bower, you two will visit Marshal Yates to inform him of our presence and assignment. Barring any trouble, we shouldn't need his help. Preacher, Brewer, and I will team up to check if the shipment has been scheduled. Lewis, you'll head to the weigh station to gather information on whatever you can find. Sam and Will, you all follow any leads you can uncover. Any questions?" Gabe asked, his eyes scanning the room, meeting each man's gaze with steely resolve.

"And one more thing," Gabe added. "Marshal Northrop wants our badges kept out of sight. Any questions?"

"Seems clear enough to me," one of the men replied, with the rest nodding in agreement.

"Perfect," Carson said with a grin, rubbing his hands together. "Boys, I'm famished. Let's grab a steak on the government's dime."

Laughter filled the room, melting away the tension as they gathered their gear. With a renewed sense of purpose, they headed out, eager to get some hot food and prepare for the challenges that awaited them.

The following morning, the sky was clear, and the eight lawmen made their way to the Huntoon livery to retrieve their horses, trudging through the grayish-brown silt and mud. No words were exchanged as they split up to complete their assignments. Lewis headed west to the weigh station, past the Capitol Iron Works. The weigh station was a labyrinth of holding pens. Near it was its own borough. It was as bustling as a small town and covered almost as much land. It had its own livery stable, tavern, and bank. Merchants lined the street with shops, taking advantage of cash flow from cattle sales.

After arriving at the weigh station livery, Lewis decided to leave his horse and walk around. The unpleasant, pungent smell of manure and wet cattle yards hung in the air as he strolled towards a nearby tavern. Its weathered door creaked as he pushed it open and saw several cattlemen there having breakfast.

The tavern was crowded already, a murmur of conversations filling the room. The cattlemen eyed him warily as he moved through the room, his presence noted by all. He scanned the room, looking for an empty table, when he heard someone say, "You're welcome to sit here, friend, if'n you don't mind the company."

"I don't mind if you don't," Lewis replied. He removed his hat and took a seat. Just then, a waitress walked over to take their orders.

"What will it be, Mr. Erwin?" she asked the young man.

"I'll have the regular, Jennie," he replied.

"Alright, and for you, sir?" she asked, turning to Lewis.

"I'll stick with just coffee, ma'am."

"Ma'am!" she scoffed. "Call me Jennie, or you'll get nothin' at all, mister."

Lewis smiled at her brash way. "Alright, Jennie, I'll just have coffee."

"You'll eat what I bring ya," she said before returning to the kitchen.

"Don't give no mind to Jennie," Erwin told Lewis.

"Don't mind her. She takes good care of us. She's a little rough around the edges, but you'll get used to her."

"I'm Farrell Lewis, by the way."

"Just call me Hannon," Erwin replied.

"What do you do, Hannon?"

"I work for the Double J and help at the weigh house when shipments go out," Hannon replied.

"The Double J Ranch owned by J.T. Fergusson, you mean?" Lewis asked.

"That's the one," Erwin responded.

"How long have you worked for the Double J?"

"About a year. I came into town on a cattle drive and decided to stay. Mr. Fergusson was good enough to give me a job. I plan to have a ranch of my own someday," Hannon said.

"What about you, Mr. Lewis?"

"I'm here on business from Kansas City, looking into the cattle business. Maybe you can show me around."

"I'm headin' over to the weigh house right after finishin' off my breakfast. You're welcome to tag along if you like."

Just then, Jennie served their breakfast, telling Lewis, "Them's the best steak and eggs in Kansas, mister. If it ain't, it's on me," she told him proudly.

"Thank you kindly, ma'am … I mean, Jennie," Lewis gratefully said.

She stood over Lewis until he took a bite and immediately agreed with her opinion.

"Jennie, it is the best steak I have ever tasted," he declared.

Jennie beamed with pride. "Told ya," she replied and bustled off to attend the next table.

Lewis savored his steak, being hungrier than he thought.

"You mentioned that Fergusson fella," Lewis said as he took a sip of his coffee. "You know James Fergusson by any chance?"

"I know him, but not personal-like," Hannon replied. "I reckon he's one of J.T.'s cousins. Don't know much else about him. If you want to meet him, he will be here in the morning weighing in a herd going to Wyandotte City."

"Where do you reckon he'd be today?" asked Lewis.

Hannon chewed on a piece of steak as he thought for a minute. "His favorite haunt is a tavern west of town, not far from the Double J," he replied. "You might catch him there this evenin'."

Lewis quickly polished off his steak, eggs, and coffee, rose from the table, and thanked Hannon for the excellent company. "Hannon, I appreciate you for sharin' your table with me. I'll have to decline your offer on the tour of the weigh station. Maybe next time."

"Hope we cross paths again," Hannon said, extending his hand.

"Hope we can," Lewis replied, dropping three silver dollars on the table. "It's on me, my friend." The jingle of silver caught Jennie's ear, and Lewis nodded gratefully as he tipped his hat to her.

Hannon looked pleasantly surprised at the gesture. "Well, it's been a pleasure meetin' you, Mr. Lewis. Thank you kindly."

Lewis turned to Jennie. "Thank you, Jennie, for your warm hospitality."

She waved off his thanks as she walked over to pick up his money. With the information he needed about Fergusson's possible whereabouts, Lewis bid them farewell and made his way back to town.

Across town, Carson and Bower's assignment was to visit Marshal Yates. They walked into the marshal's office and were greeted by a deputy.

"Is the marshal in?" Bower inquired.

"Yes, sir. He is in that office. I'll fetch him for you if you like," the deputy said. The deputy knocked on the door.

"Who is it?" the marshal yelled roughly from inside.

The deputy opened the door. "There's two fellas here to see you, sir."

"What do they want?" he demanded in a tone of aggravation. Suddenly, Carson stepped around the deputy and walked into the office. The marshal stood up with an ill-tempered look because of Carson's intrusion.

"Marshal Yates, I am Lieutenant Carson, U.S. Army. This is Deputy Marshal Jim Bower of the Western District of Missouri." The marshal looked them over, noticing that Carson was not in uniform.

"You don't look like a lieutenant," he replied to Carson. "And how do I know you are Northrop's deputy marshal?" he insisted. Bower showed his badge, and Carson showed him his credentials.

"Alright, gentlemen, I'm known as an impatient man. I don't take kindly to anyone barging into my office uninvited, much less into my jurisdiction. State your business. This had better be important."

Carson started from the beginning. When he got to the part about having seven lawmen from Missouri in his territory, he became infuriated.

"Are you telling me you have five more deputy marshals from Missouri in my territory?" he thundered, his voice echoing off the office walls.

"Six, sir, to be exact," Bower replied coolly.

The marshal slammed his fist on his desk. "That no good, over-reachin', sorry Northrop! How would he like it if I sent seven of my deputies into his territory? If this don't beat all," the marshal yelled, with a few choice words added. Northrop and Yates didn't cotton to each other one bit, as they say in the South. He thought Northrop liked to throw his weight around too much, having a habit of crossing jurisdictional lines.

Yates pointed his finger at Bower, narrowed his eyes, and warned, "Unless you have a warrant, Deputy, you ain't takin' nobody from this territory."

Bower reached into his vest pocket and presented the warrant. Yates swiped the paper from his hand, put on his glasses, and read the document. When he saw it was signed and notarized by District Judge James Yager, he tossed the warrant on his desk.

"Fine!" his voice still raised with frustration. "But there had better not be any trouble. The last thing I need is a bloodbath. Do we have an understanding?"

Bower picked up the warrant and placed it back into his vest pocket but didn't guarantee anything, especially since he had just pulled rank over him.

"Marshal Yates, Marshal Northrop, and the U.S. Army, thank you for your cooperation," Bower said before they departed.

They were about to mount their horses when Carson started

laughing. "Did you expect that warm reception?" Carson asked with a grin and lighting up his cigar.

"Oh, yes. I've never met Yates, but Northrop has dealt with him before. From what I've been told about him, this was a good day. He was actually very cordial."

Carson laughed as he took a draw from a cigar, pulled their horses around, and said, "Let's find Gabe and the others and see if they had as much fun as we have."

As Carson and Bower returned to the hotel, the Pawnee brothers, Will and Sam, rode out of town toward the Double J Ranch, thinking they could shake a few bushes closer to the ranch. Riding northwest of the city, the vast expanse of the countryside unfolded before them, with sprawling flatlands dotted by homesteads, orchards, and grazing cattle.

Along the way, they noticed a solitary tavern, or at least what looked like a small gathering place for cowpunchers. Surrounding it were a handful of buildings. Will and Sam decided to hang around to see what they might find out from the locals. The sun was getting hotter, so they found cool shade to picket their horses and walked down the street toward the tavern. Both Will and Sam were imposing figures.

The street was empty that morning for the most part. It lay quiet, save for a few souls going about their morning routines. Yet, there was one who paid particular attention to them. He was sitting on the boardwalk in front of the tavern, sheltered by the porch shade. He watched as Will and Sam approached him. Will paused to scrape the mud from his boots. They nodded to acknowledge the old black gentleman who was missing his left leg just above the knee and a blind left eye. His weathered features spoke of a life that paid a price for living on the frontier.

"Is the tavern open?" Sam asked the man who studied the pair through his one eye.

"It's open, but it's cooler out here," the old man replied. He took a twist of tobacco and cut a plug with his knife. "Care for a chew?" he offered.

Sam accepted, while Will, who usually had a cigarette in his mouth, politely declined. The old man spat into his spittoon and then asked, "What brings ya'll to Topeka?"

They wondered how he knew they were from out of town. "I may have just one eye, but I can tell strangers when I see'em. You ain't white. I'm guessin' Pawnee or maybe Osage Injin. You're lookin' for somebody. I'm guessin' that the fella or fellas you're lookin' for ain't friends of yours," the old black gentleman surmised.

Sam and Will just looked at the old man, amazed at his accurate appraisal. He continued. "Them horses you rode here on ain't for cattle drivin'. And from the looks of them holsters and revolvers, I'm guessin' you two are lawmen."

"Maybe you can help us," Will said without denying a word of the old gentleman's assessment. "We are looking for one of the Fergussons."

"Which one. There ain't a one of 'em worth shootin'."

"James," Sam replied.

"James, you say. He comes here when he's in town. There's a pretty little gal in yonder he fancies. He's in town, or you two wouldn't be here. You might find him here tonight."

"What's your name?" Will asked him.

"Just call me Ezra," he said, spitting and wiping his mouth with a tobacco-stained rag. He then folded it neatly and wiped the sweat from his bald forehead.

"Ezra, we are obliged for your help. Can we trust you to keep this between us?" Will asked.

"I ain't got no dog in this fight," Ezra grinned.

"Is the gal you spoke of holed up in yonder?" Sam asked, nodding toward the tavern.

"Reckon so," Ezra replied, leaning back in his chair.

"What's her name?"

"Lillian Bass."

"Much obliged, Ezra. We have no quarrel with her," Sam reassured.

"That's good to hear," he said. "She's a sweet girl, and I'd hate to see any harm come to her."

Will and Sam entered the tavern. Since it was an early hour of the day, only a couple of ranch hands were seated at a table next to the back wall. They glanced up when the Pawnee brothers sat near the door at one of the tables. Lillian also noticed them when they sat down. She was stunningly beautiful, a tall, slender woman with eyes as dark as her long hair. She walked over to the table and couldn't help but notice that these two were different.

"Pawnee?" she asked them. She could tell by their distinct features. She pulled up a chair and joined them at the table.

"What band is your people?" she asked them.

"Ours is the Tapage Pawnees," Sam replied.

"Yours?" he asked.

"Xaui, the Grand Pawnees," she said proudly.

"What are you called in Pawnee?" Sam asked her.

"My grandmother called me Pahaat Ta, Red Deer."

"I was called Kaac Skiri, Gray Wolf," Sam said.

"I am Taaka Pahuru, White Owl," Will added.

Lillian felt an instant connection. "Let me fetch you some coffee," she offered warmly, heading back to the kitchen. Sam and Will exchanged knowing glances, realizing she could be their link to James Fergusson. They knew they had to tread carefully, maintaining only a casual acquaintance. The bond among the Pawnees ran deep, regardless of band, especially as their nation dwindled under the relentless pressure of U.S. Government treaties for their land.

It was only a few minutes before Lillian returned with their coffee. Their conversation flowed between English and their native tongue, filled with memories of childhood experiences and cherished traditions. However, the mood shifted when Lillian expressed her disagreement about their people's surrender of tribal land, dismissing Will and Sam's firsthand experiences and their views on the advantages of adapting to a changing world. As the hour passed, Lillian had to excuse herself. "Cowhands will be arriving in a few hours for dinner," she said regretfully, clearly having enjoyed their visit.

"Good meeting you, Pahaat Ta," Will said.

"Likewise, Kaac Skiri and Taaka Pahuru," Lillian replied with a smile before returning to the kitchen.

"We have what we need," Sam said. "Let's find the others and let them know."

On the way out, they thanked old Ezra. "I'm sure I'll see you again this evenin'," Ezra said.

Earlier that morning, as the other lawmen were on their assignments, Gabe, Preacher, and Brewer crossed the river, heading to the spot where they expected Fergusson to reserve a couple of train cars for shipping cattle. They followed the tracks northwest until they arrived at the bustling depot, teeming with cattlemen and cowhands. Gabe took charge, "Preacher, come with me." Brewer stayed outside, keeping a watchful eye.

Inside, the depot was crowded and lively. Two men were working the desk. One of them was busy with paperwork, his back to the door. The other man spotted Gabe and Preacher and stepped forward.

"Yes, sirs. How can I help you all?" he asked, eyeing them curiously.

"There's a shipment heading to Wyandotte City from the Double J Ranch. I was wondering if it's been scheduled," Preacher inquired while Gabe kept a sharp eye on the door and the people who were there, ready in case James Fergusson happened to be there or walked in. The attendant checked the ledger.

"Not yet, sir. Do you want to schedule it now?"

"No, but much obliged for your help," Preacher replied.

As they stepped outside, Gabe suddenly found himself face-to-face with someone who looked strikingly familiar. Shocked, Gabe blurted out, "Davis!" He stood nearly toe-to-toe with the man, having almost walked right into him. The name slipped from Gabe's lips before he had time to think.

Gabe stood there, frozen with shock and confusion. The man wasn't Russell Davis—known in truth as Alan Kilpatrick—but Jake, his identical twin. The color drained from Gabe's face.

"Pardon me," Kilpatrick said, giving Gabe a puzzled look as he stepped around him. Preacher and Brewer, noticing Gabe's sudden strange behavior, exchanged concerned glances. "Is that him?" Preacher whispered.

"No, wait here," Gabe instructed, steadying himself with a deep breath. He wiped his brow with a bandana and stepped back inside.

"Kilpatrick!" Gabe called out. The man turned to face him.

"Alan?" Gabe asked.

"Alan was my brother," Kilpatrick replied. Gabe approached him cautiously.

"You're Alan's brother?"

"That's right."

Kilpatrick's curiosity and unease grew. "How do you know my brother? He was killed a few years ago in Kentucky," Kilpatrick said.

"Sorry to hear it," Gabe responded. "When I saw you, I thought it was him. Sorry to bother you." Gabe turned and left, feeling Kilpatrick's eyes on his back. Once outside, he quickly mounted his horse.

"Let's go. Now!" Gabe urged; his voice laced with urgency.

Preacher and Brewer, still confused, followed Gabe's lead. They rode hard, Gabe's heart pounding and hands trembling. After a couple of miles, Gabe pulled up and dismounted, needing a moment to compose himself.

"What happened, Gabe?" Brewer asked.

Gabe recounted the events of the shootout of '68 with Alan Kilpatrick, who was then known as Russell Davis. Meeting Alan's identical twin, which Gabe had never known existed, felt like seeing a ghost.

"This complicates things," Gabe said. "I have no doubt he's working with Fergusson."

"Let's get back to town," Brewer suggested. "Maybe the others have had better luck."

With a nod, they mounted and rode back, Gabe's mind racing with the unexpected twist in their pursuit.

Alan Kilpatrick stood on the porch deck; his eyes fixed on the direction the strangers had ridden. The wind carried the dust away, leaving behind a feeling Kilpatrick couldn't shake.

26

Gabe, Preacher, and Brewer arrived back at the Papendick Hotel after stabling their horses. The sun was high. The sun and wind had dried the rut-carved roads. A dust devil swirled across the street. Gabe and the other two stepped onto the porch when they noticed a commotion. To the left of the main entrance was a man roughly scolding a boy. He had a tight grip on the boy's arm and was slapping him. The boy was yelling and tried to get away from him, but he couldn't break free. Gabe quickly intervened.

"What's the problem?"

"You stay out of this, mister. This is none of your affair," the man scolded.

Gabe showed his badge. "I'm making it mine, mister. Let the boy go," he said firmly, inches from the man's face. The man let go of him, and the boy tried to run away, but Gabe caught him by the back of his trousers and lifted him off the ground.

"You can leave now, mister," Gabe told the man.

He left but gave Gabe a nasty look, spat on the porch, and cursed. "Dirty little negro thief," he mumbled.

Gabe turned his attention to the boy who had calmed down, especially since he couldn't get any traction. Preacher and Brewer found it amusing while it lasted and entered the hotel.

"Now," Gabe said to the boy, "what did you do to make that man angry with you?" Gabe held on to his shirt in case he decided to run.

"I didn't do nothin'," the boy replied in protest.

Gabe noticed a bucket of water and a brush on the porch beside a chair. "Is that yours?" Gabe asked him. The boy looked at the bucket.

"Yes, sir."

"Do you clean people's boots for money?" Gabe asked.

"Yes, sir," he replied, his face downcast.

"Do you ever try to steal from people?" The boy was timid about answering the question. Gabe knew the answer.

"What's your name, son?"

"Gabriel," he replied.

"Gabriel, huh. That's my name, too. Where's your mammy and pap?"

"I ain't got none," the boy replied.

"No family?"

"No, sir."

"Where do you sleep?"

"At the livery stable. Mr. Huntoon lets me stay there."

"Gabriel. You're not going to be homeless for long. Will you trust me to help you?" Until then, he kept his face cast down, but then he glanced up at Gabe for the first time, unsure whether to trust him.

"Are you hungry?" Gabe asked. Little Gabriel nodded.

"You stay here. I'll get you something to eat." Gabe went inside after getting Gabriel something to drink, bread, fruit, and boiled eggs. When he returned, he gave the food to Gabriel and sat down next to him while he ate.

"I might have a home for you, Gabriel, back in Warrensburg. Would you go back with me?" Gabriel looked at him for a moment, still unsure about him. He was only ten years old but had experienced enough to be careful about trusting people. However, there was something about Gabe that caused him to feel differently.

"Yes, sir. I'll go wich'ya," Gabriel replied with a smile.

"You have to make me a promise, though," Gabe said. "No more stealing. Do we have a deal?"

"Yes, sir."

"Good. I'll be seeing you around." The two Gabriels shook hands, and Gabe went back inside. Walking into the dining room, he saw Carson and Bower seated with Preacher and Brewer. They were talking about Gabe's little encounter outside.

"Looks like you made yourself a new friend out there, Gabe," Brewer said with a chuckle.

"He's an orphan. I think I can find him a good home in Warrensburg," Gabe replied.

"What made you take that on for yourself?" Brewer asked him.

"I don't know. His name's Gabriel, same as mine. In the Bible, Gabriel is God's messenger of good news. Everybody needs good news, even little Gabriel, I reckon." They nodded, appreciating his charity.

They spent the next hour discussing what they had learned from their day. Soon after, Lewis entered with the Pawnee brothers, who shared their findings. By mid-afternoon, they put together a plan.

"Well done, gentlemen," Gabe began. "We will go back to the tavern this evening. Hopefully, old man Ezra will still be there. Sam, you will ask if he's seen James. If he hasn't arrived, we'll wait and watch for him. Either way, Brewer and Lewis will go in first. Carson, Bower, and I will follow once we know he's there. Preacher, Sam, and Will, the three of you will stay across the street out of sight. When I identify Fergusson, I will signal and step aside for him to be apprehended."

After discussing different scenarios and with the plan in place, they waited until evening.

Gabe walked out of the hotel, finding little Gabriel sitting on the edge of the porch petting a stray dog. Gabe settled in the rocking chair and asked, "Who's your friend?"

"I call him Bo," Gabriel replied.

"I had a dog, once. I named him Tip. He was a good rabbit dog," Gabe said, reminiscing about former days. "Gabriel, when did you lose your parents?"

Gabriel hesitated for a minute. "My mammy died of the fever a while back. I never knew my pap. I been alone since then. Mr. Huntoon found me in the cold one night. He told me to stay in the livery stable." Gabe took an apple from his pocket and a stick of licorice and handed them to him, which brought a big smile to Gabriel's face.

"I have to be gone for a little while this evening, but I will try to bring you something later at the livery stable," Gabe said as he stood up to leave.

"Mr. Gabe," Gabriel said respectfully. Gabe turned and responded,

"Yes?"

"Not since my mammy did somebody care so much."

Gabe smiled and went back inside the hotel.

The hour had come for the eight lawmen to leave. They met in the hotel's drawing room to walk through the last details of the plan. They stepped outside to a warm evening. The sun had set in a clear red sky. It was Saturday night, which meant the town was getting lively. They walked to the livery, mounted their horses, and rode northwest of the city, the Pawnee brothers leading the way. When they were about twenty yards from the tavern, Sam proceeded alone while the rest remained behind, waiting. Sure enough, Ezra was seated in his usual place. Sam rode up close to the tavern porch.

"Hello, young brave." Ezra greeted. 'I think I know who you're lookin' for."

"Is he here?" he asked. Ezra nodded and looked toward the door indicating that he was inside. Sam went back to tell the others. "He's here."

They rode cautiously to the tavern, tension high as Gabe prepared to spot Fergusson before being seen himself. The tavern was lively, with music playing, and a thick cloud of smoke hung in the air. The smell of whiskey, beer, and cattlemen filled the room. Gabe motioned for Preacher and Lewis to enter first. After a minute or two, Gabe, Bower, and Carson followed. Cowhands lined the bar to the right while tables were crowded with poker players and whiskey drinkers. Although it was unusual for ladies to frequent such places, a few were present. As Gabe moved through the crowd, he realized that finding James without drawing attention to himself would be a challenge.

Carson and Bower snagged a table near the door, while Brewer, Preacher, and Lewis leaned against the bar. Gabe kept his hat low, scanning the faces in the raucous crowd. Doubt crept in as he wondered if Fergusson had slipped away unnoticed. Just as he began to lose hope, James and Lillian descended the stairs, arm in arm, heading towards a table occupied by two other men.

Just as Gabe prepared to signal the others, his eye caught a man at the table, his back turned but bearing a striking resemblance to Kilpatrick. A chill ran down Gabe's spine. Time was slipping away. He needed to alert the others, but hesitation held him back. The tension mounted as they watched Gabe closely, expecting him to signal Fergusson's presence. Instead, Gabe approached the table.

"What's he doing?" Bower asked Carson.

"He knows what he's doing," Carson replied. "I hope," he added, taking a nervous draw from his cigar.

Sweat beads covered his brow and ran into his beard. Gabe stepped up to the table without anyone noticing him standing there.

Gabe spoke the name "Frank Tate," using James' alias in a low voice to see if that would get his attention. It did. James set his glass on the table and looked up to see who it was that had spoken that name, but he didn't recognize him. Looking more into Gabe's eyes, he suddenly knew who he was.

"Gabe MacCallan? Is that you, my friend?" James exclaimed loud enough for all around him to hear. He stood up, eagerly shaking Gabe's hand, and slapped his shoulder. "What brings you to these parts of all places?"

James noticed Gabe's lack of shared enthusiasm, and his expression changed to a look of concern. Gabe had concealed his badge on the inside of his vest, which he revealed to James.

"U.S. Deputy Marshal," James said with a confused look, which got more attention from those seated at the table.

"James, you are under arrest," Gabe told him. "Come with me. Quietly. Don't try anything. The room is full of deputies, and there are more outside."

"My, my, Gabe. I'm impressed," James replied, realizing this was not a joke.

Troubled with the situation, Lillian arose from her chair and walked slowly around the table, keeping her eyes on Gabe. The other two men at the table sat observing quietly.

"James, what is this about?" Lillian asked, working her way between James and Gabe.

"It's nothing, sweetheart. This is an old friend of mine from Kentucky."

When James said that, Jake Kilpatrick stood up, throwing his chair to the floor. The crowd was now quiet, and all eyes were on Gabe and James.

"Keep your seat, Jake," James said, with his hand outstretched toward Kilpatrick. At that moment, Jake remembered running into Gabe at the shipping depot earlier that morning.

"That's why you thought I was Alan. You knew him. You are the man who killed him," Kilpatrick said, his face flushed with anger.

"I didn't kill him," Gabe said. "Besides, he pulled his guns first. James has the scar to prove it."

"Gabe, you've made a big mistake by coming here," James said with genuine concern. "I don't want you to get hurt. Think of Hannah."

"Come with me peacefully," Gabe demanded. "If this is all a mistake, this will be settled quickly."

The room grew eerily quiet as all eyes turned to them, the deputies on high alert. Brewer, watching the crowd, slipped the leather strap off the hammer of his gun.

After a tense moment, James finally spoke. "Alright, I'll go with you," he said slowly. "But on one condition—no cuffs."

"No cuffs," Gabe agreed. He took James' gun and led him to the door, the others backing out of the room to ensure no one had any other ideas. As they stepped out and began crossing the street, the sound of hurried footsteps erupted behind them. Jake Kilpatrick burst out of the tavern, with Lillian close on his heels. Jake stepped onto the dimly lit street, squaring up to face Gabe.

"MacCallan!" he shouted in anger. "You're lyin' about my brother. You killed him!"

Gabe and James turned to face Jake. Gabe spoke calmly but firmly, "Your brother was involved in the murder of my friend. We reap what we sow, Jake. It's godly justice. Don't make the same mistake as your brother. He sowed the wind and reaped the whirlwind."

"Jake!" James intervened, his voice firm and authoritative. "The deputy is right. Your brother's death was by his own recklessness. Turn away and go back inside."

Jake was consumed with rage. He looked like a man who wanted revenge, but Gabe wasn't going to let him have it. Because of how this had unfolded, a sick feeling settled in the pit of Gabe's stomach. Gabe could see his rage slowly turn into a stone-cold expression. Jake's hand moved swiftly for his gun. Suddenly, a barrage of gunfire erupted, thunderous echoes erupting from eight revolvers.

It was over within seconds. Jake Kilpatrick lay dead face up in the street, but he did not die alone. Kneeling over the other body lying in the street, his lifeless eyes were closed. He had given his life to save Gabe's. When Jake went for his gun, James Fergusson shoved Gabe aside, stepped in front of him, and received a bullet to the heart. He died instantly. Lillian rushed to James, weeping over his body. She looked up and recognized the Pawnee brothers walking toward her. "Murderers! You killed him," she cried and lowered her head in grief. The crowd that gathered was silent.

Gabe was stunned because he had been spared a bullet that would have taken his life. The thought of how close he came to never seeing Hannah and Alec again on this side of heaven shook him to the core. What troubled him more was the selfless sacrifice made by the man who used to be his enemy.

Preacher walked over to Gabe, who knelt on the ground and laid his hand on his shoulder. "The scripture says, 'Be not deceived; God is not mocked: for whatsoever a man soweth, that shall he also reap.'" But the scripture settling most on Gabe's mind at the moment was, "Greater love hath no man than this, that a man lay down his life for his friends." Gabe wept.

As Gabe stood and turned to walk away, he realized that his revolver had never left his holster. He wouldn't have stood a chance. When he walked by old Ezra, he remarked, "God ain't done with you, Deputy." Gabe stopped and glanced up at him. "He ain't done with you," Ezra repeated. Gabe stood there for a moment without any expression, still stunned by what had transpired, and walked away.

The eight lawmen and the lieutenant mounted their horses and returned to the hotel, not one of them saying a word.

27

It was well past dark when the lawmen reached the livery stable. Little Gabriel, who usually stayed hidden when strangers came around, emerged from his hiding spot to greet them.

"Are you hungry, my little man?" Gabe asked him. Gabriel was glad to see Gabe and nodded yes. Too many people came into his life and were suddenly gone. That almost happened again that evening. "I'll be back shortly," Gabe assured him. "It's best if you stay here for now."

On returning to the hotel, Preacher told Gabe, "You're a good man, my friend," handing over twenty dollars. "Monday morning, get the boy some new clothes and shoes."

Gabe nodded, grateful. "I'm goin' to worship in the mornin'. Come with me."

"I'd like that," Preacher replied with a smile. "We need to spend some time with the Lord and his good people."

By Monday morning, news of the shooting and the eight lawmen from Missouri had spread throughout West Topeka. James was buried in the family cemetery on Sunday, while Kilpatrick was laid to rest in the public cemetery. The Fergusson clan was thirsty for vengeance because of the killing of one of their own. At the Double J Ranch, an angry group gathered, demanding revenge.

"Them lawmen is still in town," one of them said. "They have to pay for what they did."

J.T. slammed his fist against the table, his face red with anger. "We're not going to do anything. You got that?" he ordered. "Do you want lawmen from the whole state of Kansas to come down on us? It's bad enough to have that fool, Marshal Yates, breathing down my neck." He glared at each man, eye-to-eye. "We are leaving it be. Do you hear me? Leave…it…be!"

Though the men in the room weren't pleased with his decision, they dared not go against J.T. and left it at that.

Back at the hotel, Gabriel sat on the edge of the porch as he usually did when Gabe exited the hotel. "Hey, Gabriel. I have a surprise for you today. We're going to get you dressed up and ready to go. Gabe had arranged for Gabriel to bathe before purchasing new clothes and shoes. They found a place selling children's clothing and purchased shirts, trousers, and shoes. Gabe had him proudly stand before him, dressed in his new outfit. "Let's see you now," Gabe said with a smile. "You look like a Philadelphia lawyer." Gabriel beamed with pride, admiring his new shoes, trousers, and shirt. It changed his whole demeanor. He felt like somebody important now.

"We are leaving for Kansas City this afternoon. I have some business to take care of there, and then we will leave for Warrensburg. Are you ready?" Gabe asked.

"Sir, will I have a new family?" Gabriel asked.

Gabe responded to him with a smile, "Call me Gabe. Yes, you will have a new family."

This pleased Gabriel very much, but one last thing remained to be done. Gabe and Gabriel visited Dr. Huntoon, the owner of the livery stable, to let him know that Gabriel would be going to his new home.

The clock inside the hotel struck ten. The summer sun beat down, intensifying its scorching heat upon the town. Carson and Bower returned to the hotel, having completed their visit with Marshal Yates.

They found Gabe and Gabriel sitting on the porch, ready to leave. Carson walked up with a big grin and a cigar in the corner of his mouth, as he always did.

"How was Marshal Yates this morning?" Gabe asked, smiling back at him.

"Well, let's say he was not happy. I thought he would have a stroke before we left, but he knew his hands were tied. An old goat like him has to butt heads to make himself feel better."

"Are we finished here?" Gabe asked.

"As far as I know, we are. Lewis, Brewer, and Preacher are staying to follow up and ensure that the Fergussons behave. The Pawnee brothers headed back to Missouri early this morning."

"Master Gabriel," Carson asked, "are you anxious to get on the train?"

Gabriel grinned and nodded.

"Well then, let's make our way to the depot," Gabe said.

By five o'clock that afternoon, they were back in Kansas City unloading their horses. Bower returned home to his family after promising to meet Gabe and Carson in the morning. Carson returned to the Broadway Hotel as Gabe and Gabriel went to see Red Kinsley.

"Gabriel, the man we are about to visit is an old friend of mine," Gabe said. "I will need you to stay with him for a day or two."

They arrived at Kinsley's house, and Gabe knocked on the door. There was no answer, and it seemed deserted outside. He knocked again. Finally, the door creaked open, revealing Miss Mary, the housekeeper.

"Mr. Gabe?" She looked surprised to see him and puzzled at the sight of Gabriel.

"Miss Mary, is Red here?" Gabe asked, removing his hat.

"No, sir. I don't expect him until Wednesday."

That presented a problem for Gabe. He scratched his forehead, wondering what to do.

"What can I do to help you, Mr. Gabe?" She could tell he was in a difficult spot.

"Miss Mary, this here is Gabriel. I'm taking him home with me, but I needed him to stay here for a day or two."

"He can stay with me," she offered.

"Are you sure?"

"Oh, my Laudy, yes!" She smiled warmly.

"I'll be alright, Mr. Gabe," Gabriel said confidently. "I know you will be back."

"I will be back by Wednesday, if not before," Gabe assured him.

Leaving Gabriel in Miss Mary's capable hands, Gabe returned to the hotel after taking Midnight to the livery stable. He paid for his room and saw Carson sitting alone in the drawing room. Gabe walked in and sat down.

"Have a cigar, Gabe. I know you don't drink," Carson offered.

Gabe gratefully accepted, though he and tobacco had a history of mutual dislike, having raised so much of it in his life.

"You know, Gabe," Carson said, sipping his brandy and smoking his cigar, "you made an indelible impression on the deputies last week. Tomorrow, I will recommend to Marshal Northrop that you keep that badge."

"Carson, that's just the brandy talking," Gabe remarked.

"No, I am quite sober," Carson insisted.

"You should consider it," Carson continued. "You will be near your wife's family and have already established a good rapport. The marshal and his deputies value your leadership. I can't think of one reason you shouldn't keep that badge."

"We will see. Only God knows," Gabe replied.

Carson paused briefly, "You are a strong believer in the providence of God, aren't you, Gabe?"

"I am," Gabe replied. "I might not be able to explain it, but I believe the British poet was correct when he wrote, 'God moves in a mysterious way, his wonders to perform.' Whether we acknowledge his ways or not, he accomplishes his purpose."

Gabe paused and continued, "You know that little boy I'm bringing home with me?"

"Gabriel?" Carson answered.

"Yes. He may have been our real purpose here. However, it took tracking down a wanted man to bring us to him. We witnessed two things last week that go hand-in-hand," Gabe explained, "judgment and salvation. It was judgment day for James Fergusson and Jake Kilpatrick and salvation for Gabriel. Their destinies are sealed forever. Gabriel's life and his family tree will be changed forever."

Carson listened and asked, "Do you remember when you asked me if I feared God?"

"I do," Gabe replied.

"To fear God means to respect his way. Am I right?"

"That's right," Gabe replied, wondering where he was going with this.

Carson continued, "When I saw Kilpatrick challenge you in that street, I had no doubt that you could handle the situation, but when I saw Fergusson push you aside and step in front, I knew then that you had Divine protection. Argue what you will about how God does what he does, but too many things happened at that moment to be by chance. I must confess. I have more respect for our Maker's way than I did. And as for Gabriel's destiny? Well, I have to agree with you."

With that sober reflection, they sat silently for a few minutes, each lost in his own thoughts. Then Carson leaned forward in his chair and broke their silence. "Let's see what's for supper."

That night, Gabe opened the scriptures to a familiar place, read, and slept more peacefully than he had in a month.

Gabe and Carson met in the dining room for breakfast the following morning to plan their day. Carson, dressed in his officer's uniform, looked every bit the part.

"We need to pay a visit to Jared Fergusson today, but first, we'll stop by the marshal's office," Carson said, slicing into his steak.

"Alright," Gabe agreed, sipping his coffee. "Let's finish our steaks and get started. I want to get home."

After breakfast, they rode to the Federal Building. Walking up the long, winding staircase to the second floor, they headed down the hallway. Gabe entered the grand hall ahead of Carson. The heels of their boots echoed from the hardwood floor as they walked in unison. They entered the marshal's office, where Jim Bower was already speaking with the marshal, who didn't look pleased.

"Here they are," Bower announced to the marshal. "Come in, Deputy MacCallan and Lieutenant Carson. I have already briefed Marshal Northrop."

"Have a seat, gentlemen," Northrop said in an unwelcome tone. The marshal rose from his chair and walked around to the front of his desk. His appearance said he was not in a good mood.

"I have one question, Deputy MacCallan." Northrop's voice echoed around the room with the sound of authority. "You were specifically ordered to identify Fergusson, not to apprehend him. Am I correct?"

"Yes, sir," Gabe responded, suddenly feeling as if he landed himself in the hot seat, which neither he nor Carson were expecting.

"Are you in the habit of disobeying orders, Deputy?"

"Sir, I am not in the habit of disobeying orders. May I have permission to speak, sir?"

"It had better be good, young man," he said in frustration.

"At that moment and in that room, sir, I knew that if the other deputies apprehended Fergusson, he might have resisted, which would have escalated the situation inside a tavern full of Double J cowhands."

"But it did escalate. Correct?" the marshal interrupted.

Gabe started to continue, but the marshal asked again. "Correct?"

"Correct, sir," Gabe responded.

"Continue," the marshal ordered.

"I managed to convince Fergusson to surrender peacefully. He cooperated by telling those who were with him to stand down. The man who confronted me was his partner, Jake Kilpatrick. He had a brother who was shot and killed in a confrontation with me and my sheriff back in Kentucky. He blamed me for his brother's death. There was no way I could have known that Kilpatrick would be at the table with Fergusson."

The marshal interrupted again. "And that's precisely why you should have followed orders."

"Yes, sir," Gabe replied respectfully.

"If I may jump in here, Jameson," Bower interjected, "Deputy MacCallan handled himself and the situation professionally. He did everything he could to prevent a confrontation. With all due respect, none of us could have walked Fergusson out as peacefully. What happened with Kilpatrick could have happened, regardless."

Marshal Northrop's demeanor shifted as he stepped behind his desk. Gabe removed his badge and respectfully placed it on the desk. Northrop picked up the badge, paused momentarily, and said, "I need another good deputy that will think on his feet, assess a situation, make a decision on the spur of the moment, and defend his actions. Deputy MacCallan, this badge is still yours if you accept it."

A grin could be seen on Carson's face, but he stayed out of the discussion.

"With all due respect, sir, I don't want the job," Gabe replied.

Carson was surprised by Gabe's response but remained silent. Northrop looked sternly at Gabe, narrow-eyed and with a clenched jaw.

"That's another reason why I'm offering it to you," Northrop replied. "You're not a man who seeks glory for himself."

Gabe continued to decline the offer. "I have a good position as a deputy sheriff back in Kentucky."

"All the more reason to leave. Exit when no one wants you to leave," the marshal added.

Gabe thought for a moment. "May I talk it over with my wife back in Warrensburg?"

"I'll give you two weeks," Northrop replied as he tossed the badge back to Gabe.

"I will need to return home to Kentucky," Gabe added.

"I'll give you six weeks to report back," Northrop responded, making his last concession. "You are still U.S. Deputy Marshal MacCallan in the District of Western Missouri. I'll see you in six weeks."

"Thank you, sir," Gabe said with honor and relief.

Gabe and Carson didn't say a word until they exited the building.

"I really thought you were in big trouble," Carson remarked.

"Well, I appreciated the backup you offered," Gabe replied sarcastically with a smile. Gabe removed his hat and wiped the sweat from his forehead. "I've never been reprimanded that way, not even in the military. But I had it comin', I have to admit. He was right. Now that I think about it, he wanted to establish our relationship to see how I would react."

Just then, Bower walked out of the building, grinning. "Northrop didn't beat you up too badly, did he?"

"My backside is a little too sore to get into a saddle, if that's what you mean. I would have done the same, so I should have expected it," Gabe replied. "I appreciate you coming to my defense."

"Northrop can be a hardnose," Bower said, "but you won't find a better man in Missouri as a lawman or a better one to work for. I've known him for twenty years. He's a good judge of character. I hope to see you next month."

"We will see," Gabe replied. They shook hands and parted ways.

"Let's find out if he is in a forgiving mood," Carson replied with a grin. "If not, you and I will own a lot of beef."

Upon their arrival at Jared Fergusson's place, the towering Irishman stood steadfastly at his post. They rode up, dismounted, tied their horses, and stepped onto the porch. Carson looked up at Ennis. "Top of the mornin' to you, Ennis. How are you, my friend? Is Mr. Jared in?"

"He's not to be disturbed," Ennis replied in his deep Irish voice.

"That's too bad. We have unfinished business and were hoping to see him. Are you sure we can't see him?" Carson asked as he took a cigar from his vest and handed it to the Irishman.

"Maybe he'll not mind," Ennis said with a smile. He knocked on the door. Jared answered, "Who is it?" Ennis opened the door, allowing Carson and Gabe to enter.

"Thank you, Ennis," Carson said and tipped his hat.

"Gentlemen, come in, come in," Jared said as he noticed Carson in his uniform and Gabe with a badge on his shirt.

"Jared, my name is Deputy Marshal Gabe MacCallan, Western District of Missouri. This is Lieutenant John Carson, U.S. Army." Jared sat down, wondering what this was about.

"I am sure you heard about what happened in Topeka last Saturday night," Carson said.

"I heard from J.T. yesterday," Jared said. "Are you about to tell me you had something to do with that?"

They offered no expression or an answer to his question, but Jared could see the answer in their eyes. Carson began to tell his side of the story. "I've been on the trail for several years to find two men. One of them was James Fergusson, who was unfortunately killed Saturday night." Jared took a drink from his coffee, swallowed hard, and held the cup with both hands.

"James came back here several years ago looking for work and a place to stay," Jared said. "J.T., being kin and feeling a sense of obligation, gave him a place to hold up and work. It didn't take long for James to climb the ranks. I didn't trust him, but J.T. did, so I kept my mouth shut."

Jared's mood changed to frustration. "I figure you are here for your down payment since you revealed who you are."

"That's why we are here," Gabe replied.

"You used me to get to James. You misrepresented yourselves. That's called fraud and falsifying a legal document. Am I right?" Jared accused with a raised voice.

"I'm sure you would prefer to give us our money than to become entangled in legal matters that involve two jurisdictions and the U.S. Army. After all, it is only a hundred head of cattle, and they are still in your possession," Carson replied.

Jared set his cup down hard on the desk without taking his eyes off Carson. Jared was not one to invite trouble. He rose and walked to a safe in the corner of the room, opened it, counted the cash, and gave it to them.

"Thank you, Mr. Fergusson."

The signed agreement was beneath the handful of cash, which Carson promptly tore in two, placing it into his vest pocket with the money.

"Now, if you don't mind, gentlemen," Jared said. "I need to find a buyer for a hundred head of cattle."

Gabe and Carson left his office. Ennis was still at his post. Carson reached into his vest pocket and took out two cigars. "Ennis, I doubt that we will see one another again. I think you and I could have enjoyed a nice bottle of bourbon," Carson said. "Take care, my friend." Ennis accepted the cigars, nodded, and smiled.

Gabe and Carson returned to Carson's room at the hotel to settle their business.

"Here's your pay, Gabe. This should also cover all of your expenses. I also added a little for any expenses Gabriel needs. Please give my best regards to your wife and family. I'll be taking the train west this afternoon."

"Back to Arizona?" Gabe asked.

"For a while. I might retire in Denver. I'll contact you and let you know." Gabe put out his hand. "It's been a pleasure serving with you, John."

"The pleasure has been mine, young man," he replied as they shook hands. "You will make a difference in this world. I'm proud to know you. I expect to hear great things about you."

Having completed their mission, Gabe and Carson bid each other farewell and departed. Gabe's mind focused now on Gabriel and returning home. It was almost noon, and Gabe spent the remainder of the day purchasing tickets, gathering train schedule information, and preparing for their departure.

The next morning, Gabe returned to Red Kinsley's place. Kinsley was relieved of his commitment regarding the cattle deal but was ready to fulfill his part if necessary. He and Gabe bid farewell as friends, assuring Kinsley they would likely meet again soon.

That morning, Gabe and Gabriel boarded the train departing from Kansas City for Warrensburg. Gabe felt a mixture of emotions as he held both badges in his hand, one as a Deputy Sheriff and the other as a Deputy Marshal. After a long train ride, they reached Warrensburg. Gabriel was fast asleep and had to be awakened. They managed to arrive home before nightfall.

28

The family was excited to see Gabe standing unexpectedly at the front door. Their surprise deepened when they discovered who he had brought along. After many hugs and taking Alec into his arms, who was glad to see his father, Gabe introduced Gabriel. Gabe didn't have to explain that Gabriel had been orphaned. Everyone made him feel at home. They all settled in, enjoying a hearty meal before retiring for the night.

Gabe and Gabriel left to see Miss Lizzie at the Adair House the following morning. She was thrilled to see Gabe when she came to the door.

"Mr. Gabe, what a pleasant surprise. Please come in. I have just finished making some biscuits and gravy. Will you have some?"

"You know I can't pass up your biscuits, Miss Lizzie," Gabe said, even though he and Gabriel had just finished a big breakfast.

"Now, who is this with you?" Lizzie asked as she smiled at Gabriel.

"This is Gabriel, Miss Lizzie. I hoped you could help us find a good home for him."

She looked with concern at Gabe. "Where did you two meet?"

"We met in Topeka last week," Gabe replied.

Lizzie thought for a minute as she poured coffee for Gabe and milk for Gabriel. "How old are you, Gabriel?" she asked him.

"My mammy died a year ago. She say I be nine-year-old."

"What happened to your mammy?"

"She died of the fever."

Lizzie thought for a minute more. "He can stay with me," she said. "It's decided. He can stay with me."

"That's what I hoped you would say," Gabe responded with a smile.

"Yes, sir," she continued, "I could use a man's help around here." "Gabriel, what do you think? Would you like to live with me in this big house?"

Gabriel looked around the house, grinned with a big grin, and replied, "Yes, ma'am!"

"There," Lizzie said, "it's settled."

Gabriel found himself in a loving home where he could grow in the nurture and admonition of the Lord, receiving an education in the same way Miss Alice did for Lizzie.

Gabe had already shared the news of his opportunity as a U.S. Deputy Marshal in the Western District with Hannah and her family. Hannah was surprised by the news, but pleasantly so, because she would like to live closer to her family.

The following week, they made their way back to Kentucky. Gabe resigned as a deputy sheriff, a decision that Sheriff Nathan didn't particularly like but understood. Gabe's family was overjoyed to be reunited with Alec and understood the opportunity was too good to turn down.

Hannah had the task of breaking the news to Doctor McKinney. After she told him that they would be moving to Kansas City, he said, "Before you go, I want to give you something." Doc McKinney walked over to a narrow cabinet in a corner. He opened a drawer at the bottom, took a small box from it, and handed it to Hannah.

"What is this?" Hannah was a little confused by the small box in her hand.

"Open it," he said. Hannah opened it to find a pendant.

"It's the staff of Asclepius," he explained. "You know about Asclepius from your studies in medical history. He was considered the most skillful physician in ancient Greece. My mentor, Doctor George Nesbitt, a brilliant Scottish doctor, gave me that pendant. I want to pass it to you."

Overwhelmed with emotions, Hannah embraced Doctor McKinney with a hug, reflecting a bond akin to that of a daughter to her father, and she kissed his cheek.

"Go," he said gently, "before you have us both in tears."

After a two-week stay with Gabe's family, they embarked on their journey back to Warrensburg. Gabe gave Whirlwind to Eli, Hannah's brother. Gabe faithfully reported for duty on the assigned day of his return. Eventually, Gabe and Hannah settled on the east side of Kansas City. Hannah continued her medical practice as a registered nurse while waiting for the opportunity to become a doctor, which she eventually did.

As time passed, Alec became the oldest of three boys and one girl, Kinsley, Carson, and Alice. Gabe became well-known as one of the best lawmen in Missouri and was respected for his godly justice. A favorite scripture underlined in his father's Bible proved to be true, Romans 8:28, which reads, "And we know that all things work together for good to them that love God, to them who are the called according to his purpose."

Author's Note

While this is historical fiction, two significant truths were woven throughout the story. First, those who hold steadfastly to their faith in Christ and live in reverence toward God are beacons of light in a world of darkness. As such, they are in constant conflict with darkness, even though they do not seek confrontation. They want to live quietly as servants of God, raise their families, and be good neighbors.

In the story, Miss Alice states, "Whenever light enters a dark room, the darkness flees. It flees and struggles to return." The struggle between light and darkness is the tribulation we experience as long as we are lights in a dark place. We may want to run from the struggle, as Gabe wanted to do, but it will always follow us. When Gabe acknowledged this for himself, he became a formidable foe to elements of darkness. The same One who said, "*I am the Light of the World*" also said, "*In the world ye shall have tribulation: but be of good cheer; I have overcome the world.*"— Jesus of Nazareth.

The final to consider is the relationship of godly justice, judgment, and salvation. When people sow the wind, they reap the whirlwind, says the prophet Amos. This is true for a simple reason. There exists an Almighty Judge who seeks justice in the affairs of men. Because God created us, he has the right to rule. He has set moral boundaries. Godly justice is invited when these boundaries are ignored. When we sow the wind, we ultimately face the whirlwind of judgment. However, in the realm of divine justice, mercy is always preferred if it can be granted. Mercy seeks salvation and deliverance. Mercy triumphs over godly justice.

—*R. Darrell Wallace*

Chronology

April 20, 1865
Gabe leaves the military and goes home to Kentucky

May 12, 1865
Gabe arrives in St. Louis and Warrensburg

May 13, 1865
Gabe confronts bushwhackers at Miller's harness shop

May 14, 1865
First Sunday at the Tabernacle
Gabe meets Hannah

May 17, 1865
Shootout at the Adair House

May 21, 1865
Second Sunday at the Tabernacle and Miss Alice's counsel with Gabe

June 6, 1865
New Constitution of Missouri adopted

July 1866
Gabe decided to stay in Warrensburg
He and Hannah became a couple

July 27–28, 1866
The Black Water Ghost enters the story

July 29–30, 1866
Shootout with Lile and his men
Shootout at Devil's Branch
Ben's tavern is shut down

September 1866
The wedding and departure for Kentucky
Kinsley leaves for Kansas

October 1866
Gabe and Hannah leave for Kentucky

1867
Gabe becomes deputy sheriff

Spring 1868
Gabe and Hannah's son, Alec, is born

June 1868
Hannah begins her nursing career

October 1868
Quinn Howard is murdered
Shootout with the Walbert brothers
Shootout with Russell Davis

December 1868
Frank Tate leaves

Late spring 1871
Lieutenant Carson arrives in town

May 20, 1871
The MacCallans arrive back in Warrensburg

May 24, 1871
Gabe travels to Kansas City with Lieutenant Carson
Gabe is deputized as U. S. Deputy Marshal

May 25, 1871
Gabe reunites with Red Kinsley in Wyandotte City

May 26, 1871
James Fergusson is found

May 27, 1871
Gabe and the lieutenant travel to Topeka with six deputies
Gabe meets little Gabriel

May 28, 1871
James Fergusson and Jake Kilpatrick are killed

June 1, 1871
Gabe and Lieutenant Carson report to Marshal Northrop
Gabe is offered a position to remain as deputy
Lieutenant Carson leaves for Arizona

June 2, 1871
Gabe and Gabriel arrive in Warrensburg

June 5, 1871
The MacCallans travel back to Kentucky

June 19, 1871
The MacCallans travel back to Warrensburg

July 13, 1871
Gabe reports for duty as U.S. Deputy Marshal, Western District of
Missouri, Kansas City

www.ingramcontent.com/pod-product-compliance
Lightning Source LLC
Chambersburg PA
CBHW041746010726
47507CB00008B/301